THE STEINWAY SEVEN

By Badees Nouiouat

The Steinway Seven

Copyright © 2026 by Badees Nouiouat

This novel is entirely a work of fiction. The names, characters, and incidents portrayed in it are the work of the author's imagination. Any resemblance to actual persons, living or dead, events, or localities is entirely coincidental.

ISBN: 979-8-234-07003-6

Editing by Marufa Hoque and Sarah Jaffe
Art by Agija Mikelsone

www.badeesnouiouat.com

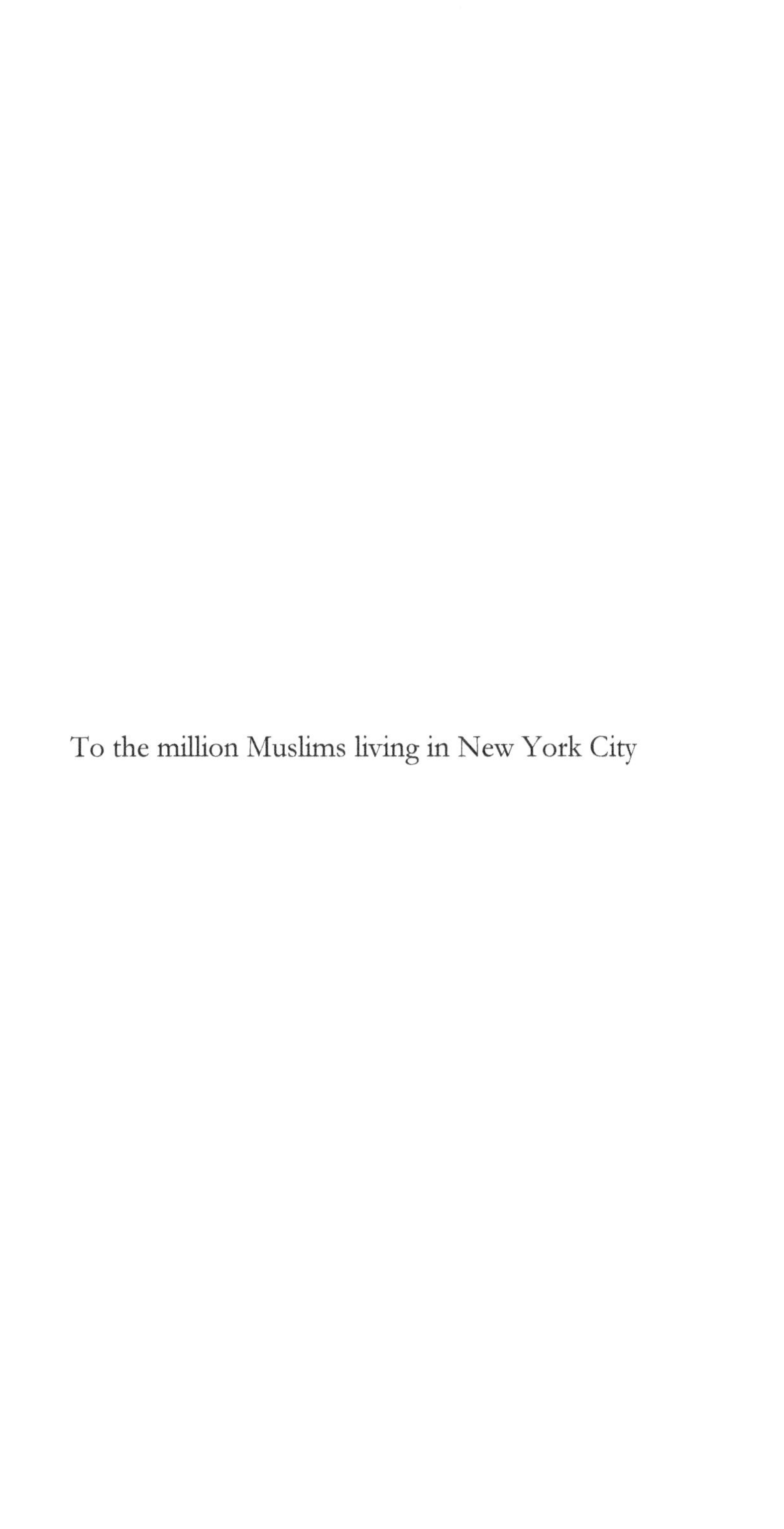

To the million Muslims living in New York City

Chapter 1: Yasin

Allah, you created me free…please return me to freedom once more, Yasin prayed in his consciousness. He wondered if one of his ancestors, enslaved and packed on a ship to America, ever made the same prayer.

He was sitting on the floor of an NYPD van, his wrists cuffed behind his back and his ankles shackled to a rusty hook in the wall. His eyes were closed, desperately trying to cling to a hazy vision of his wife and teenage son, to whom he hadn't spoken or sent money since he was first jailed at Rikers. Then, the van rolled over a large pothole, and Yasin's head was jerked up, banging the stainless-steel wall behind him. He opened his eyes in defeat.

It was night outside. The only light in the van came from a flickering LED bar in the ceiling. Yasin looked around and blinked a few times, waiting for his eyes to adapt to the darkness. He heard the voices of two corrections officers chatting about baseball in thick New York accents. They were sitting on chairs bolted to the floor, their batons hanging loosely at their sides, guarding the exit from the prisoners. Yasin's eyes now fully adjusted, he decided to take stock of the other prisoners around him, knowing he might have to share a cell with one of them soon.

Directly in front of him sat a thin man with a receding hairline and wire-rimmed glasses. He was the only prisoner in the van that had been outfitted in a straitjacket. His light brown hair had grown long on the sides, but his large bare forehead reflected the LED light above him. He caught Yasin's gaze for a moment, and Yasin looked away, a shiver running down his back. *Audho billah, he looks like the devil himself. I'll remember him as Psycho.*

Beside Psycho sat a large Black man who looked like he could be a heavyweight boxer. He was asleep, and his whole body heaved whenever he took a breath. *He looks like Muhammad Ali*, Yasin thought. When he was a child in Guinea, his uncle would tell him stories about seeing Ali during his first tour in Africa. *I'll call him Stinger. Sting like a bee.*

On the other side of Psycho was another Black man, with a light brown-reddish complexion. There was a tattoo of two playing cards on his neck—a Queen of Hearts and a King of Diamonds. He was mindlessly staring at the floor, giving Yasin permission to observe him for a while. *Let's name him Red, like Malcolm.* The Autobiography of Malcolm X was the only book at Rikers that was in French.

The first person in the row opposite Yasin was near the rear, seated next to one of the officers. He was also asleep, and every now and then his head would start to dip near the knee of one of the officers. When it dipped too low, the officer would shove his knee up, into the man's drooping head, and he would wake angrily, cursing, then silently seethe until he began to doze off again. Yasin was glad not to be near him. He wouldn't want to be within striking distance if there was a real fight. *Wake up, Droopy. Watch your head.*

Next to Yasin, on his right side, was an old Latino man, with a gray beard and shaggy hair. He was sitting cross legged, and his head hung low while he rocked gently side to side, whispering softly to himself. *The Whisperer,* he thought. *Or maybe, just Whisper.* Whisper seemed to be in his own world, not a threat to anyone, almost like a homeless man on a busy street. However, from his recent experience in jail, Yasin knew that sometimes those types of people were the most dangerous, because they were the people you least suspected of anything.

And finally, the last inmate other than himself was on his left side. He was a young man, the youngest in the van, and he looked ethnically ambiguous. Yasin couldn't tell if he was Latino, Arab, or simply mixed. He had two tear drop tattoos below his right eye, the side that Yasin could see clearly. He also had a tattoo above his right eyebrow that read "krooked." Yasin smiled internally while thinking of the nickname *Typo.*

The prison van began to pick up speed, and Yasin realized that this wasn't just another facility transfer. They were on the Rikers Island Bridge. This time, it was heading off the island, three months after Yasin had been stripped away from the outside world.

Following their court convictions, Yasin and the six other prisoners in the van were now being transferred up the river to the notorious Sing Sing correctional facility. They were each sentenced for varying crimes, but all had been deemed dangerous enough to be sent to the maximum-security prison, about an hour's drive up from New York City.

Despite the conviction, Yasin knew he was innocent. He wasn't so sure about the other prisoners around him. He scanned through their faces again, looking at them one by one while he repeated their nicknames. *Psycho, Stinger, Red, Droopy, Whisper, and Typo.*

He accidentally said the last name out loud.

"You say something?" a corrections officer grunted at Yasin, his hand reaching for his baton. Yasin closed his eyes and shook his head. The officer looked at his colleague and snorted.

Just then, the van turned sharply to the right, causing Typo knees to slam into Yasin's back. The van picked up speed, jerking erratically. It continued to take off until the two officers looked at each other in alarm. Yasin watched them in panic, trying to read their faces to understand what was happening. The van must have been clocking eighty miles an hour. The officers started speaking rapidly into their radios, but the signal seemed jammed. Then, something slammed into the van's side and it jerked violently, careening off balance, and flipping three times until it landed on one side. The officers' heads slammed into the steel walls of the van and they both fell unconscious.

Yasin's side of the van had become the ceiling, and now Yasin, Typo, and Whisper, still shackled to the wall, hung a few inches suspended from the top. Yasin howled in terror as he dangled in mid-air, the smell of smoke filling his lungs. Everyone was shouting and praying to whoever they believed in. Everyone except Psycho.

Psycho began to laugh, first slowly and silently, then shrieking maniacally as the rear doors of the van were jammed open. Two men in white ski masks clawed their way in, clambering into the overturned vehicle and shoving the two unconscious officers out of the way. But with Yasin, Typo, and Whisper dangling from the ceiling, they couldn't reach Psycho. Using bolt cutters, they began to work.

Typo was cut loose first. He watched the masked men, wide-eyed for a moment, then looked down at the unconscious officers. "See ya suckas!" he shouted as he jumped out of the vehicle.

The first masked man came to cut Yasin loose next, while the second masked man went to Whisper. Whisper got loose before him. He muttered something under his breath, crawling clumsily over the unconscious officers and out of the vehicle. Yasin watched Whisper disappear, nervously excited and terrified over the prospect of freedom.

Then Yasin was finally cut loose. He fell a few feet to the bottom of the van, right on top of Stinger. He moved his hands and fingers freely with wonder. *Am I really free to go?* He tried to get up and follow the others out, when he realized that someone was holding on to him. Stinger had pincered Yasin's thigh between his thick legs and wouldn't let go.

"You're not leaving until I'm loose," Stinger grunted between gritted teeth.

With their obstacles removed, the masked men moved urgently, cutting loose the now hysterically laughing strait-jacketed Psycho; first his legs and then his hands. Then one of them held Psycho's head and shoulders and the other held him by his feet. They carried him out carefully, like movers carrying a precious piece of art, and they took him to a black Mercedes SUV, stowed him in the trunk, jumped into the back seats, and then the driver slammed the gas pedal.

Once the sound of the screeching tires faded, Yasin looked up at the menacing Stinger, who nodded towards the bolt cutters that were left behind by the masked men. Yasin gulped and tried to make a move towards it, but Stinger still held onto him.

"I'm going to get them!" Yasin pleaded. Stinger let him go, but still he glared at Yasin, the whites of his eyes glowing in the darkness of the van. Yasin crawled over on his knees and reached for the bolt cutter. With trembling hands, he grasped the tool and put all his might into cutting Stinger loose. After several immense efforts, Stinger ripped the broken shackles off and scrambled out of the van. Just as Yasin was about to follow him, Red and Droopy began to shout and beg him for help. He sat, paralyzed, weighing the situation. *Do I have to?* Seeing their desperate eyes, Yasin picked up the bolt cutters again and rushed over to cut Red loose, praying that the police wouldn't arrive before he was done. After freeing Red, he was moving over to Droopy when one of the corrections officers began to stir.

"Hurry!" Droopy shouted, noticing the officer's movements. "Cut me loose, punk!"

With fumbling fingers, Yasin managed to cut one of Droopy's hands free before the officer began to move again.

"Gimme!" Droopy screamed, yanking the bolt cutter from Yasin. He wielded it in his free hand and slammed it on the back of the officer's head, knocking him out cold once again. This time, a pool of blood began to grow on the floor of the van. Yasin shuddered at the sight of the blood and left the bolt cutters with Droopy, crawled out of the corrections van, and fell hard onto the pavement. Droopy cut his other hand loose and tumbled out next to Yasin.

"Bet you wish you didn't mess with me!" Droopy spat on the face of the officer he had struck and ran off into the night.

Yasin got up and dusted himself off. For a moment, time seemed to stand still. The street they were on was a dead end, and it was eerily quiet. There was a slight chill in the air, and nothing stirred, except for the leaves in the trees gently rolling in the silent wind. Cars of varying levels of decay were parked in front of closed mechanic shops around him, their shuttered garage doors smothered in graffiti. *Should I really run for it? What if I get caught again?*

Yasin realized that no matter what his intentions were so far, he was now considered an escaped fugitive with two badly injured officers beside him. He had already been condemned to rot for decades in a horrible prison, and if he got caught again now, nothing would change. In fact, things would probably get worse with added felonies. So he might as well try his best to escape.

He began to walk briskly off in one direction. Then he looked down at his clothing, and realized that anyone would immediately notice he had escaped from jail. All the stores would be closed at this hour, he figured, and besides, he had no money to buy anything. He looked back, and an idea came to mind. *I have no other options.*

Yasin approached the officer who was severely injured. He flipped him over softly, and saw that his clothes were stained with blood. *Not him.*

Yasin now went to the other officer. The wail of a siren knifed through the still air. Yasin's hands began to tremble again as he quickly went to work. He took a gray jacket off the officer, and began to remove the white dress shirt underneath. Deftly working through the buttons, he slipped the shirt off both of the man's arms, and used it to replace his baggy orange prison shirt. Skipping the pants, he swapped his prison-supplied sneakers with the officer's shiny loafers.

In his new outfit, Yasin ran off in the same direction toward the next street. "Steinway St." the sign read. It sounded vaguely familiar—he knew that he was somewhere in Queens. He ducked into an empty bus stop and finished buttoning up his new dress shirt. The fire truck whizzed by, making a sharp turn in front of him. Sitting extremely still, he waited for the truck to disappear, then sprinted straight down Steinway, hoping to find an area with a crowd. The street was dark and lifeless, but he was getting closer to sounds of nightlife. Finally, Steinway Street merged with Ditmars Boulevard, and he found throngs of people strolling along, and he slowed his pace down to match them.

Yasin gradually caught his breath and tried to blend in. His crisp white officer shirt was clearly mismatched with his baggy orange jail pants, but people around him didn't seem to notice. They were coming out of bars, eating gelato on benches, and dining in quaint outdoor seating arrangements. They were living life, carefree.

Yasin's eyes glazed over as he witnessed the scene. A Mexican restaurant had live music playing. Outside an Egyptian restaurant, a middle-aged man was speaking animatedly—he was holding up a phone on video call. An Albanian club played techno music, with two tall pale men, crisply dressed, guarding the doors.

After a few minutes, Ditmars met another busy street: 31st Street. Looking left, he immediately recognized the subway sign that told him the name of the stop: Astoria-Ditmars Blvd. *Should I take the subway?*

As he weighed this thought, a gang of police officers appeared by the station, running up the subway steps. "This station is closed!" they shouted, barring people from going up. "This station is shut down!"

Yasin was about to cross the street when a police cruiser swerved in front of him, barreling towards the subway station. In desperation, he turned back and pushed his way into a small crowd of people on the sidewalk and stood still, staring at the floor. After a moment, he looked up and realized that he had accidentally gotten in line at a halal food truck.

"Habibi, for you," Yasin heard. He looked up to see the kind face of an Arab man in his fifties, with his hand outstretched. In his gloved fingers, a warm piece of falafel was extended. Yasin shook his head no.

"I don't have any money, brother," he said.

The man's smile stayed. "Don't matter," he replied. "Just take."

Yasin again shook his head no, but a young woman next to him spoke up. "He gives them to everyone," she said. "Just take it."

Yasin's mouth watered as the savory aroma of the falafel penetrated his nostrils. He hadn't eaten anything enjoyable in months, ever since entering Rikers. *Fine, I'll take it.*

Yasin reached forward and took the falafel from the man. He held it to his lips, and smelled it tenderly. *I'm never going back to those moldy salami sandwiches.* The purportedly halal options at Rikers had given him food poisoning on more than one occasion. He took a small bite of the falafel and steam emerged from inside. The falafel was crispy on the outside, and pillowy on the inside, with a hint of spice.

The Arab man in the cart smiled with satisfaction. "Habibi," he said, "Ramadan Kareem!"

Yasin looked up at the dark sky and noticed a fledgling crescent moon, peeking behind the translucent clouds.

Chapter 2: Saif

At Madison Square Garden, the graduates of the NYPD's Police Academy marched in single-file formation to chairs set up on the massive hardwood floor. Once the class of 583 graduates had taken their seats, the police band marched in, filling the stage. They played patriotic songs like The Star-Spangled Banner, Amazing Grace and America the Beautiful. When they finished, the NYPD Police commissioner, followed by her deputy commissioners and other NYPD leadership, took their seats on the stage.

Saif watched quietly, his eyes large and bright, soaking in the atmosphere. Less than a year ago, he was sitting at home—a college dropout and hopelessly unemployed. Now, he was officially being inducted as one of New York's finest. He looked up at the stands to see his mother but it was too dark to make out faces.

The commissioner rose, and Saif quickly scrambled up as well, along with all the new officers. The commissioner stood at a wooden podium emblazoned with the logo of the NYPD, her deputies seated on either side of her. She tapped on the microphone to make sure it was on.

"Let's give our band another round of applause." The commissioner paused, and the arena thundered with vigorous claps. The new officers also clapped, straight-faced, evenly and in unison. At the sign of their senior officer, they halted.

The commissioner continued. "And now, we invite Officer Chen, for the singing of the national anthem."

"Att-en-tion!"

Three senior officers in full uniform, carrying the flags of the United States, New York City, and the NYPD, in order, marched in. They were bookended by soldiers carrying official NYPD-issued rifles. Then, the young Officer Chen marched in, a solemn look on his hairless face, and he approached the podium.

"Pre-sent All!"

Every police officer in the room, including the new recruits, whipped their arms up, placing their right hands beside their heads in a salute. Officer Chen immediately began to sing, quite beautifully, his body standing firmly still, but his mouth moving animatedly with the words.

When he finished, the officers relaxed their hands to their sides. The audience, made up of friends and family of the new officers, clapped and whistled passionately.

The commissioner next announced that the graduates would be taking their oaths to officially become NYPD Police Officers. They chanted the oath in unison, repeating sentence after sentence with the commissioner, their voices echoing in the arena every time it was their turn to speak. Saif spoke firmly and loudly. His mind flashed back to his training, and he felt proud of himself for completing the brief yet rigorous police academy.

But as Saif chanted the oath, he was internally in turmoil. He had grown up hating the NYPD. Throughout his childhood, Saif and his friends had disrespected police officers at every turn, cursing at 'the pigs' in their neighborhoods and on their streets, seeing cops as bullies, racists, and thugs. He was consciously aware of this tension within him, but he didn't dare to let his mind linger on it. He focused his mind on the words they were saying and reassured himself that he was free to evolve as a person, and his past didn't have to dictate his future.

"So help me God," the new officers concluded. It was time to walk the stage.

The newly minted officers stood in front of their seats, waiting patiently as line by line went forward to the foot of the stage. Saif was in the third row. When it was their turn, his heart suddenly raced, as it did when he knew people would be looking at him. He let his muscle memory lead him, marching perfectly in form when the third row began to move. He wanted to look up for his mother, but his head stayed perfectly straight.

"Saif Belkacem."

Saif stepped forward onto the stage and marched towards the middle. He posed with the commissioner, each of them holding half of his certificate, took the commissioner's hand into his own white-gloved one in a firm handshake, and then marched off the stage. As he wound his way back around to his seat, he looked up, and locked eyes with his mother for the first time, who smiled tearfully down at him. His heart softened, and he remembered why he was doing this all in the first place.

After two-year-old Saif's father died, his mother moved them from Algeria to New York City. Over the years, she worked tirelessly to provide for him, working two minimum wage jobs while he went to school. In his childhood mind, he was going to one day go to college, get a good job, and retire her for good. But after a year and a half at Queens College, he lost his financial aid due to poor performance, and his self-respect started to chip away day after day of watching his mom go to work while he sent online job applications into the void. Enough had been enough. With his new police officer starting salary of sixty thousand dollars, he was finally going to be able to help cover the bills, and hopefully, allow her to retire from work.

Once all the new officers had received their certificates and taken their seats, the band started playing again. Confetti fell from the ceiling, in colors red white and blue. Saif smiled around at his fellow new officers and admired the show. He looked up again at his mother, who waved back at him.

When the band concluded their song, the mayor arrived and took to the stage. The crowd began to cheer loudly as he approached the podium. He smiled broadly at the new officers, having been a police captain once himself, and sighed in reminiscence after taking the microphone.

"I remember when I was in your shoes," he began, "young and hungry to make a difference in the community.

I congratulate you today, and I am grateful to have New York's best and brightest working to defend our city."

Saif smiled and applauded with the others. It felt good being called one of the 'best and brightest'.

The mayor continued. "As I have said time and time again, my priority as mayor is ensuring the safety of our citizens, and I am investing heavily into bulking up our city's police department, in your numbers as well as your resources. Put simply, we need more cops, such as yourselves, and I applaud you for stepping up to our city's needs." The audience cheered, and several deputy commissioners nodded in approval.

The last bits of confetti fell, and Saif brushed a few pieces off of his lap.

"This is the greatest city in the world, and our safety is key to our greatness. In these times of social media virality and social justice causes, there will be more scrutiny on you than ever before. You must exercise the utmost discipline, and your loyalty must be unwavering and unquestioning."

The mood became serious, and the new officers nodded solemnly.

"But don't forget that millions of New Yorkers see you as their heroes, and have deep respect for their police force. Do not let the voices of a few color your perception of many."

There was a smattering of claps among the audience. While Saif glanced back at his mother, a tall man with a bushy gray mustache entered the stadium, briskly walking toward the stage. The officer guarding the stage moved to block his way. The mustached officer bent forward and whispered into his ear, then walked onto the stage, heading directly to the seated NYPD commissioner. In the meantime, the mayor continued to speak.

"No doubt there will be many celebrations today, and for good reason, as there is much to celebrate. I will just leave you with one parting message, and one parting gift."

The mustached officer was speaking rapidly in the ear of the NYPD commissioner, and her eyes were growing larger as he spoke. Suddenly, she rose.

She whispered something, and then the mayor turned back mid-speech. *We have a situation.* She mouthed these last words, but Saif was sitting close enough to read them on her lips.

"Okay, let me wrap it up," the mayor said in a low voice to her, but the microphone caught some of it and everyone heard. The commissioner rose to stand near him as he concluded his speech. By now the whole arena's eyes were on her, not the mayor.

"Congratulations again, and I leave the floor to your commissioner." The mayor concluded early, and he took his designated seat on the stage.

The arena fell silent after a brief applause. Then the commissioner spoke.

"A recent development has come to my attention." She paused and took a breath. "Due to the gravity of the situation it is important that I address it here, and then we will have to immediately take action." She spoke carefully and slowly, despite the urgency in her words. "In the early hours of this morning, around 12:13 AM, a transportation van leaving Rikers Island was hijacked with seven convicts on board. They were on their way to be imprisoned at the Sing Sing Correctional Facility in Ossining, New York State. Two correctional officers were attacked and the seven convicts have all escaped custody."

The crowd collectively drew their breath, and the sound of this raised the hairs on Saif's arms.

"What I've said to you now has been highly confidential information unreleased to the public. Unfortunately, against our best efforts, I've just learned that news of the escape was leaked to the media. This means we will have to conclude our graduation early—and postpone any planned festivities."

The crowd was stunned. Then, the part of the arena with family and friends of the graduating officers hummed with hushed whispers. The new officers looked around at each other with startled expressions. This was not how they expected their graduation to go.

"The last thing I will say to you all," the commissioner continued, "is that in the attack, two officers, such as yourselves, were harmed, and—" her usually solid voice cracked at this point, "—and one officer has succumbed to his injuries." The grieving commissioner steeled her face and set her eyes on the graduating class of police. "Today is a firm reminder of the danger that is associated with your jobs, and also a reminder, that this is a fight between good and evil, and your first order, as of today, is to find the criminals who have killed your brethren, and leave no stone unturned until justice is served."

Every officer in the building, from Saif and his fellow graduates, to the most senior deputies, stood up instantly, whipping their hands to their heads in a solemn salute. "Understood!" They barked, their voices echoing through-out the arena.

Chapter 3: Yasin

The train station crawled with cops. Sirens wailed from every direction. It was nearly two in the morning, and the streets were becoming emptier. Yasin quickly backed into a nearby donut store to take cover.

"We're closed, sir," a familiar voice called out from behind him.

Yasin whipped around and saw Stinger, wearing a mint green apron that was far too small on him. He was wiping down the counter with a wet towel when he froze.

"Whose apron is that–" Yasin asked.

"Shhhh!" Stinger hissed, ducking behind the donut display. Yasin ran around the counter and squatted next to Stinger.

"What are you doing here?!" Stinger growled.

"I should ask you the same thing," Yasin said. "What poor person did you attack to get that uniform?"

"Says the guy wearing shiny police shoes," Stinger snapped. His anger was hard to take seriously alongside the apron that barely covered half of his chest. "Listen, you need to get out of here, as far away as you can."

"I know, I'm not dumb," Yasin shot back. "Have you seen the cops out there?"

Just then, the door swung open, and they heard the sound of footsteps. "Hello?" a young voice rang. Stinger clasped his thick hand on Yasin's face, smothering his breathing. After a moment, the girl asked again, "Anyone there?"

Then, they heard her light footsteps again, and the door opened once more. Yasin ripped Stinger's hand off his face and took a much-needed gasp of air.

"Listen, take the bus, it should still be running. Get out of Queens as fast as you can. And cover your face— here's a mask," Stinger said, taking a blue cloth face mask out of a dusty box that looked like it hadn't been used in years.

Yasin took the mask and prepared to leave. "All right, thanks—"

"Wait!" Stinger hissed. "What happened after I left?"

"Everyone forced me to free them." Stinger nodded. "Droopy, I mean, the guy next to you who kept falling asleep, he hit one of the officers," Yasin continued. "He was bleeding too much."

"How bad?" Stinger asked. "Like about to die bad?"

"Maybe," Yasin shrugged.

"That's not good. If he dies, the cops will be after us for revenge. And all of us could be charged with his mur-der."

Yasin gulped. He knew he was innocent of the crime that put him in Rikers, but could he be guilty of this other very real crime? He recalled that it was he who had given Droopy the murder weapon.

"By the way, this guy who hit the cop, he's going to be looking for you," Stinger warned. "If he realizes that the officer he attacked died, and you were the only witness, he'll try to kill you too."

Yasin felt his stomach churn and took a deep breath. "Okay, I'm leaving now," he whispered, and dashed out from behind the counter. He took a side exit that led onto a quiet dark street. He smoothed his white dress shirt as he walked and ran a hand over his messy beard. Going into Rikers he had hardly any hair on his face, as he usually kept just a thin line of hair along his jaw. Now, he had patches of hair growing all over his face. He knew its appearance could ring alarm bells. He put on the musty mask Stinger gave him.

Down and down the road he walked, and he kept his eyes peeled for a bus stop. The streets were dark and empty, but he took extra steps to avoid street-lamps and stay in the shadows. He came up on a park, where a few people were hanging out. He crossed the street. Behind the park, he could see the blue light of a bus stop, with a crowd of people around it. *How could it be so busy at this time?* Walking up to the bus stop slowly now, he tried to act cool. *I'm just like anyone else, juuust trying to get home.*

When he arrived at the bus stop, he could see the train station a few streets away on a raised platform, as the stations often were structured in Queens. On top of the platform, armed police were gathered, speaking to each other and keeping watch below. Yasin fixed his gaze on the floor, not daring to look up at them.

"What's going on?" a raspy female voice said. "I was on the train and then they kicked us off and said there was a security situation."

"I was not about to wait around to find out," a woman replied impatiently. "Where is this bus at?"

"I heard it was a criminal on the loose," a teenage boy piped up. "They were definitely looking for someone at least," he added, seeing unconvinced faces around him.

"This bus better hurry up," the second woman said. "And I'm not paying for it, I already tapped for the subway."

After a few minutes of silence, the M60 bus arrived at the bus stop, and the people in line smothered the entrance. Although the bus was nearly empty, the waiting crowd was so large Yasin worried if he'd be able to fit in. He fought his way into the thick mass of people.

"Pay to ride!" the driver shouted, confused at the size of the crowd at this time of night.

"We're not paying again!" a woman shouted, and others muttered in approval.

"They just kicked us off the train," another man grumbled. The driver sighed and made a wave with his hand as if to signal everyone on.

"Just pack into the back, don't leave any space until everyone is on," he called out.

Yasin found himself a seat near the middle of the bus, snugly fit between two older women. There was a man with a sleepy young boy standing right in front of him, holding the bar with one hand and trying to keep his son between his legs with the other. Yasin felt bad for the young father and offered him to take his seat. The father looked grateful and nodded. He raised his son onto the open seat. Yasin stood beside the father and held the bar as the bus sped up. He prayed silently that it would go far from where they were. When he opened his eyes, he saw the bus had merged onto the highway, leaving Queens for Manhattan. He took a deep breath with his eyes closed and thanked God, knowing he would be putting a river between himself and the massive number of cops now swarming through the area.

The bus's first stop in Manhattan was on 125th and 1st Avenue, on the east side of Harlem. Yasin was elated. Before his arrest, he used to live in Harlem. He knew the streets as well as any cab driver, especially 125th Street, where he used to sell trinkets and counterfeit bags to pedestrians.

The bus continued to make stops all along the breadth of 125th Street, and Yasin thought about where he wanted to get off. He figured a bus stop positioned at a distance from the train stations would be best, guessing that the cops could be monitoring the subway entrances, if not now then soon. He decided to get off at Eighth Avenue, knowing he could walk straight to his old apartment on 144th Street from there. He wondered how his old roommates were doing, though to be fair, calling them roommates was a stretch. They rarely saw each other, spending most of their waking moments outside working. But still, he hoped they were doing well, and knew that at this late hour, nearly everyone should be home.

He walked briskly from the bus stop to the apartment, an eerie feeling overcoming him as he crossed the familiar streets. Before being arrested, he never would have predicted that the sequence of events that followed could happen. He was an undocumented immigrant, yes, but he had never committed a serious crime. He had never done drugs, let alone sold them. The major drug trafficking violation he was convicted of, he never could have expected.

As he skipped up the front doorsteps, he heard noise inside. It was now nearly four in the morning. *What are they up to in there?* His hands casually reached for the doorknob, unconsciously knowing the door would be unlocked, like it always was. But to his surprise, the knob didn't twist. He pulled down his mask and raised his fist. *Knock knock.*

Yasin heard feet shuffling, and the door swung open.

"Yasin? What are you doing here?"

"Suleyman!" Yasin cried, running up to hug him.

"Yasin is back!" someone called out from inside the two-bedroom apartment. Yasin walked in with Suleyman and found the other four roommates seated on the ground on a plastic sheet. Several plates were arranged around to share. They were having Suhoor, the pre-dawn meal before the first day of Ramadan fasting began.

"Yasin, sit down, eat with us," Amadou gestured, grinning ear to ear. Feeling ravenous, Yasin grabbed a whole boiled egg and bit into it head first, while the others watched him in disbelief.

"How are you, my brother? We've missed you," Amadou said. "The last thing I heard is you were…" and he trailed off.

"Convicted and sentenced to twenty years in prison," Yasin finished the sentence. "Where should I begin?"

Everyone leaned in. Yasin recounted the events of the night, from the attack on the van, to the masked men who saved Psycho, the freeing of the other inmates, and the bloodied officer. With each development, the group reacted with increasing astonishment.

"I still don't understand why they arrested you in the first place," Amadou said finally. "We all know—" and he looked around for approval, "Yasin is as clean as they come. You are our big brother, our role model," he said, looking at Yasin.

Yasin sighed. "I am just as confused as you are, my brother. All I remember is I was selling my things at my usual spot next to the 4-5-6 train, 125th and Lex, when Suleyman came by," Yasin recounted, waving a hand in Suleyman's direction. "Suleyman was watching for cops and he came running to tell me the police were doing sweeps. I quickly wrapped up my things and ran, and the police chased me down to the subway. They took everything and handcuffed me while they looked through everything. Then suddenly they started shouting and more cops came down. I couldn't see clearly but it sounded like they found something in my bag. I was thrown in a car and taken to a local jail, and then the next day they sent me to Rikers for three months—the worst three months of my life." He shuddered, recalling the filthy prison cell, the scary inmates he had to deal with, the disgusting food, and more things he didn't wish to remember.

"What was it, that they found?" Suleyman asked. "Drugs?"

"Yes, drugs," Yasin continued. "I have no idea how it got in my bag. They said they found fentanyl pills, almost five pounds. During my trial, the police said the pills are connected to a gang in the Bronx. They accused me of being connected to their gang."

"Did you have a lawyer?" Amadou asked.

"The city gave me a free lawyer. We denied everything of course, but the useless lawyer did not fight for me."

"That's crazy," Suleyman said. "Do you think the police planted the drugs on you?"

Yasin hadn't thought about the possibility of being framed, but couldn't rule it out.

"I don't know, maybe," he said. "But that is the least of my concerns now. The cops are going to search every inch of this city looking for me. And I have nowhere to go."

The men finished their meal in silence, and then Amadou announced that time to stop eating had come, and their sixteen hour fast had begun.

They rose to prepare for prayers at the nearby mosque. "Yasin, you better stay here," Amadou warned. Yasin nodded and sat down again. Then Amadou came closer to him.

"Yasin, how is your family doing?" he asked in a quiet voice. "Your wife and your son? Are they able to survive?"

Yasin's eyes fell. "My wife's brother is doing what he can to help. But he has his own family as well. I don't know what to do." His voice cracked as he spoke.

Amadou put his hand on Yasin's shoulder. "Trust in Allah my brother. He will make a way out for you, in sha Allah." He pulled Yasin in for an embrace, and then quietly left the apartment, glancing back to meet Yasin's watery eyes as he exited.

Once they all left, the apartment felt extremely quiet. Suddenly, Suleyman came back in.

"Yasin," he said. "I don't think it's safe for you to be here. The cops might come looking for you. You know, they came here a few days after they arrested you. They asked us about you."

Yasin's sense of safety evaporated.

"What did you tell them?" Yasin asked.

"We told them the truth of course, that you're inno-cent. But anyway, you should leave. Go as far away from here as possible. You should leave the country if you can." Suleyman pulled out his wallet now and began to pluck out bills. He counted a hundred dollars in twenties and walked over to Yasin. "Listen, take this, buy a bus ticket, go to Canada, and don't look back."

Yasin furrowed his eyebrows. "What do you mean, 'go to Canada'?" he repeated. "How will I get over the border? I don't have papers, or have you forgotten? You're the only one out of all of us who does, since you got married to that Teresa. And we all know you married her for the papers."

Suleyman towered over the sitting Yasin, anger flashing over his face. "Don't you dare bring up my Teresa. My green card is arriving soon, and you will not ruin this for me. I don't want anything to do with you, felon. Get out of the apartment and don't come back!" Suleyman stormed out and the door slammed shut with a bang.

Yasin was now, effectively, homeless.

Chapter 4: Saif

Saif clocked in at the Queens 114th precinct for his first day as an officer. It was six in the morning, the day after graduation. He knew it wasn't going to be the typical cop's first day.

The other new recruits were huddled up in the center of the office. An administrator directed Saif to join them. "Your orientation will be in conference room two in ten minutes," she said.

Saif looked around at the other recruits who were assigned to his new precinct. He was lucky to get his first choice in Astoria. It was only a short walk from the apartment he and his mom shared on Steinway Street.

Jessica, Elias, Justin, I don't know, I don't know, Emmanuel, Rachel…and I think that's Yaakov. In all, they were nine new officers at the 114th precinct. It was not typically a busy precinct, and nine was a smaller class than many others. But the 114th precinct was extra full this day because many senior officers had been relocated to create a special task force to find the escaped fugitives.

"We're moving to conference room four," the officer leading their orientation announced, as he nudged his way through the traffic to where the new officers were seated. "I've never seen this place so full. Follow me," he said. He walked in another direction, carrying a cup of black coffee so full that it looked like it was going to spill. They stopped in front of a small conference room without enough chairs for the group.

"Let's do a standing orientation," the officer said, and instructed them to remove all chairs from the small room.

"Good morning!" He started over, speaking in a dull voice. "My name is Captain Mancini of the 114th precinct, and I am leading your orientation today. On behalf of the NYPD, I'd like to welcome you to your new home." He paused, and became energized again, like he had gotten the boring part out of the way.

"Now, this isn't any old average day at the 114. You have been selected to represent the very precinct where the biggest jail escape in decades has taken place. That means you have the chance to make a name for yourselves by playing a role in finding these criminals." Captain Mancini's small black eyes sparkled as he spoke. "I would have done anything to be in your position as a fresh recruit…" he trailed off.

"Anyway, back to your orders for today. You will be placed on patrol duty at several major intersections in Astoria. Stay at your posts and do not move. Major Cases has shut down the area north of Ditmars Boulevard. The FED is already taking positions all over the city—"

"Captain, the Feds are involved?" Yaakov butted in.

"No, not the Feds, the FED: The Fugitive Enforcement Division. They have multiple units all over the city, and the North Queens unit is actively investigating already."

Yaakov nodded deferentially.

"The Feds will probably be called in too if we don't catch these maniacs soon," Captain Mancini continued. "Everyone is trying to get a piece of this pie. But remember, if you see any signs of the missing fugitives, you are to alert me immediately."

"Yes sir!"

"Your first assignments will be automatically emailed to you momentarily," Captain Mancini concluded. "Check in with the tech department to pick up your computers, and you will find your new email addresses set up for you."

The new officers walked out in a single file line. Saif found himself leading the group. He walked through the now even busier precinct to the far end, near the evidence lockers. It was there that unused tech was stored.

"Can I help you guys?" a bald man with round glasses looked up from his computer, seeing the young group. "Ah yes, new recruits?" Saif nodded to the man, who was treating him like the leader of the group. The man closed his laptop and took it under his arm. "Follow me," he said.

Saif walked forward first and the rest of the new officers followed him. They went into a large dark storage area with dozens of locked cabinets stacked high around the edges of the room. The bald tech manager stopped in front of one of the cabinets and began sifting through his keys, trying one occasionally until one of them turned.

"Here we go," he said to himself, opening it all the way to reveal rows and rows of laptops standing sideways, plugged in to charge. He set his own laptop down on a nearby table and began to unplug and lift out computers one at a time, stacking them neatly on the table. After a while he counted out the number of laptops he took out and looked up, counting the number of new officers. "One too many," he mumbled to himself, and he put one of the laptops back in, then closed and locked the cabinet.

"One for each of you," he said, "and don't take any extra or I'll call the cops."

Saif found the joke so unfunny that he nearly burst out laughing.

"No need to laugh, I know I'm hilarious," the man said, raising his hands in defeat. The new officers smiled kindly to reduce the awkwardness in the room.

"Now, when you open your computers, you will be prompted to make a secure username and password. You will use the same details to join our email system. If you have any issues, I am always available for trouble-shooting. Even though I'm not legally allowed to carry." He made finger guns when he said the word shooting.

"Good one," Saif said encouragingly.

Saif took his computer and went back out into the crowded office. The desks all full, he went into the break room and sat on a round table, empty except for some mugs half-filled with last night's coffee. *Easy enough*, he thought as he set up his computer. Several emails were already waiting in his inbox. He scanned through them for anything about his first day's assignment. Then he saw:

NEW OFFICERS: DAY 1 ORIENTATION

Saif clicked on the email from the Captain and looked for his name. *Saif Belkacem & Elias Dimas - Steinway and 30th Ave.* He instantly knew the block that he was assigned. In fact, he lived right around there. Saif looked up to see if he could see Elias, who he was partnered with, but couldn't. He closed his laptop and went to look for him.

Elias was standing against the wall trying to balance his laptop on one hand and type with the other. "Did you see? We're on patrol duty together," Saif informed him.

"Nice!" Elias smiled. Though they knew each other from high school before starting at the police academy, Elias mostly had hung out with the Greek kids while Saif hung out with the Algerians and Moroccans. But during the police academy they had been some of the only recruits from Astoria, and they both had wanted to be stationed near home after graduation.

"Let's go sit down," Saif said, seeing Elias struggling to type. Some seats had opened up since many of the task forces had already deployed.

At that moment, the NYPD commissioner strode into the precinct, two aides at her side. The whole building became silent.

"Everything ready?" she looked at Captain Mancini, who hurriedly came to her side.

"Yes, commissioner, the presentation is prepared," he said.

At the push of a button, a projector screen began to descend at the front of the room. The local NYPD officers who remained turned toward it expectantly. The commissioner flipped through some pages on a clipboard that she was handed by Captain Mancini.

"In about an hour and a half, details of the escape will be broadcasted on all major news channels in the city. We have dispatched the names and photos of the seven fugitives to local affiliates of CBS, NBC, FOX, and ABC. The New York Times and New York Post are publishing our press release at exactly seven AM. I will be leading a live press conference at One Police Plaza alongside the mayor at eight o'clock." She said this all breathlessly, so fast that Saif barely had time to digest the words. "This precinct is the closest one to where the escape occurred. We are taking steps to ensure that each NYPD officer here is intimately familiar with the details of the case, so that you may capture them as quickly as possible."

The commissioner detailed all that was known about the escape, then clicked to a new slide. On the screen, seven photos now appeared, and with a second click, names appeared below them. There were three profiles arranged in two rows, and one profile at the bottom, with a short description under each name.

"First, we have the most dangerous of them all: Stephen Hoffmeyer, convicted of blowing up a low-income healthcare clinic in Jamaica, Queens. Hoffmeyer was charged with multiple counts of first-degree murder, conspiracy, use of explosives, and his attack killed eleven people and injured twenty-four others; he was set to serve eight life sentences at Sing Sing Correctional Facility. We believe that the recent escape was orchestrated by Hoffmeyer and his associates, as he is the most high profile case on our list."

Saif looked at Hoffmeyer's photo and shivered. Stephen Hoffmeyer's thin lips were spread in a wide smile in his mug shot, but his eyes were flat and dark. His forehead was riddled with red acne, going all the way back his receded hairline.

"Next up," the commissioner continued, moving a pointer to the next photo, "we have Amir Johnson Jr., convicted of multiple counts of armed robbery and assault." Saif moved his eyes to the Black man in the second photo. He had a large head and a broad neck. "He was set to serve twenty-five to life at Sing Sing."

Everyone shifted their attention to the third photo, of another Black man with a reddish-blond patch on his afro. He stared angrily in his mugshot. "This is Terrence Howard. He was set to serve one life sentence for the murder of his girlfriend in Brooklyn last year." Saif saw what looked like two red playing cards tattooed on his neck.

"In the next row, we have Derek Mahan, charged with multiple drug offenses and assault of a police officer. He was set to serve seventeen years." Saif thought Derek looked like someone he went to school with. In his mugshot, he seemed sleepy, his eyes barely open.

The commissioner moved the pointer to an older Hispanic man in the middle of the second row. "Luis Almanzar, set to serve fifteen years for repeated attempted sexual assault in public areas. He has been in and out of prison for a few decades now. His file also has records of being held in mental health facilities." Luis looked unstable, carrying a scraggly beard and staring with an unfixed gaze.

"This is Malik Clark, who was picked up after a string of bank robberies across The Bronx. He was set to serve eight years, with the chance to get just three years if he cooperated with us in capturing the rest of his accomplices, but quite frustratingly he refused to speak." Saif thought Malik looked like the youngest fugitive yet. *I could catch this clown myself.* Malik even had a goofy tattoo over his eyebrow—he had misspelled crooked as krooked.

Now, Saif's eyes moved towards the last fugitive, which was confusing because the name below the photo had a question mark beside it.

"This is, we believe, Yasin Bamba," the commissioner said hesitantly. "We don't have much information about him, due to his illegal migrant status. He is estimated to be around forty years of age, of medium height, originally from the west African country of Guinea. He was picked up for drug trafficking charges in Harlem while running an illegal stall on 125th street. In his merchandise we found five pounds of fentanyl pills. His sentence was elevated to twenty years once we found a link between the pills and a drug bust last month on 145th street. Some of you may be familiar with that case."

Saif looked at the photo, seeing the fear in Yasin's large eyes. *Just couldn't help yourself, could you?* Saif thought. He usually had sympathy for migrants in New York City, technically being an immigrant himself, but that sympathy went out the window when people broke the law.

"You all have been sent emails with this presentation," the commissioner concluded. "Your local police chief will give you further instructions." She handed her bundle of papers to Captain Mancini and left promptly with her aides for her press conference at HQ.

The precinct prompt cleared up. Captain Mancini reappeared from his office to find the rookies seated at a few desks.

"You all by now have received your assignments for the day. Along with monitoring your street for the fugitives, you will be tasked with placing flyers of those seven men throughout your area." He gestured towards a huge stack of one-page prints on a table. "Take some and leave immediately for your assignments."

Saif and Elias were soon walking a few blocks over to their post at Steinway and 30th Avenue. It was a brisk ten minute walk from the precinct. At five minutes to seven in the morning, the street hadn't quite woken up yet. Empty coffee cups and takeout food boxes collected in nooks and corners where the wind had swept them.

"Have you been there before?" Elias asked him, pointing at the darkened sign of a popular shawarma spot they had just passed. Saif nodded.

"Yeah, it's pretty good. But that one over there—" he pointed ahead, "is more worth it for the money." Elias looked where Saif pointed, mentally taking note.

"Hey, shouldn't we start sticking these on the wall?" Saif suggested. The two officers began taping the flyers with faces of the seven fugitives on street-lamps, bus stops, and telephone poles along their way. The big fearful eyes of Yasin began to burn into Saif's mind; the more he stared at them the more he wondered who this man was, and what led him down a path of crime.

They soon reached their post and did a quick visual sweep. Saif scanned around for anything suspicious. The few people outside seemed to be early morning commuters headed to work. None of them seem prepared for what was about to become breaking news.

Chapter 5: Yasin

Pink sunlight shone through the broken blinds when Amadou and the other roommates returned to their apartment. Amadou found a scrawled note on his pillow from Yasin.

> *Amadou, I apologize in advance for taking your clothes. Suleyman said the police might come so I had to leave quickly. Please get rid of my old clothes and keep my return a secret. I don't know if I will see you again my brother. Stay safe and don't worry about me.*

Amadou found Yasin's old clothes lying in the corner in a heap. While he began to tear up the note Yasin left him, he heard loud banging on the front door.

"Police, open up!"

Amadou scrambled to his feet, putting the paper shreds in his pocket. He searched wildly around for a way to hide Yasin's clothes. Commotion ensued in the living room when the other roommates, who were all undocumented immigrants themselves, ran for cover. Amadou grabbed Yasin's pants, shirt, and shiny black shoes and threw them into his dirty laundry basket.

"We're not here to arrest anyone," a police officer announced, kicking down the door of the apartment. A police hound led the way for two armed officers. "We are looking for a fugitive. Someone who used to live at this address."

Amadou found his roommates backed up against the wall, staring with terror at the wolf-like dog in their apartment.

"What is this about?" Amadou feigned ignorance.

The police officer with the dog struggled to maintain a hold on the leash.

"We are looking for the man in this picture, Yasin Bamba," the first officer shouted over the din of the dog's barks. Amadou squinted, as if the chaotic sounds of the room obstructed his vision. "We know he used to live here."

"I haven't seen him," Amadou shook his head.

"Has anyone here seen this man recently?" the officer looked around.

The men shook their heads violently.

The officer sighed. "Listen up, I know some of you guys don't have your papers. But this is a serious investigation, and if you cooperate with us, we will not take any action against your status here. If you see this man, you must alert us immediately. We have all your information, and we can inform ICE about your whereabouts should you choose not to cooperate."

"We will cooperate to the best of our ability, sir," Suleyman promised.

"Good. We are located at the 32nd precinct on 135th street. And remember, harboring a fugitive will get you not just deported, but thrown in prison for a long, long time." The two officers and their dog left the apartment. The men on the wall collapsed onto the ground, too stressed to worry about the mess the police had made in their home.

"That damn Yasin," Suleyman muttered through gritted teeth. "I will not let him ruin my path to citizenship."

Amadou looked at Suleyman helplessly, wondering what Yasin would do now.

Yasin was tired. He hadn't slept in nearly twenty-four hours, but he had nowhere to go. In his traditional clothes, borrowed from Amadou, he fit in the neighborhood quite nicely. As Yasin walked along 145th street, he saw men in religious attire, heading home after Fajr. Since he didn't pray Fajr yet himself, he decided to find a mosque.

After walking up a flight of broad stairs, he entered a brownstone home that had been converted into a mosque. The building was nearly empty now with only a few men left inside, seated on the floor hunched over copies of the Quran, their soft voices filling the room with a calming hum. Yasin went to the bathroom and washed up. He rubbed the dust and grime that had collected on his hands and arms during the night, then washed his face, the cold water refreshing on his eyelids. He took off the sandals he had taken from Amadou and rinsed his feet thoroughly with soap. He had a vivid flashback to Rikers, when he had his prison-issued sandals stolen by another inmate and had to walk on the filthy floor of the shower rooms, and his mouth screwed up in visceral disgust.

Alhamdulillah, I am out of there, he thanked God. Despite how worried he was about getting caught again, this moment of freedom was enough reason to be grateful.

Re-entering the mosque's prayer room, Yasin stood at the front and prayed Fajr alone. He entered a place of calm and peace as he recited verses of the Quran to himself, relishing the atmosphere. Then he progressed to the phase of prayer where he bowed his head on the ground. While letting gravity draw his forehead into the plush carpet, he felt utterly powerless, and tears came to his eyes.

Allah, I need your help. I don't know what to do. I know I haven't always made the best decisions, but please, help me, take care of me, protect me. I have hope in nothing and no one but You. You are capable of everything. Please, give me a way out of my situation, and guide me forward.

He finally raised his head and continued his prayer, making no effort to wipe his tears, while they slid slowly down his cheeks and disappeared under his chin.

After prayer, he found himself having the whole mosque to himself. He felt his eyes trying to close in tiredness and drew himself against a wall. There, he allowed his eyes to rest, and wound up sleeping for several hours, until two men entered the mosque for afternoon prayers.

"I told him, if he doesn't want to work, let me use his account!" one man complained. "What good is his account if nobody is using it?"

"ICE is looking for him, brother, wouldn't you hide too?"

Yasin's ears perked up. He could understand some of the words that the men spoke, but it wasn't his mother tongue.

"Brother, if I'm on my bike doing deliveries, how will they get me? I would rather be mobile rather than just hide in one place."

"What if the phone can track his whereabouts?"

"How will they know which account he is using? All of us are using fake names in the first place!"

"Hmm, maybe you're right."

The men sat down and nodded in acknowledgment to Yasin, who was watching them. They were young men, maybe in their late twenties, and they each carried a large square bag, brightly colored and emblazoned with a delivery app logo. One of them pulled a charger out of his pocket and dragged himself on his knees to an outlet, then plugged his phone in.

"Scary times we're in, scary times," he murmured to himself. The first man got up and prayed quietly by himself, as he awaited the congregational prayer.

More men began to filter in, and soon the call to prayer was made. Yasin looked around but didn't recognize anyone from when he used to live in the area. He had walked down to central Harlem, and the neighborhood here was populated with immigrants from Senegal. Though there were many similarities between the Senegalese and Guineans, Yasin could tell by small differences in their clothing, their language, and their towering height that they were not Guinean.

After prayer, Yasin approached one of the men he had overheard earlier.

"Assalamu alaikum," he said. "I was wondering how I could become a delivery driver. I'm sorry but I heard you saying something about using fake accounts. I don't have papers so I was wondering if you could help me do the same."

The man looked for his friend from earlier and then looked back at Yasin.

"I don't know. Maybe my friend Idris can help you." The man saw his friend and beckoned for him to come. Idris approached them with a curious look on his face.

"My brother, what's going on?" Idris asked.

"He wants to do delivery," the first man replied.

Idris looked at Yasin up and down for a moment and understood his situation.

"I guess you just got here and you're looking for work. We have a man we work with. His name is Guillermo. I can connect you with him."

"That would be much appreciated, brother," Yasin said. "Where is this Guillermo located?"

"He's usually in Chinatown. There's a mosque nearby there, where we all hang out. Come with us tonight and we'll take you to him."

Yasin was concerned when he heard Chinatown. He didn't know if being in downtown Manhattan while the entire NYPD would be looking for him was a good idea. Idris seemed to recognize his unease, but not the reason behind it.

"Listen, I get it. Many of us were in your shoes before. We're just trying to put food on the table. Come break your fast with us tonight at Madina Masjid in the East Village and meet some of the brothers. If you wanna go forward with this, we'll take you to Guillermo. He can get you set up with a bike and a phone, and you could start making money as soon as tomorrow."

"Sounds good, brother. Thank you so much," Yasin said, bowing his head slightly in appreciation.

Idris smiled and left with his friend.

Maybe if I work for a few days, Yasin thought, *I can make some money and find a way out of the city. And being on a bike is better than being on my feet...*

Chapter 6: Saif

Steinway Street was finally beginning to wake up. On a light pole near Elias and Saif, a woman wearing hijab was hanging colorful plastic lanterns and crescent moons. "What's going on today?" Elias asked Saif. "Is there some type of festival happening?"

Saif thought for a moment. "It's Ramadan," he said slowly. "Today is the second day of fasting." Saif hadn't planned on fasting this year. He didn't last year either, though his mom thought he did. He flashed back to the Ramadans of his childhood, waking up at four or five in the morning, eating Algerian specialties like masfouf, a sweet couscous dish with milk and raisins his mother only made in Ramadan, and later, breaking fast at the mosque with his friends. But something changed last year. After dropping out of school, in a pit of depression and drug use, he decided he wasn't going to do hard things for God until his life got better. Not until things were fair. He eventually lost touch with those childhood friends from the mosque, and now his new social circle was made up of people from the NYPD academy, and he didn't feel any social pressure to be a good Muslim.

"Are you fasting?" Elias asked, reeling Saif out of his own thoughts. Noticing a grimace, Elias pulled back. "I mean, not trying to be offensive, just curious."

"Yeah—I mean no," Saif mumbled. "Not this year."

Saif watched men wearing their thobes and djellabas as they milled about from store to store, reminding him of a past version of himself, and he wondered if he was missing out on anything by leaving that world.

"Let's put up some more of these," Elias said, handing Saif half of his stack of flyers. Saif grabbed them wordlessly and wandered over to the nearest pole.

"What's that?" a Muslim woman who was taping decorations asked him. He looked down at her and smiled. "Seven men escaped from jail around here last night. Oh, and Ramadan Mubarak!" He felt self-satisfied for a moment, then realized the poor delivery of his words. Her mouth opened in shock.

"Here? In Astoria?"

"Yes, but don't worry, we're searching for them…" His voice trailed off while she ran into a nearby storefront dialing a number into her phone. *I'm such an idiot…*

Saif shook his head and continued down Steinway, away from the Arab end of the street and towards the Hispanic side, posting flyers wherever he could. At the bottom of the flyers, big red words announced a 10,000 dollar prize for any information that may lead to the capture of the fugitives. Saif stared down the seven men on the flyers, and they stared back in their mugshots. He wondered who would be the easiest to capture. His eyes rested on Malik Clark, the young man with the 'krooked' tattoo over his eyebrow. Somehow, something about the way Malik looked irked Saif. He realized that he saw some of his own features in Malik's face. *If I see him, he's dead meat.*

Suddenly, a loud scream whisked Saif's attention away. A young man on an electric scooter was fleeing the scene of a collision. An older man lay on the ground, struggling to get up. The young man on the scooter whipped by Saif at full speed, and for a moment, Saif caught a glimpse of his face. It's him!

Saif mounted a chase on foot, darting between double parked cars and slow-moving traffic. The man on the scooter noticed his pursuit and tried to shake him off, making a sharp turn onto a side street.

"Stop now!" Saif shouted, "You're under arrest!" The image of Malik Clark filled his eyes, like a vivid waking dream, and visions of glory back at the precinct filled his chest. The man on the scooter made a sharp right into an alley, and Saif's adrenaline powered his legs ever closer. The scooter suddenly hit a pothole, and the young man was thrown forward violently, but somehow he managed to stay on his feet. He ran and cut back toward Steinway, throwing a chair from a cafe into Saif's way. Saif deftly leaped over it, like a hurdler in the Olympics, and closed the gap to ten feet. Seeing his chance, he lunged forward in a full-bodied tackle, grabbing the young man from behind in a bear hug and smashing him into the concrete sidewalk.

He reached for his handcuffs and caught his breath for a few moments, holding the man down on his stomach and clasping his hands behind his back with his free hand.

"Elias! Where are you!" Saif shouted, looking up. A crowd had formed around him and his detainee, and people were whispering to each other.

"Is he one of the escapees?" he heard. "Did you see how that cop threw him down?" someone said.

Elias finally arrived and Saif breathed a sigh of relief.

"I got him, the Clark kid," Saif gloated with a wide smile.

"What the hell are you talking about," a muffled voice said. "I didn't do nothing, it was an accident."

"Shut up!" Saif barked, cuffing the man and putting his knee over his back.

"Let me see his face," Elias said, pulling out a flyer to compare it to.

Saif flipped him over, and uncertainty wormed its way in.

"I don't think it's him," Elias whispered. "He doesn't have the tattoo."

While Saif and Elias thought of what to do next, a chant began to rise around them. "No cops, no KKK, no fascist USA! No cops, no KKK, no fascist USA!"

Saif looked up at Elias in fear. Day one as an officer, and he was already the target of a protest.

Then, a bunch of teenage boys appeared on scooters, pointing their phone cameras at Saif, while chanting obscenities.

"Back! Back up!" Elias screamed, pushing them away from the scene. Saif was locked in fear, his eyes large and glazed over.

"AYO THAT'S SAIF!" one of the teenage boys suddenly recognized him. The boys fought through Elias to get a closer look, then began to jeer.

"YO IT'S REALLY HIM!!"

"I can't believe he became a pig! Pigs are haram!"

"You're a sellout! You disgusting rat!"

Their faces poked forward one at a time from either side of Elias, like a popup box clown from a horror movie.

"You're not one of us! If I ever see this bum again it's on sight!"

Saif felt indignation rise in his throat at the last threat. He adjusted his ruffled police uniform and straightened his badge.

"You better not speak to me like that, if you know what's best for you," he said darkly, whipping out his NYPD-issued baton. He cracked it on his hand menacingly as he approached the teenagers.

"This guy thinks he's tough just because he has a little badge and a stick," one of the boys taunted. "Bro, we KNOW who you are! You're soft as hell!" The others broke into delirious laughter.

"Saif, stay there," Elias warned. "Don't do anything stupid—"

"You damn Arab kids are always causing problems. Nobody wants you here, if you haven't noticed. Some of us actually contribute to society. I wish I could get my hands on you and put you in your place!"

"Bro talking like he's not Arab himself!" The teens erupted in jeers and kept filming Saif. Elders who had gathered around now stepped between Saif and the teenagers, trying to de-escalate. Saif tried to swat a phone out of his face, but missed.

"Saif, go unlock his handcuffs," Elias called. Saif's heart was pumping so fast his vision was blurring. He felt his anger boiling, but knew he had to control himself, or else the videos might go viral and get him fired on his first day on the job.

"Fine," he said after a moment, and he turned back to free the young man, who went off running immediately, clutching his right arm, sobbing.

"We better go back to the precinct," Elias said. The two officers pushed through the crowd and walked briskly onto a quieter street. When they arrived at the precinct, Captain Mancini was waiting outside.

"What the hell are you two thinking?!" he screamed. Saif felt extremely guilty.

"Elias had nothing to do with it, sir," he said, standing straight and trying to seem responsible. "I made a mistake."

Captain Mancini chewed on his upper lip for a moment. "Listen, kid. There are two types of cops. Some are overzealous, undisciplined, egotistical, and always go too far. And there are others who are just as ruthless when they need to be, but they know how to handle themselves. They stay cool headed, they think rationally, and they make the right calls." Captain Mancini looked Saif and Elias in the eyes. "If either of you want to last a long time in this career, you will learn to be the latter."

Chapter 7: Yasin

Clear skies and warm weather were forecasted, but a sudden thunderstorm rippled through from the southwest and blanketed the city in thick rain. Yasin was still in the mosque, late in the afternoon, when a loud *crack!* startled him onto his feet. He looked out the window and saw puddles rapidly forming on the sidewalk.

From his vantage point, Yasin could see green poles and railings, which told him a subway stop was located just outside. Then, as he was watching, two cops ran up the stairs from the flooding subway station, jumping two steps at a time, sheltering their heads from the oncoming rain. Other people were running too, taking cover; the rain had started so abruptly and was so heavy that people barely had time to hide under the nearest store awning before getting fully soaked.

Yasin was getting to the stage of fasting where hunger felt all-consuming. He was thinking of the offer the Senegalese men had made him earlier. Aside from the opportunity to work as a delivery driver and make some money, they had also invited him to share iftar with them down at

Madina Masjid in the East Village, and he didn't yet have ideas on how he would find food to eat. The twin motivations of work and food guided him to another thought. *If it's raining so hard that the police have evacuated the station, I might be able to get in and take the train unnoticed.* He prayed that once over the turnstiles, there would be somewhere to stand not completely flooded.

Adrenaline began to flow as he conceived his risky plan. He took the hundred dollars Suleyman had given him and packed it safely in the waistband of his pants to stay dry, then slipped on the sandals he had borrowed from Amadou. As he leaned outside, mist sprayed onto him from the rain pounding the pavement a few feet away. Yasin lifted his pants to his knees. *One…two…three!*

As he ran out into the open, a booming thunderclap shook the street. It was so loud that it felt like a cannon went off in the neighborhood. Yasin darted through the mass of people, leaping over pools of collected rainwater, until he reached the subway entrance. Water was thundering down the steps leading to the station, like a mighty river.

He hesitated for a moment, then remembering his mission, he skipped down three steps at a time, and at the bottom he plopped down into a pool of dirty water a foot and a half high, nearly reaching his knees. Grimacing as he felt filth and grime swirl around his sandaled feet, he trudged over to the turnstiles, reached one leg over the bar, lifted his body fully over, and then brought his other leg to meet the first. Once inside, he waded over to a bench and stood on it, watching the water flow down onto the rusty tracks.

Two minutes later, Yasin was on a packed Brooklyn-bound 4 train. The train car smelled like rain water mixed with subway juice. Someone's wet umbrella dripped onto Yasin's sandals. He discreetly checked for a bump in his waist-line—the money was still there. At the next stop, more people got on. At the stop after that, half the subway car emptied and seats opened up, but water had pooled on all the benches and it didn't seem like a good idea to sit. Two more stops, and he was at fourteenth street next to the East Village. Madina Masjid was only a short walk away.

Yasin carefully observed the subway station for cops, but there were none to be seen. He knew it was the right stop, but he didn't know how to get to the mosque from here. Emerging from the station, the first thing he saw was a halal cart.

"Salam brother, do you know where Madina Masjid is?" he asked the man behind the counter.

"Yes, go straight down fourteenth, and right on First Avenue," he said in a strong Egyptian accent. "You won't miss it."

Yasin adjusted his soaked face mask and followed the man's instructions. After a few minutes, he turned right, and a couple blocks later, the rows and rows of electric bikes and scooters with delivery boxes attached to them told him that he had arrived.

It was nearly sunset. Yasin had now fasted the first day of Ramadan, and survived his first day as a fugitive. He entered the mosque and pushed through throngs of West African men to get to the restrooms, where he washed up and prepared for prayer. He rinsed his parched mouth, making sure not to swallow any water and risk his fast.

In the main prayer hall, local elders were setting down plastic sheets in neat rows when Yasin entered.

"Assalamu alaikum brother, ramadan kareem!" An elderly Bengali man handed Yasin a trio of dates and a small bottle of water. He accepted them graciously and found a seat between a father with his son and a young group of friends. They chatted loudly, excited to eat and drink after nearly sixteen hours.

Yasin watched the timer on a wall-mounted TV count down to sunset. The seconds passed like minutes, and the minutes like hours. Finally, the countdown ended, and a man went up to the microphone and began to recite the adhan. That was the signal for everyone to begin eating.

Yasin was peeling the pit out of his third date when Idris caught his eye from across the room. He waved Yasin over, and Yasin took his water and date pits over to Idris and his friends.

"I'm glad you made it brother. Everyone, this is Yasin, I met him earlier today in Harlem. He just arrived, if I remember correctly."

Yasin had been in the US for over four years, but he nodded so he wouldn't have to explain the misunderstanding.

Idris now focused his attention on Yasin.

"So, have you decided on becoming a delivery worker?" he asked.

"Yes, I have."

"Good, I will take you to Guillermo after we eat iftar." Yasin noticed that the men around him were eyeing him peculiarly. Idris sighed.

"I should be clear that Guillermo pays a fee for anyone who brings him new workers. It is quite lucrative which is why people might be staring at us right now."

"You didn't tell me that before," Yasin said.

"No, I didn't. I didn't want to scare you away."

"So this was a way to make money for yourself, then."

"Why can I not make a little extra money if you yourself have admitted you're looking for work?" Idris argued.

"Fair enough," Yasin muttered.

"It's ok then? You'll come with me to see Guillermo?"

Yasin nodded, and shook Idris's outstretched hand.

The man who gave the adhan now stepped forward and performed the iqamah, which meant prayer was to begin immediately. They took a final sip of water and then lined up for prayer.

During prayer, all Yasin could think about was if he was making the right choice by pursuing such a public job while the NYPD were searching for him. But getting some dollars in his pocket could open doors for him later on. *Allah, if this is a good decision, please make things easy for me. And if it's not good for me, please put barriers in the way for me.*

After they prayed, the local Bengali elders who ran the mosque made a short appeal for donations, and then young men wheeled in trolleys with multiple shelves that were loaded with individual containers of food. Volunteers also directed people who finished praying to sit back at their places on the floor beside the plastic sheets. Yasin sat with Idris and his friends and they patiently awaited their food.

"I wonder what they're serving today," one of Idris's friends said.

"It's always the same, curry and rice," someone else replied. "At least it's free."

Someone came by and handed Yasin a black plastic container with a clear lid. It was divided into three sections: one large one and two small ones for sides. He opened the container to find a bed of rice in the large part, with a tube shaped, spiced kebab on it. In the other two pockets were a brown oily curry with a chunk of meat in it and an okra and tomato stew.

He closed his eyes and thanked God for the sustenance, then dug in. All the sounds of chatter from earlier had dissipated. After a few minutes of silence, people began to speak again.

"Yasin, tell us about yourself," Idris said, trying to bring him into a conversation with the others. They looked at him expectantly as he finished a bite. Yasin chewed slowly, giving himself time to decide what he wanted to divulge.

He swallowed his bite. "Why don't you brothers go first?" he deflected. "I am curious to learn more about you all."

Idris took the lead. "Most of us here are from Senegal. We came all within the last few years. I arrived two years ago myself. That's my blood brother Ismail," he said, pointing to a man who had similar features. "He left home about eight years ago and made his way here. I was able to join him a few years later. But his journey was not as easy as mine."

Yasin looked at Idris's brother, who had been silent until then. He had dark skin and yellow eyes, and he looked far more aged than Idris, who looked young and vibrant. There were creases around his eyes and lips however, that spoke to a time when he used to smile often.

"I arrived here almost eight years ago after a six-month journey," Ismail began, his eyes distant in thought. "Alhamdulillah, I made it safely—not everyone with us survived the trip." Idris and the other young men watched Ismail speak with a quiet reverence, like one does to an elder, though Ismail was just a few years older than them.

"I had a job in our town as a sheep herder. But not for regular sheep. These were called the Ladoum sheep, and they were a prized breed that people paid thousands, even tens of thousands for. I raised these sheep in the countryside and sold them to collectors to compete in competitions and shows." Yasin was familiar with the Ladoum sheep. He had never seen one in person, but he knew they were very large, sometimes up to a man's shoulders, and rarely used for food.

"One day, I was working when a man, a wealthy man from Mauritania, came looking for me. People had told him about a particular sheep in my possession. This sheep was tall—nearly six feet tall, the tallest one I ever had. He was also heavy, over four hundred pounds, and muscular too. He fathered many sheep for me, and was my prized possession which I never intended to sell. But this man, this wealthy trader from Mauritania, was determined to purchase him from me." Ismail paused. "I named that sheep Mansa Musa." His eyes sparkled wistfully. "However, that day, the Mauritanian trader made me an offer I could not refuse, no matter how attached I was to my Mansa. I did not tell my father, who had entrusted me to raise the flock, and I took the money. It was a small fortune—I could have lived on it for years without raising another finger. But with money, came trouble."

Idris watched his older brother nostalgically as memories of home played vividly before him.

"Not long after the sale, people in the town began to speak. 'Mansa is gone,' they whispered. 'What happened to Mansa Musa?' Everyone knew about him because he was the envy of the other Ladoum breeders. Then people began to spread rumors. 'There was a visitor from the north,' people said. 'Perhaps he convinced Ismail to sell his prized sheep?' When word spread about the Mauritanian, people started to watch me closely. They wanted to see if I had suddenly started spending money. They observed everything from the way I dressed to the motorbike I drove. I knew that this attention could lead to nothing good, especially if the wrong people got wind of it. And soon enough, they did."

"They tried to rob you?" Yasin asked.

"Yes, some people did. They didn't try to take my money though, because I had entrusted it to a good friend in the capital, an accountant who was well connected in the professional world. But the robbers, these thugs dressed in masks, came to the farm and stole over thirty Ladoum sheep from me. That was over half my flock. It was a devastating blow to my livelihood. My father was furious when I told him. He was in Mali at the time, and when I sent him a message to inform him of the robbery, he told me he was returning at once and he didn't want to see me when he got back home."

Idris hid a wry smile when Ismail mentioned their father, but quickly returned to seriousness.

"I was in the enviable position of having full pockets, but I had nowhere to go. My people had gotten the idea in their mind that a wealthy man had come and paid me a huge fortune, and robbers were still targeting me, trying to find the cash. And my father had effectively banished me. So I phoned my friend in the capital and asked him what I should do. He told me I should come visit him and we could talk about it. So I took a bus to Dakar and didn't look back."

"He didn't even say goodbye to me," Idris recalled, and the group laughed. Ismail, though smiling, looked regretful.

"When I arrived in Dakar and met my friend, I did not know what he would suggest, but I had decided in my mind that I would do what he said. So when he told me to go to

America, I was surprised, but I did not hesitate. I had no bags to pack, nothing to take with me. With the money I had entrusted to him, I was able to get a false passport, and he booked my whole journey there." His brow furrowed as he tried to recall the extensive trip.

"The first part of the trip was the longest in distance, but the smoothest. From Dakar, I flew to Algiers, Houari Boumediene Airport, named after the famous Algerian war hero. Then, I flew to the crowded Istanbul airport. My last flight, over thirteen hours, was to Bogota, Colombia. This was the first portion of the journey. It was tiresome, but there were no problems."

The men around Ismail nodded, remembering similar travel routes. Then they made grim expressions as they awaited the next part of the story.

"Had you flown before?" Yasin interrupted.

"No, it was my first time on a plane," Ismail said. "Luckily, the French I knew was enough in navigating the airports. It was a different story on the ground in Colombia. Nobody spoke French, and of course nobody spoke Wolof. I didn't speak a word of English at the time, nor Spanish. I only had the description of a man who would be waiting outside the airport." Ismail shook his head. "I remember, it was a scorching day, but he was dressed in a long, black leather coat, like some type of movie character." Idris and his friends chuckled.

"Once I found him, he took me to a bus that was half filled and I waited with those people for hours until it was crammed full. I didn't speak at all, and not just because I didn't know the language. My friend from Dakar had given me some US dollars to keep with me for the trip, and I had folded them very small, wrapped the bundle up in plastic, and tucked it into my lower lip, like a piece of chewing tobacco. So I kept my mouth shut.

The bus finally left the capital city and we rolled over gravel roads all the way to a small town on the border of Colombia and Panama. There, we were left on the ground and told to wait. Again, hours went by until a short man with suntanned skin arrived. He said we would have to wait until dawn to leave. We laid down in the open on the dry grass, but I was anxious and could not fall asleep. As soon as rays of sunshine spread across the sky, the short man reappeared and led us on a trail into the jungle and we marched for a while until I heard a roaring river. My sandals started to sink into the wet soil and large, thin mosquitoes swarmed around my face, much like during the rainy season back in Senegal. We were loaded onto a long, narrow boat and he led us down the snaking river. The thick jungle suffocated the air on either side of us. The boat's driver was on high alert, watching both sides of the riverbank for signs of something, I never knew what. But I did hear that there were vicious predators that lived in that jungle: jaguars, crocodiles, snakes, and more." Yasin was both captivated and terrified as Ismail recounted his journey. But he wasn't prepared for what Ismail said next.

"As we continued through the jungle, I grew close to another man in the party. He was an elderly Latino man who had shared some fruit with me. He never spoke a word to me, and neither did I to him, but we established a brotherly relationship of looking after one another. At some moments during the trek that followed our boat ride, he leaned on me for support, especially when leaping over large rocks and tree roots. We trekked through miles of jungle and emerged in a small town, a tiny town of no more than fifty wooden shacks where indigenous people lived. There, the locals had been prepared for our arrival. Our guide took us to a makeshift market where food was being sold; plantains prepared in every way: fried, boiled, mashed, yellow plantains, green plantains, you name it. They were also selling clothing; they called it 'American style': jeans and basketball jerseys and sneakers. My fatal mistake was thinking we were already near the US border. I took out my hidden US dollars and bought myself a whole American outfit, thinking that I would fit in once we arrived. I then took some cash and ordered a plantain feast. I invited my elderly friend to come share a meal with me. He suggested we go near the edge of the forest so others wouldn't stare at us and our food. As we approached the trees, he said he would go gather some fresh water from the river to drink. He took a few empty mango skins and disappeared into the jungle. I waited for him to return for several minutes but he did not come back. I began to worry that a jaguar had eaten him, and I went looking for him. After a few moments, I felt a sharp pain in the back of my head, and felt something dripping onto my back. I turned around and my vision began to blur, but the last thing I remember is seeing my elderly friend standing above me with a bloodied stick. The next moment I woke up, I checked my lips, and to my horror the rest of my money was gone, and I never saw that man again."

"That horrible old man!" Yasin exclaimed. The men around Ismail had heard this story before, but even they were shaking their heads in disgust as if just hearing it for the first time.

"Alhamdulillah, our guide found me before I lost too much blood. The old man was caught and exiled from our group, and a kind villager I previously purchased food from tended to my wound and gave me a herbal brew to help me recover. I will never forget their kindness. We began our travels again in the weeks that followed. I marched, sat in buses, and rode on boats through a list of countries until I arrived in Northern Mexico, at the border town of Hidalgo. I had lost forty pounds during the journey. I was once a healthy young man in Senegal—" Ismail balled up his fists and pumped his chest. "Strong as an ox I was." Then he lifted one arm in a weak flex, showing proof of his unformed biceps. "I've never recovered since then."

"And how did you get to New York?" Yasin asked.

"From Mexico, the last task was crossing the Rio Grande. On the outskirts of Texas, our Mexican guides told us where to cross the river and disappeared. Everyone made a crazed dash. I ran ahead of the others and didn't look back. The river swept me off my feet but I knew how to swim, and I landed somewhere down the river in Texas. My friend back in Dakar, who had organized the whole thing, told me once I was on land in Texas, to get arrested as soon as possible. The Governor of Texas was not a fan of illegal immigration, but he hated the Democrats more. So after a few days in a detention facility, we were put on a bus directly to New York City, leading me to be here before you today."

"Every time I hear it I get goosebumps again," Idris said, staring at his brother in awe. The others murmured in agreement. "Did you go through the Darién Gap too, Yasin?"

Yasin now felt comfortable opening up a little. "You know, my journey mirrors Ismail's closely. Though alhamdulillah, I didn't get attacked, but I did get very sick in the Panamanian jungle."

"We're glad you are here safe and sound," Ismail said. "You are part of our family now, and we will take care of you."

Yasin bowed his head slightly in gratitude. He looked around and the only people left in the mosque were some local Bengali elders who had begun cleaning up.

"Should we help them?" Yasin suggested. The men rose together and gathered their dirty napkins, empty containers, and water bottles, then carefully rolled up the plastic sheets they had eaten on, keeping the crumbs inside. The elders were very pleased, their job having been cut in half.

"All right Yasin, are you ready to go see Guillermo?" Idris asked. Yasin nodded. They said goodbye to Ismail and the others and went out into the cool night. Yasin lifted his blue cloth mask over his face.

"Guillermo's going to need to see your face," Idris warned.

"Just until we get there, then I'll take it off," Yasin said, looking up and down the bustling East Village streets for signs of cops or video cameras.

The two men walked briskly towards Chinatown, to the west of Madina Masjid, with Idris leading the way. They soon passed the Canal Street station, where several men were selling counterfeit goods on the street side. Yasin's heart began to pump faster, and he felt himself sweating all of a sudden.

"Are you okay?" Idris asked. "Don't worry. He's not going to hurt you, Yasin."

Yasin tried to ignore the flashbacks playing through his mind. He tried not to think of Suleyman running towards him, warning him of cops on their way, and being handcuffed to a post at the subway station while cops searched his goods. He wiped his damp forehead.

"I'm fine," he said at last.

Idris led him to a door next to a dumpling restaurant on Canal Street. He pressed the buzzer for the sixth floor. "La casa del lobo," he announced. After a moment the buzzer went off, and the door unlocked.

"Just let me do the talking," Idris said. Yasin nodded. They trudged up six floors of stairs. Finally, they knocked on the door of apartment 6B.

"Hola Guillermo," Idris said after the door opened.

"Guillermo?" Yasin whispered. "That man looks Chinese."

"Korean, stupid!" Guillermo shouted, slamming the door shut.

Chapter 8: Saif

Two days after the wrong suspect incident, Saif and Elias clocked in at the 114th precinct. The commissioner was going to address every station via live broadcast with some updates on the investigation.

"Um, I'm sorry about what went down a couple days ago," Saif told Elias. "I've had time to let it sit and I feel like I just handled everything horribly."

Elias laughed, relieved Saif had finally addressed the situation. "You were tweaking big time, bro. What was going on with you?"

Saif sighed. "I don't know man…" He fell silent, unable to express what he was feeling.

"It's alright," Elias said. "That was just day one. Let's start fresh."

"Attention!" Captain Mancini announced. "Before the commissioner gives it away, I would like to applaud Sergeant Roberto and his team for the capture of one of the fugitives, Amir Johnson Jr., last night. He was found hiding out in a donut shop, funny enough, out of the blue…I'll let him tell the story."

Captain Mancini leaned over to Sergeant Roberto and whispered that he had two minutes before the live broadcast with the commissioner began. The sergeant nodded, grinning as he looked up.

"Good morning officers. Let's see…I could make up a dramatic story of how we caught our dangerous suspect after a shootout in broad daylight, but the truth is much funnier. We—" and he gestured in a half circle towards another three officers, "were just stopping by for some coffee. Our usual spot, the one on twenty-third that has the officer discount, was closed for some reason. So we went around the block to this other spot. I was in the cruiser while the others went inside, when I saw a huge man making a run for it from the side door. I flicked on the siren and chased him down." By this time, Sergeant Roberto was nearly crying trying to hold back laughter. "He was still wearing this tiny little apron," he wiped a tear, "with these cute donut drawings all over it—" and the sergeant finally lost it. Everyone else in the room laughed too. Captain Mancini waved him off the podium, seeing he wasn't going to stop laughing anytime soon.

"All right, back to business. Remember there are still six other fugitives out there. Dangerous, dangerous men— well, maybe not Amir Johnson, but mostly dangerous men," he smiled. "Now let's give our undivided attention to our fearless commissioner."

The bald tech manager fiddled with an HDMI cord. Then his laptop wallpaper, which was the NYPD logo on a blue background, appeared on the projector. He clicked on the live link in his email and a new window popped up. The officers watched the black screen, waiting for the live feed to begin. Then, the commissioner appeared, seated on a table with deputy commissioners on either side of her. She stared at the camera, then looked to her right and nodded to someone out of sight. "NYPD officers, thank you for tuning in to this live update on the case. I know you are all working hard to the best of your abilities," she began. "I have some exciting updates for you, but I want to stress that the job is not over. Until we catch all seven of these men, I want you to stay focused and alert on your assignments."

The mood at the 114th precinct was one of calm anticipation, with people still clapping Sergeant Roberto on the back, along with the other officers who were involved in the arrest.

"Today, it's my pleasure to announce that two of the men have been caught and arrested," the commissioner continued.

Suddenly, everyone in the room was paying rapt attention, and whispers filled the room.

"Two?"

"Who's the second?"

"Shh, we can't hear her!"

"In Queens, 114th precinct officers picked up Amir Johnson Jr., found hiding out in a donut store on Ditmars Boulevard in Astoria. He is currently in a high security convoy headed for Sing Sing Correctional Facility."

Officers smiled again in Sergeant Roberto's direction, but went back to watching the high-resolution feed of their commissioner impatiently.

"In Brooklyn at 4:32 in the morning today, detectives from the Fugitive Enforcement Division found Derek Mahan sleeping on a bench in Prospect Park."

"Dammit!" a female cop shouted. Others groaned in dissatisfaction.

"Settle down!" Captain Mancini ordered, not taking his eyes off the screen.

"Mr. Mahan is now being prepared for transfer to Sing Sing. Again, I want to thank our brave officers for keeping our city safe and returning these dangerous criminals back to where they belong: in prison. Remember, the job is not done, and it will take everyone—whether you are a local beat cop or a special teams detective—to restore order and safety on our streets." After an extended pause, she raised up an open hand. "Five men remain." The live broadcast abruptly ended and the screen returned to black.

"Those lucky pricks," Sergeant Roberto blurted. "He was asleep, it shouldn't count!"

Saif didn't dare call out the hypocrisy of having just as easy of a capture.

"Why are they so pissed? It's all the same as long as we're capturing these guys, right?" Elias whispered to Saif.

"Maybe there's a rivalry between our divisions?" Saif said.

Jessica popped up from behind them and shook her head. "Nah, that's not it. Basically, if we catch the fugitives ourselves, we could get more funding, but if the FED catches them, they'll get a huge chunk of cash from the city. They're a pretty small department, because situations like this don't happen very often. Since everyone's eyes are on this, there's a lot of money at stake to make sure it doesn't happen again."

"I see," Elias said. "That's why the higher ups seem the most annoyed about it."

Jessica shrugged. "It's always about money."

"Jessica to the rescue again," Saif laughed. At the police academy, she was always helpful when they were studying for their written exams.

"Listen up everyone," Captain Mancini shouted. "As you all heard, the tally is now tied up, one-one. I know we're at the 114th precinct, so we won't be running around Brooklyn looking for fugitives, but I want to make sure that not a single person is caught in Astoria if they're not caught by us. We need to own these streets. No messing around, no distractions. Am I understood?!"

"Yes, sir!"

Saif soaked in the renewed energy at the precinct. "It's a new day," he said to Elias.

Elias fist-bumped Saif. "New day!" They suited up and left together for their daily assignment. As they approached the same block on Steinway where the incident happened, Saif steeled himself, preparing for hostility from the public. People stared at them as they walked, but Saif wasn't sure if they recognized him or were just staring at them because they were police. Eventually, they reached their post, where the street had remained blocked off with a big blue wooden barrier from the day before.

"All right, today you check licenses, and I'll direct traffic," Saif said. He dragged the barrier to the side, leaving just enough room for a car to pass. Cars were only allowed to continue down Steinway Street and towards the service road that led to the highway if the driver showed their license.

"Stop!" Saif called out to the first driver who arrived, while raising his palm flatly. The driver pulled up slowly beside Elias.

"License please," Elias instructed. The old Arab man behind the wheel didn't understand. "License!" Elias said, louder.

Saif sidled up to Elias. "I don't think he speaks English," he told his partner. Then he leaned toward the driver. "Salam, ammu," he said. "Endek el permis?"

"Wa alaikum assalam," the man replied. "Eh huwa bermi?"

"Permis," Saif repeated. "Fih ismek, wa tswira ta'ek."

"Ahh," the man said, raising his eyebrows. He reached into the glove compartment and pulled out his Green Card.

"Ask him for his license," Elias prodded.

"Whatever, this is good enough," Saif said. He knew his Arabic wasn't good enough to continue the conversation. Elias shot him an impatient look. "What? He's obviously not one of them," Saif complained.

"Saha," Saif told the driver, tapping on the hood lightly. The man smiled and drove carefully past the half-moved barrier.

"So you speak Arabic pretty good then?" Elias said. "You always told me you were bad at it."

"Come on, that was basic stuff," Saif admitted. "And I still couldn't talk to him well. All I know is the Algerian dialect, and he probably speaks the Egyptian dialect."

"How different could it be?" Elias asked.

Saif laughed. "You'd be surprised."

The next car that came by was blasting an upbeat Egyptian pop song. Saif squinted his eyes to see who was behind the tinted windows. His heartbeat quickened when he noticed several heads with the same curly hairstyles. He waved them over to Elias, trying not to look at them directly. The car crept forward slowly and then the driver hit the brakes and rolled down the windows.

"Yoo, it's the legendary Saif!" the driver snickered, giggles emanating from the back seats.

"Who even are you?!" Saif snapped. Then he remembered what the captain had said about two kinds of cops, and tried to be the better kind.

"Chill, chill," the teenager said, turning down the blasting music.

He looked familiar but Saif couldn't place him. "I heard about that case you guys have going on. Seven killers on the loose?"

"Yeah," Elias called out, approaching the still car. "Actually, not all killers." He looked at Saif with caution in his eyes. Saif stayed silent and didn't move.

"If you've heard about it, and you know there are seven highly violent men on these streets, then don't make our job harder than it is," Elias warned.

The driver put his hands up in defeat. "I'm not trying to make light of the situation, officer," he said earnestly. "I just want to know more about what's going on. I'm a citizen, right?"

"You're right," Saif said. "You have a right to know what's happening. Luckily, two of the men have already been captured."

"Who are they?" someone in the back seat said, rolling down the window. It was a young teenager, no more than thirteen or fourteen, wearing sunglasses and a chain around his neck.

"One of them is named Amir Johnson, and the other Derek Mahan. It's on the news already."

"What did they do?" asked another kid in the backseat, who looked like a copy of the kid next to him.

"One of them was convicted of…armed robbery, and the other for drug charges and assaulting a cop." Saif looked up at Elias, who nodded in confirmation.

"That's it?" the kid asked. Seeing the stern face on Elias, his smile dropped. "Just kidding."

"Any other questions?" Saif asked. The kids shook their heads.

"You better find the rest of them," the driver said as he rolled away. "Put my tax dollars to work!"

As soon as he cleared the barrier, he slammed the gas and the tires screeched loudly and the music went back to full blast.

Saif shook his head at Elias. "As if those little wannabes pay taxes."

Elias laughed. "They seem like good kids though."

Saif secretly thought the same. It seemed like only a moment ago he was as carefree and goofy as them. He missed having fun. He remembered his old friends, who he used to run up and down Steinway with, stocking up on snacks from the corner store and riding on Citibikes two apiece. Now, he hadn't spoken to those guys in years, ever since they graduated high school and slowly drifted apart. He was an adult now, and adults had to make a living. Being a cop may not have been his first choice, but he had made a decision and he had to ride with it.

Chapter 9: Yasin

"Guillermo!" Idris shouted, knocking again. "Come on, it was an honest mistake!"

Yasin smiled sheepishly. "You should've told me he wasn't a Latino," he whispered. Idris raised his index finger to his lips.

"Guillermo, please," Idris called. He wasn't willing to let his fat commission go this easily.

The door cracked open.

"Come on, give him a break, he's fresh off the boat," Idris pleaded.

Guillermo appeared again, looking fully composed. "I can get you a phone, but you have to find your own bike," he said.

"That's okay, that won't be a problem," Idris said, taking Guillermo's hand into a dap and walking in. Yasin followed. He felt he was supposed to be happy, and that Idris expected him to be grateful, but the truth was he was not a new immigrant, fresh and unknown, excited to make his first dollar. He was a fugitive, and there were thousands of NYPD officers searching for him at that very moment.

"Gimme a few minutes to get the phone set up for you," Guillermo said, disappearing into a back room. Yasin got comfortable and took in the place. Guillermo's home was messy, but Yasin could tell it was swanky when it was clean. There was eclectic art on the walls, a furry magenta rug under their feet, and a pair of parakeets, one green, one yellow, sitting motionless in a nearby cage.

"One of these should work," Guillermo said when he emerged. He had a bundle of iPhones in his hands. One by one, he unlocked them, opened a dizzying procession of food delivery apps, and checked profile details within each app.

"This one is clean," he said, handing a phone to Yasin, who took it hesitantly, looking at Idris. Idris gave him an encouraging smile. Yasin swiped across the home page, exploring the layout and UI of different apps.

"Make sure you know the name and details of the account you use, so if a customer asks for the name, you have the right answer," Idris suggested. "Sometimes, customers will report delivery workers who seem different from their profiles."

Guillermo nodded in agreement. "They've been getting mad strict on us lately," he added. "Anyway, my usual rate is fifty bucks a week per phone. You can only put twelve hours on each account per day, because the apps started capping hours worked. If you want a second phone it will be a hundred dollars. And all tips go to me."

"One phone should be fine for now," Yasin said, still scrolling through the apps. "Wait, how am I supposed to pass as Hong? Born in 2001? I'm almost double his age!"

"Just be Hong," Guillermo grinned.

Yasin stared at him dumbfounded. "I guess your name didn't fit your face either."

Guillermo's smile dropped and he picked up a business-like tone.

"Hey, when the cops go around sniffing for someone named 'Guillermo', they're not looking for an Asian man are they?" he said, tapping his index finger to his forehead. "Anyway, getting paid with a prepaid card good with you? I can do cash too, but it will cost you extra."

Yasin looked at Idris. "What do you do?"

"Oh, I have a bank account. I get my earnings deposited directly." Idris said.

Guillermo smirked greedily. "A lotta new guys go with the prepaid debits. I only take ten percent for those. Cash is fifteen."

Yasin had had a bank account before he was arrested, but he never got his wallet back from Rikers. Regardless, now it was impossible to use.

"I'll go with the cash." Yasin said.

Guillermo's eyebrows rose, but his smile widened. "If you swing by once a week I'll get you paid."

Yasin nodded and rose awkwardly. He reached a hand out to shake Guillermo's.

"Hold your horses, buddy," Guillermo snapped. "If you want to take that phone with you today that's gonna be fifty bucks."

Yasin patted his waistline, looking for the tucked hundred dollars Suleyman had given to him a few days ago. He couldn't feel it. *Could it have slipped out of my pants on the stairs up?* His chest constricted in fear.

"You better not have wasted my time. One of you's gotta pay me before you leave," Guillermo snarled, eyeing Idris.

Idris looked at Yasin with concern. "Do you have the money?"

"Found it," Yasin breathed at last, finding it in the back of underwear. He held up the sweaty bills towards Guillermo.

"That's revolting." Guillermo held his nose while taking the cash from the edge with two overgrown fingernails. He walked back to the other room and returned with a fifty dollar bill.

Yasin tucked the money inside his pants again, on his hip.

"If he works for more than two weeks, you'll get your commission," Guillermo told Idris. Then, he led them out the door and left them in the hallway.

"Ok, now let's get you a bike," Idris said. They walked back to Madina Masjid. Idris went straight to the bike rack outside. It was dark, so he pulled out his phone and turned the flashlight on, looking for a certain bike. They were all so crowded on the racks that it was taking a while.

"Which one are you looking for?" Yasin offered to help. Idris didn't answer for a few moments.

"Ha, this one is my bike. I will allow you to borrow it for tonight. Just so you can get a feel for this job."

"Thank you, my brother," Yasin said. "And after that?"

"After that, you can pay me to rent it by the day, or if I'm using it, you can rent from one of my friends. When these bikes are all sitting here locked they're useless." He looked at Yasin kindly. "Don't worry, I'll give you a low price. Ten dollars a day."

Yasin did the math. If he rented the bike for seven days a week and was paying fifty a week for the account, then to even see a cent of profit he'd have to earn over a hundred dollars. Idris noticed his face deep in thought.

"Like I said, today is free. And if you find a better deal, no pressure. Do what suits you."

Yasin pulled out the phone from Guillermo again. "So I pick up an order through the app, show it to the restaurant worker, and then the app will show me the way to the customer's house. I just hand the food over and move onto the next order. Is that all of it?"

"You got the basics of it. I will just add some tips. First, never leave my bike unlocked anywhere. It will be stolen faster than you can say your shahada. Second, this time of night is prime for delivery. I start my day around two in the afternoon, and finish around two in the morning. Third, keep switching between the apps to see what's available. Sometimes when one app gets really busy, they will pay an extra bonus for each delivery. That will boost your profits."

"Got it," Yasin said. Night time seemed a good time of day to do deliveries while staying unnoticed. He saw a helmet buckled to the seat. "Do you mind if I use your helmet?"

"Sure, go ahead. I don't really wear it anyway. Any other questions?" When Yasin didn't answer, Idris turned toward the mosque's front doors. "I'm going to go inside and pray for a bit before knocking out."

Yasin hesitated for a moment. Then before Idris disappeared he called out.

"Do you know any place where I can sleep tonight?" He felt a wave of embarrassment, being so needy in front of someone he barely knew.

Idris sighed and turned back to Yasin.

"You don't have anywhere to sleep?"

Yasin shook his head.

"Weren't you up in Harlem earlier? I thought you had an apartment there or something."

"I was just visiting a friend." Yasin tried not to flinch at the lie. Well, it was a half-truth, he considered, remembering Amadou.

"I guess for now the best thing you can do is sleep at the mosque, so you're not homeless at least. The Bengali elders on the board here don't allow it, but it's Ramadan, and they might have sympathy. I'd recommend working at night, and napping inside during the day, so they don't try to kick you out at night."

"Okay, I'll try that."

"I'll see what I can do for something more long term. Maybe my brother Ismail can help. A lot of people owe him favors."

"Thank you so much again, brother, for all your help today."

"No problem." Idris turned around again, silhouetted in the doorway. "Don't lose my bike!" Then he went inside the mosque.

Without Idris, the buzz of East Village nightlife became more apparent. Yasin opened his phone and scanned through the apps. Jobs kept popping up on his screen, but as soon as he had looked over the details, an error appeared saying they had been taken. After a few minutes of frustration, he just accepted the next order that arrived immediately, then looked at the details. *22 dollar payout. Pickup: Little Italy Pizza, East Village. Delivery: Park Slope, Brooklyn.*

"Brooklyn?!" he exclaimed out loud. "I can't go that far." *Cancel button…cancel button….*

Yasin found the cancel button and canceled his pickup. Then, a button popped up.

You have two cancellations remaining this hour.

"What?!" He returned to the home screen and tried to review details before accepting an order, but they disappeared almost immediately again. Training his eyes to look for just the destination, he was able to accept an order that he saw with a delivery destination in nearby Chelsea.

"Seven dollar payout?!" He sighed and settled onto Idris's bike, double checked the pickup location, and kicked off into the night.

Chapter 10: Saif

On a quiet Saturday afternoon, Saif awoke from a luxurious sleep. He felt fully rested for the first time in a while. The NYPD was paying overtime during the search for the seven men, and he had worked five days in a row, twelve hours a day, collecting as much money as he could before reaching a point of exhaustion.

As he rose and walked to the bathroom, he felt the weight of the last few days settle in his knees with each step.

"Wesh bik?" his mom called out from the living room.

"I'm fine, Mama. Just tired."

She tsked and went back to her TV show. It was a series retelling stories from early Islamic history, commissioned by Saudi Arabia for release during Ramadan. She usually watched her shows with a huge bowl of sunflower seeds beside her, but since she was fasting, she kept her hands busy with a knitting project while she watched.

"Saif, I need to start cooking soon," she said when she heard him leave the bathroom. "Since you're finally eating iftar with me today, I need you to pick up some groceries."

"Okay, write me a list," he called back from his room. With his long work schedules he hadn't been home for iftar yet this Ramadan. He checked the time on his phone. He was hungry, but sunset was only a few hours away. *I guess I'll just fast today,* he decided.

He came out a moment later fully dressed. It was the first time in a week that he was going out in something besides his police uniform.

"Bring me a pen and paper," she said.

"How about you just text me?"

She glared at him.

"Sorry, I'm just saying it would be easier." Saif took a seat next to his mom and asked for her phone. He already knew the password, so he quickly navigated to their shared Whatsapp chat and handed the phone back to her. "Just type here what you need. I'm heading out."

He slipped into his shoes, grabbed a couple of empty bags, and skipped down two flights of stairs, exiting onto Steinway Street.

Their first floor neighbor, Taher, was chilling outside their building, a cigarette in hand. He was a Tunisian guy in his mid-thirties, and though he wasn't paid to be a door-man, he was always standing outside the front door. "Saif, shnuwa hwalek, labas?"

"Hamdoulillah labas," Saif replied. That was the extent of most of their conversations.

Saif turned left and walked down Steinway. He had seen the street through a different lens over the past week. It was hard to separate this new perception from the way things felt before. He caught himself looking at random people as potential threats, mentally analyzing how they looked and walked. He scrutinized the alleys as potential hiding spots. His hand felt drawn to his waist, as though ready to pull out a phantom Glock at a moment's notice.

Saif stood still for a moment and closed his eyes. He shook his head like a wet dog shedding water and opened his eyes. The new Yemeni coffee shop across the street finally opened. A toddler scootering past him softened his heart. The Ramadan decorations glittered in the sunlight. It was the Steinway of his youth again.

There was a new, large grocery store that stocked Arab goods and halal meat near his home, but Saif opted to go to Ammu Ali's humble mini mart instead. He had been going there for years, and though Ammu Ali's groceries were slightly inferior to its modern competitor, seeing Ammu Ali was always nice. Saif checked his chat with his mother to see if she had sent him the list. She had.

-One package merguez
-One sack of potatoes
-A bunch of parsley
-One can tomato sauce
-One can hummus
-Gazouz you choose

Saif tried to guess what his mom had planned for iftar based on the ingredients she had asked for. The merguez was self-explanatory; Ammu Ali's prepared sausages were a main course in themselves, but he wasn't sure if she was planning to serve them alongside the potatoes or cooked in a tomato sauce. The chickpeas and parsley were probably for making harira soup, so probably the tomato sauce was for soup too. So most likely dinner was harira soup to start followed by merguez and freshly fried potatoes. Though that was a frequent dinner in their household, it never got old for him.

"Salam, Ammu Ali," he said as the bell above the door tinkled.

"Wa alaikum assalam." Ammu Ali smiled his familiar smile. "Labas wala labas khoya?"

"Labas," Saif grinned. "Wenta?"

"Hamdoulillah." Ammu Ali turned his face to meet Saif's right cheek, and then his left.

Saif navigated the small store with its narrow aisles, knowing the exact location of items as if a map was downloaded into his brain. Despite its size, there was a wide array of products crammed into the store's loaded shelves. He deliberately avoided the imported chips section, which was sure to heighten his hunger. *I forgot how hard grocery shopping is while fasting.*

Last on the list was soda. *Hmm, Hamoud or Selecto,* he mulled. Selecto, the cola-like product with a distinct banana flavor, was his favorite. But he knew his mom liked the lighter, lemon-lime flavored Hamoud. Unable to make a decision, he took a small bottle of each.

"How's your mother?" Ammu Ali switched to English when Saif arrived at the counter. Years ago, Saif's mother used to bake Algerian desserts and sell them in different stores down Steinway. She left them on counters just like the one right in front of him, staged as a delicious upsell to customers.

"She's good," Saif said.

"I'm still waiting for her to start making those kalb el louz again." Ammu Ali reminisced as he packed up Saif's groceries. "I remember when they used to sell here like hotcakes."

"Maybe she will again soon." Saif smiled. He knew how much his mother loved baking. Much of Saif's ambition to become an officer and make a decent living began with wanting to give her the freedom to do what she liked doing again.

"I hope she does," Ammu Ali said. Then, his voice took a different tone. "Saif," he began cautiously, "I heard you abandoned your studies. What happened, young man? You used to tell me you wanted to be a doctor, or an engineer, or something like that."

"Wait, who told you I dropped out?" Saif said.

"Ahh, Saif, come on." Ammu Ali looked away in disbelief. "You think I don't see what happens on this street? I witnessed with my own eyes the incident with the young kid you beat up."

Saif's ears went hot with embarrassment. "What do you mean beat up? He perpetrated a hit and run!"

Ammu Ali sighed. "Look, I don't know the circumstances of that boy you slammed to the ground, but I'm just saying, I had high hopes for you, back when you were just a little boy coming here with your mama. You were a good kid, and this career choice is not for good kids with bright futures."

"I didn't ask for your expectations," Saif snapped. "What, I should open a tiny run down store to be more like you? Is that success?"

Ammu Ali stared at him silently. Then he took a deep breath. Before he could say anything, Saif tempered himself. "I'm doing what I have to do to feed my family. At the very least you can respect that, can't you?"

"Fine," Ammu Ali said. "Your life, your choices. But you don't know what I've been through. You were raised here in New York City, with all the opportunities of the world in your hands. I can, and I should hope for more from you. I watched you grow, and I'm sad to see you not reach your potential."

Saif paid and took his groceries off the counter wordlessly. Right before reaching the door, he looked back. "I didn't ask to be brought here. You did. If you're so smart, why don't you try getting a college degree? Go to Wall Street and make something of yourself." Then he turned to leave and slammed the door behind him. He decided he wouldn't go to Ammu Ali's shop anymore. The new grocery store was better anyway.

Later that night, Saif's mom set the table with exactly what Saif had predicted. They began with the soup. Saif squeezed a freshly sliced lemon wedge on top before digging in. He had in fact earned this meal—he had fasted the whole day, even if he was only awake for half of it.

"Make the dua," his mom said while he had a spoonful of soup halfway in his mouth. He took it out and said the dua in Arabic, which he recalled from childhood memory.

The thirst is gone, the veins are moist, and the reward is given, if God wills.

They ate quietly for a few minutes, then Saif reached for the TV remote. He wasn't in the mood to tell his mom about what had happened at Ammu Ali's store. She started to clear the plates while he tuned in to the TV anchors' excited chatter.

"The New York Knicks could book their tickets to the finals with a game seven win over the Indiana Pacers. Is this finally their year?"

"We're going all the wayyy," Saif cheered.

"Join us after the ad break for an interview with Coach—" BREAKING NEWS suddenly flashed in red on the screen. The two happy and hopeful anchors were replaced by a serious, middle-aged white man, clean-shaven with gray bushy eyebrows balled up in concern.

"We interrupt your program to inform you of a horrific bombing that has just taken place in Downtown Brooklyn. FBI sources say the target was the office of Councilwoman Suhaila Akter, and that this was the work of escaped fugitive Stephen Hoffmeyer."

"What?!" Saif shouted at the screen.

"Last year, Hoffmeyer was convicted of a similar attack that killed eleven people and injured twenty-four others in Queens. The NYPD says Hoffmeyer has not been apprehended as of this time. Six casualties are confirmed so far—Councilwoman Akter not listed among them. Details are emerging live as this is a developing story."

Saif stared at the TV in the center of the room in horror. His mother's trembling hands dropped a stack of plates and they fell in a loud crash into the sink. The screen played video of NYPD officers and firefighters rushing into the office building, pulling people out from thick clouds of smoke. Hoffmeyer's mugshot was shown on the screen, his familiar face smiling maniacally.

Saif looked at his mom in shock, unable to produce words. Then, she broke the silence herself.

"Saif," she pleaded, "I'm begging you. Don't go to work tomorrow. Stay home."

"I have to, Mama. It's my job."

"Your job is too dangerous!"

Saif's fear began to slip away while a sense of duty replaced it. "This is what I signed up for."

"You can find something else to do, please! Maybe…I can ask my manager at the store to hire you—"

"Mama, with these killers on the loose, nobody, no one is safe. Not you and not me."

She held his arm tightly. "I don't want to lose you too," she said.

"Isn't this what would make Baba proud?" Saif countered softly. "He gave up his life protecting his country, stopping killers from causing chaos. He was a hero, wasn't he?"

She looked at him tearfully. "Yes, he was."

"Then I have to be like him. I have to be brave. I have to make him proud."

"Just be careful, Saif. You're all I have left."

Chapter 11: Yasin

In the three days since he had begun working, Yasin had traversed the length and breadth of Manhattan more times than he could count. He felt at once vital to the inner workings of the city, and also a voiceless robot whose presence was ignored and overlooked. Even the police didn't seem to notice him.

At six in the evening, orders began to surge on the delivery apps all at once. Other delivery workers said this was typical on days when office employees were working late in Manhattan. He picked up a lucrative order for delivery to a location near Grand Central. Swinging onto his bike with ease, he pedaled over to the salad chain where the order would be ready.

"Name?" the woman behind the counter asked. Yasin just showed her the screen of his phone. She took the phone into her hands to read the details. A moment later, she left and came back with a neatly packaged salad bowl.

Yasin swiped the button to confirm that the order was picked up, then walked back to his bike and tucked it safely into his delivery bag. He looked at the address again. The grid-like structure of Manhattan that began after Houston Street made it super easy to navigate. He started to pedal straight up Lexington Avenue.

Cruising down 42nd street near the dropoff location, Yasin noticed a group of delivery workers ahead. He slowed down and squinted to see the building number. It was the same delivery address that his order listed.

He parked and locked his bike and took the delivery package with him into the crowd. He had to push his way through the mass of delivery workers to reach the wide glass doors of the office building. He swiped the app on the button indicating he had arrived. Then, a woman in smart office attire emerged from the building, staring at her phone. The crowd of workers rushed forward, pointing their phone screens at her. She barely moved, unstartled by the commotion. One by one, she looked at their outfacing phones, shaking her head before moving on to another. Then, as if finding her match, she nodded, and she and the delivery worker both swiped something on their individual phones, and she took her salad and went back into the gleaming tower.

Yasin patiently waited for his customer to arrive. Every time a yawning office worker came down, he hoped it was his, so he could move on to another order. When the clock hit seven, several people emerged, and Yasin put out his phone just like everyone else. The office workers were dressed crisply, wearing ghostly and absent expressions on their faces. When their hands brushed up against Yasin's momentarily, he felt their cool skin against his warm skin. They seemed somehow refreshed by the muggy outside air, a welcome change from the too strong office AC, while the delivery workers felt refreshed by the wisps of cool air that slipped out every time the doors opened. The delivery workers were wide awake, pouncing on the office workers with little time to spare, and their customers lazily floated from screen to screen, taking their time before returning to their mind-numbing, meaningless numbers on a screen.

Finally, a short woman with curly hair and huge hoop earrings informed Yasin that he had her order. He sighed in relief and handed her the package. He noticed that the salad toppings had fallen to one side and looked quite unappetizing, but the woman didn't seem to care.

A few hours had passed, but the bizarre experience from earlier stuck in Yasin's mind. He tried to pinpoint what was so unsettling about it. Maybe it was the zombie-like office workers that spooked him. There was a dehumanizing feeling that came with being a delivery worker, he realized. Regardless, he was grateful that it seemed to be a good disguise for him, because police officers never looked at him twice.

It was nearly midnight now. Taraweeh prayers had just ended at Madina Masjid, and Yasin was charging his phone at a wall socket in the back of the prayer hall.

"Done for the night?" Idris asked, plopping on the carpet beside him. "I'll take the bike if you're done."

"I paid until midnight today," Yasin reminded him.

"That gives you about…twenty minutes. Maybe you can squeeze a final order in?"

Yasin wanted to get up but his calves were so sore from biking nonstop since noon.

"Help me up," he said. Idris jumped up and clasped his palm firmly, lifting Yasin's sluggish body with some effort.

"Ahhh," Yasin groaned. He limped over to his shoes while he scrolled through his suite of delivery apps. He saw one pop up from a local sports bar. The name sounded familiar—he had picked up an order from there yesterday. He quickly accepted it.

On his way out, a sudden flash of light blinded him. His eyes slammed shut sharply. He blinked several times. Once his vision had returned, he looked left and right. Then, in the distance, he saw a body darting around a corner, a huge camera attached to a thick strap swinging from the person's arm.

Bewildered and concerned, he stood in place for several minutes. When he looked around, everything seemed normal. People were standing around casually as if nothing had happened. Then, he felt a buzz in his pocket.

Time's running out! Get to Louie's Sports Bar within the next five minutes or forfeit your order.

Yasin rushed over to unlock his bike and pedaled to the pickup location. He knew the drill here already. He went immediately to the entrance of the kitchen and found the same goateed bald man that was there yesterday. The bar was unusually quiet today though—he remembered something about the Knicks losing and being eliminated from the playoffs the day before. A few depressed looking men sat in one corner, still wearing their Knicks jerseys, slowly sipping beer.

"Just one second, boss. Take a seat," the bald manager said. "You can charge your phone there if you need."

Yasin looked over and saw a charger plugged into the wall with the cord hanging loose. He offered a hand gesture of gratitude and took a seat in the booth. It was one over from where the Knicks fans sat.

"What are the odds right now on that new betting app?" he overheard.

"For the next coach?" answered what sounded like an older man. "I'd wager it's–"

"No dummy," the first voice interrupted rudely.

"I don't know yet, someone just told me people were betting on this," a third, raspier voice said.

"Check then," the first voice said. "What's the over-under?"

"Bro, this isn't Vegas," a fourth, deeper voice quipped. "It doesn't work like that."

"Then how are you supposed to bet?" the first voice said. "I gotta know my odds so I can make a good bet."

"It's a different system," sighed the deep voice, as if he had no choice but to explain. "It's called a contract. You can see the percent chance of something happening and that gets assigned to a cost between a penny and a dollar. The other scenarios all get priced based on their percentage of likelihood. If one of the scenarios isn't possible anymore, its cost is divided between the others, until one scenario is left and it's worth a dollar. Then you can sell your contract back and make profit compared to what you bought it for."

"So it is basically gambling," the old voice followed.

"Relax, gramps," the first voice said. "You don't need to go to Vegas anymore to get your fix. It's all right here."

Yasin made a quick glance and saw the man who was speaking tap his phone. He looked away and pretended to see if the manager had the order ready yet.

"So what are the percentages right now," the first man to speak said, emphasizing the word 'percentages' sarcastically.

"Lemme look it up," the raspy voice said. "Ok…right now…so it's two down already, Derek and Amir, but it's been a couple days since another fugitive was found. So the odds have been pretty stable."

*Derek and Amir…*Yasin thought. *Which ones are those…*

"Anyway, it looks like Luis has the lowest percentage of being the last man standing at thirteen percent. Then it's Terrence at seventeen, Malik at twenty-two percent. Then it's a tie for most likely to survive to the end: Stephen and Yasin at twenty-four percent each."

Yasin froze when he heard his name. He suddenly felt very aware of himself. He sat still, waiting to see if he'd hear his name again.

"Dude, they're sleeping on Luis. He's probably living in the sewers somewhere," said the first man to speak.

"He looks mentally ill, bro. The cops will probably find him wandering the streets. If you're smart, you're betting on this Yasin guy," the deep voice posited.

Yasin gulped. It felt like the room was losing oxygen.

"Why him?" the raspy voice asked, intrigued.

"Cuz nobody knows anything about him. He's the perfect guy to disappear."

"That is true..." the raspy voice trailed off.

"Plus, the police probably wouldn't even be able to recognize him!" The first man laughed. "Cuz he looks like any other African dude selling fake Gucci on the street!"

Yasin involuntarily shook the table his arms rested on, and the metal napkin dispenser fell on its side loudly. The men across from him swiveled their heads and noticed him.

"Sorry dude, didn't mean to offend." But the first man laughed once more.

Finally, the manager brought out the order.

"Sorry for the wait, boss. One loaded nachos, one onion rings, and you can grab a coke from the fridge there."

Yasin realized it must be way past midnight now, and Idris would be angry. He got up quickly to grab the soda. While he did so, the manager grabbed the TV remote and flicked through the channels. He stopped on a local news channel and turned up the volume.

"The death toll has risen to eight victims following the bombing in Downtown Brooklyn last night. A mother, aged forty-four, and her daughter, aged fourteen, pictured here, have reportedly succumbed to their injuries. Stephen Hoffmeyer, the mastermind behind the terror plot, is still at large. Several other civilians are still seriously wounded and in critical condition. Live updates to come from PIX11 News."

All the voices in the bar had fallen quiet. The eyes of the four men, the manager, and Yasin were glued to the screen. But for Yasin, it was his first time hearing of Stephen Hoffmeyer's attack. Psycho's shrieking laughter from the prison van filled his ears, and his heart reached his throat in fright. His lip curled, and his eyes welled up in grief for the victims. As Yasin watched the screen, Psycho's sneering mugshot appeared, and to his disgust, his own appeared next to it, along with the other remaining fugitives. Stinger and Droopy's mugshots were covered in large red X's.

"Of the Steinway Seven, five escapees remain on the loose in New York City," the anchor continued. "Those five are Stephen Hoffmeyer, Luis Almanzar, Terrence Howard, Yasin Bamba, and Malik Clark. The NYPD is offering a staggering reward of twenty thousand dollars for information that leads to any arrest. Earlier today, the President has threatened to send in the National Guard—with or without Albany's approval."

"Yeah, I'm betting the house on this Yasin guy," the raspy voice said. "If he hasn't already, he better get the hell out of New York City."

Chapter 12: Saif

The 114th Precinct was bustling with activity the day after what the news dubbed "The Brooklyn Bombing." The attack was so shocking, so tragic, that Hoffmeyer began to overshadow the other convicts still at-large. Officers of Brooklyn's 78th Precinct had spent the night evacuating citizens and clearing off a six-block radius from the blast, but by the next morning, it was clear that Hoffmeyer had vanished once again.

After their daily briefing, Elias brought Saif a cup of fresh coffee. "I didn't get any sleep last night," he told Saif.

"Neither did I." Saif rubbed his eyes as he took the mug.

"Watch out, it's chipped on one side," Elias warned him.

Saif turned the mug around so the handle was on the left and gripped the flat side with his right palm. "I don't get how he got away again. That whole area should've been shut down immediately after the bomb went off."

"He might've put it there earlier and detonated it remotely." Elias shrugged. "Or maybe he had someone else do it, someone we don't know of. Or—" He tried to keep thinking of theories, but ran out of ideas.

"I think the commissioner's about to speak."

The officers of the precinct gathered around the projector once more to hear a live update from the commissioner. This time, when the camera turned on, the mayor was seated next to her. Flashes on the screen told them that photographers were in the room. The mayor tapped on a microphone in front of him, then began to speak.

"Good morning, NYPD officers," he said. "I am sure you all have been briefed, or at least made aware of the unfortunate attack that occurred last night. Our latest numbers say eight have been killed, and twenty-one injured. This was the work of a man who escaped NYPD custody nearly a week ago. Since then, only two out of seven fugitives have been caught."

Saif felt the air in the room stiffen. On the screen, the commissioner looked uncomfortable, shifting in her seat.

"I have received many calls since last night's attack, chiefly from the governor, who is pressuring me to bring in the National Guard. I have also received calls from the FBI and Homeland Security, who are offering me their resources in the case." The mayor paused. "I intend to accept their help."

Saif heard an outbreak of muttered curses. "Why are they all pissed?" Saif whispered to Elias. "This can't just be about money, like Jessica said."

"The more people that get involved, the less control we have over the situation," Elias said. "It's like having too many cooks in the kitchen."

It made sense, but Saif felt that there was more to it. Maybe the others didn't like the mayor going over their head. For him, restoring safety seemed like it should be the priority, no matter who helped.

"I've also received calls from personal friends, business leaders, CEOs, and other concerned citizens," the mayor continued. "This isn't just a public safety issue. This crisis is starting to put a strain on the local economy. Foot traffic has reduced dramatically on our streets. Employees aren't showing up for work. Tourists are cancelling trips. If we don't catch these seven men, and especially Stephen Hoffmeyer, we could be in a sustained economic crisis."

"Sounds like someone's worried about the elections coming up," Elias hissed.

Saif shook his head in disappointment. *How is that the mayor's first concern?*

"As I said before, I am accepting the FBI's help in finding and eliminating Stephen Hoffmeyer. I expect full collaboration from the NYPD. And the National Guard will be brought in to give citizens confidence in the safety of their city. Soldiers will be placed at busy intersections, subway stations, and major office buildings across the five boroughs. Safety will return to our streets."

The mayor stood up abruptly, and the live feed cut off. The precinct broke into chaos.

Captain Mancini's voice rang out above the clamor. "You heard the mayor today." Steely agitation punctuated the captain's words. "All resources are being deployed to find Stephen Hoffmeyer and stop him from committing another attack. Some of you will be receiving an FBI briefing regarding his known associates and potential next targets. I want to emphasize—yes, we are dealing with a dangerous man—but he clearly has a web of criminal contacts doing his bidding too. This is an organized crime syndicate, potentially a violent offshoot of the Aryan Brotherhood, which we believe Hoffmeyer joined in prison. It will take good police work to uncover how deep this rabbit hole goes. Let's get to it!"

The precinct cleared up as everyone left to their new assignments.

Jessica slumped next to Saif, her laptop open in her arms. She let out a groan.

"Uh, did you get this email, too, Jess?" Saif asked.

"Yep." She rolled her eyes. "Overnight shift? Ugh."

"Let me see." Saif scrutinized her laptop screen. He had received the same instructions.

"Let me talk to the captain and see if we can change this," he said. Jessica followed him to Mancini's office.

"Sir, I'd really like to change my assignment, if possible. I'd rather not be placed there."

"Where, the mosque? Aren't you a Muslim yourself?" Mancini sneered.

"Yeah, but—"

"Then get on with it and stop wasting my time," the captain demanded. "Do your job! Protect and serve!" He slammed his door shut after them.

"That's your problem with the assignment?" Jessica said.

After a few too-short hours of rest before their night shift, Saif found Jessica waiting at the meeting point outside the Al Iman Mosque on Steinway. The street was alive with families grabbing fresh kunafa, baklava, and mint tea from nearby shops, and the mosque's facade was layered with rows and rows of string lights.

"You look like you just rolled out of bed," Jessica teased. Saif's messy hair caught the glow from the flashing yellow and green lights above.

"That's because I did," Saif said. "I barely got any sleep last night. I was watching TV with my mom when I heard about the bombing."

Jessica's mischievous smile vanished. "Yeah, it's awful. Why do you think he did it?"

"Glad you asked," Saif said. "I haven't been able to think about anything else all day, and I have a theory. If you look at the attack from last year, Hoffmeyer targeted a women's health clinic in a working-class Black neighborhood in Queens. The latest attack is on the office of a Bengali councilwoman in Brooklyn. If I had to guess, I think the attacker is motivated by White supremacy and we're being sent here to this mosque because it could be another target."

"You really think so?" Jessica asked, surveying the area around them with a watchful eye. She pulled out a printout of the email she and Saif had received earlier that day.

"It looks like there's some type of all-night program at the mosque today," she said, reading aloud. "Probably it's for Ramadan right?" She looked at Saif for confirmation, who gave her a terse nod.

"It also says it's a youth program, so it's mostly gonna be kids and teens here. Makes sense why they wanted extra security. The request was an inbound from the youth director of the mosque."

Saif closed his eyes, trying to think who that could be. He remembered the youth director from when he was a kid himself, but he didn't know who it was now.

"It looks like the program might have already started," Jessica observed. Saif peeked through the windows of the mosque. A bunch of men were lined up in rows, praying.

"No, I don't think so. That's just regular prayers happening in there. The kids will probably come after."

Saif eyed the block for any potential danger. Despite the crowds, the restaurants weren't as full as he'd seen in Ramadans past. Usually, Ramadan was the busiest time of the year for the halal restaurants that densely packed Steinway. That meant a lot of the owners were probably losing business. Saif remembered the mayor's briefing from that afternoon.

After an echo of the imam's voice inside, the doors of the mosque opened. Men and women streamed out from two exits.

"I love their colorful robes," Jessica said. "What are they called?"

"There's a lot of names for it," Saif answered. "Thobe, djellaba, qamis…it depends on the country."

"Cool," she said.

The stream of people leaving reduced to a trickle, and then the mosque fully emptied. Saif poked his head inside to make sure. He wondered what the organizers of the night had planned.

Soon, groups of teenagers started to arrive, followed by parents dropping off their kids. Saif and Jessica checked bags for weapons and made sure people trying to go inside were actually there for the program. Jessica monitored the entrance that was labeled "Sisters" while Saif manned the entrance labeled "Brothers". A few of the adults looked at Saif with a curious expression, one that Saif wasn't used to seeing from people in the neighborhood.

"Thank you for being here, officer," a mother wearing a hijab said to him. She kissed her son on the forehead and told him she would pick him up in the morning.

When it was nearly ten o'clock., people stopped coming, and they shut the two doors. Excited voices could be heard from inside the mosque, but Steinway Street was almost quiet. By two in the morning, the last of the hookah bar patrons had went home and the street was silent.

Jessica stifled a yawn. "How are these kids still up?"

"It's the Ramadan schedule," Saif explained. "In Ramadan, kids stay up all night and sleep almost the whole day. It makes getting through the fasting easier and then at night you can eat and drink as much as you want until the sun comes up again."

"Huh. That makes sense," she said. "I used to think fasting from water all day was impossible, but I guess I've been doing that myself the last couple days."

Saif's eyebrow raised. "How come?"

"So I don't have to use the bathroom. You wouldn't get it," she laughed, seeing his expression. "You're a man."

"What's that supposed to mean?"

"I was paired up with Emmanuel the last few days, and every time I had to pee, it was such a hassle," Jessica explained. "You know how hard it is to find a restroom in this city. We were up on twenty-first street and there was nothing there. I had to take the cruiser and go to the fire station up the street every time."

"I don't see how it's any different for me," Saif said.

"Well, when Emmanuel had to go really bad he just went into the alley and…you know…"

"That's disgusting," Saif said. "I don't pee outside. I don't even pee standing up."

"How come?"

"It's against my religion," he said. He didn't know if it really was, but he thought he remembered hearing that before at the mosque.

"So you're a religious guy then?"

"Not really," Saif said. "But some things stick I guess." He tried to think of a way to change the subject. "Anything new on your end with the case?"

"Hmm, well I was working the anonymous tip line yesterday and I heard something interesting."

"What was it?"

"I don't know if it's a lead or just someone making things up," she said skeptically, "but this guy called in saying he knew something about the convict named Yasin Bamba. He said Yasin was somewhere in the East Village working as a delivery biker."

"As a delivery biker? Why in the world would he be doing that if he was on the run?"

"Yeah, I knew it was far-fetched," she said.

"It sounds racist to be honest. Just 'cause he's African."

"That's exactly why we didn't investigate it too deeply. But the caller was weirdly specific. On the phone he said to look for Yasin at a mosque on First and Eleventh street in Manhattan. I was thinking about going down there and checking it out with Detective Kaminski. Have you met her yet?"

"Do you see that?" Saif interrupted Jessica. "Somebody's coming down the street."

"What's he holding? It looks like some kind of a huge box," she whispered. "Should we call it in?"

"Wait a second, let me see what it looks like when he gets closer." Saif squinted. "Sir! I'm gonna need you to stop!" he called out. The silhouette stood still immediately.

Saif slowly started to approach with his hand hovering above his gun. He crept up closer and closer and could make out a pale, bearded face. He was carrying a tall stack of donut boxes, and on his wrist dangled a plastic bag full of bananas and other fruit.

Wait, he thought. *I know this guy.* It was an old classmate, Yahya. Though Yahya had always been nice, Saif's mood quickly soured at the sight of him. Yahya's older brother used to be one of his biggest bullies in middle school.

"Saif? Is that really you? How've you been? I feel like I haven't seen you since we graduated!"

"I barely recognized you either," Saif said with forced enthusiasm. He was starting to get annoyed at running into people he used to know while working. Maybe applying for the 114th precinct was a bad idea.

"Are you attending the all-nighter program?" Jessica butted in, all business.

"Yeah," Yahya said, turning his attention to her. "I'm the youth director here. And I want to thank you, both of you for being here." He looked at Saif with total sincerity, "The parents are so worried right now, with all the craziness going on. If we didn't have extra security this event would've been cancelled."

"Of course, sir." Jessica gave a sharp nod and strode to open the door for Yahya, whose hands looked too full to do it himself. He thanked her and went inside.

"You're a popular guy here," she told Saif.

"I wish I wasn't," Saif replied. But deep inside, seeing Yahya's appreciation made him happy. It seemed like for once in his life, people were starting to respect him.

Chapter 13: Yasin

After overhearing the conversation of people betting on his survival, Yasin felt physically sick. He decided not to go outside for a while. He hunkered down at the mosque, eating suhoor and iftar with the community, praying all twenty of the Taraweeh prayers at night, and sleeping in a corner whenever he was alone. In a stroke of luck, he accidentally discovered a secret bathroom in the basement. After his first shower in days, he changed into whatever seemed to fit him in a lost and found bucket of clothes. All the while, Yasin racked his brain for ideas on how to disappear without anyone noticing him. It was clear he needed to leave New York City. But how? If the local subway stops were being guarded by police, the bus terminal was surely being watched. And airplanes were obviously out of the question.

Periodically, Yasin peeked outside the windows of the mosque. The incident of the camera flash from a few days ago continued to haunt him. *Who was that, and why did they take a picture of me? Did they know who I am?*

His fears were heightened when he noticed a man wearing sunglasses and a camera around his neck hanging out on the street corner. Yasin even saw him facing straight at the mosque a few times.

"Idris, do you see that guy?" he asked.

"The one with the camera? What about him?" Idris replied.

"Why is he staring here like that? And what's that camera for?"

"Who cares?" Idris looked confused. "He's probably just a tourist. What's gotten into you?"

"No, I've seen him staring directly at us…" he trailed off. He was starting to question his own sanity. *Am I being paranoid, or is someone out there looking for me? Are they affiliated with the police?*

A few days into Yasin's mosque isolation, one of the local Bengali elders approached him. "Brother," he began softly, "I have noticed you here for the last several days. As you know, our masjid policy is you cannot stay overnight. I need you to find somewhere else to stay. Of course, you are still welcome to eat iftar and pray with us."

"Brother, I am homeless," Yasin pleaded, with his hands clasped together. "I have nowhere else to go."

"Brother, I am asking you nicely. I don't want to get the police involved."

Yasin's heart skipped a beat when the man said 'police'. He had to think of somewhere else to go. "No, I will find another place to stay," he said quickly. "Please, don't involve the police."

"Okay, but tonight, you should not be here. I will lock the mosque after midnight."

Yasin had to come up with a plan quickly. He looked outside the mosque into the glaring sunlight. He scanned the street up and down for the same man, the one with sunglasses and a huge camera around his neck. Then, a taxi pulled up and parked, blocking the window. A Pakistani man with a large beard emerged from the driver's seat and approached the mosque. Suddenly, Yasin had an idea.

"Assalamu alaikum," he said to the cab driver when he entered. "Can I ask you a question?"

"Wa alaikum assalam," the man replied. "Okay, what is it?"

"What's the farthest trip you would make?"

"Farthest?" The man stroked his immense beard in thought. "The farthest taxi ride I ever did was to Philadelphia."

"And how much does it cost to get there?"

"Hmm…let me check." The man opened his phone and typed into his maps app. Then he did some quick calculations.

"To Philly, I would charge four hundred."

"Four hundred?! That's a lot!"

"Hey hey, if I am going all the way to Philly, I have to charge you for the way back too. Even if it is a one-way trip, I have to come back home."

"Fair enough," Yasin said. "I will see if I have enough money. If I do, will you take me there today?"

"If you have the money, in cash, I will take you today," he promised. "We can leave after we eat iftar here."

"Great," Yasin said. He tried to do mental calculations of his own. *Have I made enough money from the delivery job to cover the trip?* Despite all his work, Guillermo hadn't paid him anything yet.

Yasin went down to the secret bathroom in the basement and assessed his appearance. His beard had grown since his escape. His hair had also grown, but it looked ungroomed, and he realized that might look suspicious. He looked around the bathroom for anything to cut it with. There were scissors on a shelf in the corner. He washed them with soap and then started to trim his hair in the sink. It was hard work—his hair was thick and the scissors were not very sharp. He cut and cut until it was short enough that the scissors could do no more. He tried to even the hair out as much as he could, and then cleaned up his beard a little bit too. Then he cleaned out the sink. In the mirror, he looked like a new man.

Yasin took a baseball cap from the lost and found bucket and took a deep breath before leaving the mosque. The man in the sunglasses was nowhere to be found. He walked briskly in the sharp sunlight to Canal Street, retracing the steps to Guillermo's apartment. At the building's entrance, he whispered the code into the buzzer.

"La casa del lobo."

After a few seconds the buzzer indicated the door was unlocked. He ran up the six flights of stairs in one go.

"Hola…Guillermo…" he said as he knocked, catching his breath in between words. The door immediately swung open.

"Yacob, right? Come in, take a seat."

Yasin didn't bother to correct him. In fact, it was better that Guillermo didn't remember his real name.

"So, what's wrong? I noticed you haven't worked in a few days."

"Nothing's wrong," Yasin said. "I just realized this job isn't for me. I want to cash out."

Guillermo looked annoyed. "I knew you wouldn't last," he grumbled. "You were soft from the get-go."

"Yes, I was soft, just get me my money," Yasin gestured impatiently. Guillermo huffed and left the room. Yasin's knee bounced anxiously. He wondered what his earnings would be. He hoped and prayed it would be enough for the Pakistani taxi driver.

"Let's see here," Guillermo was back with a laptop. "Give me your phone." Guillermo quietly counted Yasin's gross earnings across all the apps on the phone he had leased to Yasin. "In total, you've made $583.61," he said at last.

Yasin's heart leaped with joy. He had enough.

"Now, let's deduct my cut."

Yasin's heart dropped.

"245.88 are tips. As we discussed, tips go to me. That leaves you with $337.73."

Yasin closed his eyes in pain. So he would be about sixty dollars short. Maybe the taxi driver would have some mercy on him and give him a discount.

"Secondly, your dues for the phone."

"Hey, wait, I paid you fifty bucks when I rented it!" Yasin objected.

"It's a new week now, and I charge by the week," Guillermo grinned. He was enjoying this.

"Okay fine, fifty more." Yasin snarled. "Give me the rest."

"Ah, ah, ah." Guillermo wagged his finger. "Remember, I take fifteen percent if you want to be paid in cash. That leaves you with a grand total of…$244.57."

Yasin hugged his face with his hands. He felt hot tears bubble at the corner of his eyes.

"FINE! Fine, whatever, just give me my money. I EARNED THIS!"

Guillermo snorted. He retrieved a great wad of cash from his bulging pocket, counted out two hundred and forty dollars, then threw a five dollar bill on top. "Here's a little tip." Then Guillermo stuffed the remaining wad of cash back into his pocket, with some difficulty. Yasin watched the rest of the money disappear with unbridled greed. Thoughts of attacking Guillermo began to form. Before they could actualize, he stormed out of the apartment, slamming the door behind him. In the concrete stairwell between the sixth and fifth floor, Yasin leaned against the wall with his face in his hands. His back slid slowly down the wall until he was on the floor.

Nearly half an hour later, Yasin wiped his face and prepared to face the outside once more. He pulled his baseball cap over his head and pulled his mask over his nose. It was late in the afternoon, and he was starving. There were still a few hours before he could break his fast for the day. He walked back to the mosque, slower this time. He almost didn't care if he was caught. Freedom was starting to feel like a burden.

On his way back, he started to think of how he could make more money. He needed a job that was less public-facing. Maybe in a restaurant somewhere, hidden back in the kitchen. His mind raced with possibilities, but everything seemed out of reach.

When Yasin entered the mosque, he scanned over the bulletin board in the doorway for job listings. Most of the notes were people looking for apartments. But one caught his eye. It was scribbled in Arabic. He had studied Arabic formally in Guinea, when he was younger. He could read it with some focus.

Dishwasher needed in an Algerian restaurant on Steinway in Astoria. Pay is two hundred weekly. Small bedroom can be included for the right candidate.

It was perfect. Just one week of pay would make him enough to afford the taxi ride. And he could even secure a place to rest his head at night. But it was in Astoria. No matter how bad he wanted the job, he knew it was too dangerous to go back there.

Dejected, Yasin went through the next door into the main hall of the mosque. It was empty now, since there were no prayers going on, and most people would be at home resting during the last hours of fasting. The place would be full soon, but in the meantime, Yasin took the chance to take a quick nap. He lay in the middle of the carpet spreading his arms and legs out, relishing in the luxury of solitude. Then, a thought struck him. *What if Astoria is actually the safest place to be right now? The police probably searched every inch of that neighborhood and moved on now…*

Yasin jumped up from the floor with newfound energy. He went back to the note pinned to the wall in the doorway. At the bottom a contact was listed: *Interested people should contact Ali in person at his store next to Al Iman Mosque.*

Yasin had just barely stored the name Al Iman in his head when a fiery explosion inside the main hall of the mosque blew him off his feet. Shattered glass from the front door fell on his torso, just shy of his exposed neck. Smoke billowed out of the hall and suffocated his lungs. He twisted over onto his stomach and crawled out of the doorway on his hands and knees. A woman on the street screamed. A man wearing a kufi rushed into the smoldering entrance, looking for any other survivors.

"It's…empty…" Yasin managed to mumble, but nobody could understand what he said.

"Wait here, I'm calling the police," a young woman told him.

"No! No!" he grunted with all his might.

"There's nobody inside, thank God!" the man shouted as he emerged from the mosque, covered in black dust. The people in the crowd sighed in relief. Sirens wailed from a distance. Yasin wiped his bloodied face with his shirt. He took off his hat, shaking fragments of glass and drywall out of it. Then he fitted it back on and ran away as fast as he could.

Chapter 14: Saif

It was a muggy, humid summer afternoon. Officers were allowed to wear shorts in the summer, but Saif hated wearing shorts. When suiting up that morning though, he decided to try wearing them. And he was thankful he did. Elias was with him and they were managing traffic once again. The streets were eerily quiet.

"I feel like we should have caught everyone by now," Elias said, wiping the sweat off his forehead and fitting his NYPD cap back on.

"I think people here thought so too," Saif observed. "Now that Hoffmeyer's attacking again, everyone seems worried."

They looked up and down a desolate Broadway.

"Like, Broadway used to be the busiest street in Astoria," Saif said. "Now people are hiding indoors."

"Maybe it's just the heat?" Elias suggested.

"Nah, that could be part of it, but not all of it."

Elias picked up some radio chatter a few minutes later. "All units, all units, we have multiple calls reporting a possible explosion, East Village, First Avenue and East Eleventh Street. Units respond."

"Nine-Adam responding, ETA three minutes."

"Nine-Boy en route from fourteenth and third, ETA two minutes."

"Be advised, reports of smoke visible, possible structural damage. Fire Department has been notified and is responding."

"Nine-Boy on scene. Confirming explosion, appears to be ground floor of a five-story residential building. Heavy smoke, debris in the street. Fire Department is evacuating second-floor residents. Requesting additional units and ESU."

"All units, gas company has been notified. Treat it as potential gas explosion until further notice." The radio fell silent.

"That can't be a coincidence," Saif said to Elias. "It's Hoffmeyer."

Elias whipped out his phone and punched in the cross streets mentioned. He stared with his mouth agape.

"What is it?" Saif asked.

Elias turned his phone around so Saif could see. The address belonged to a mosque.

"Oh my God," Saif cried. "I knew it!"

Elias raced to find another explanation." Maybe it's just a gas explosion, like they said? It could be anything."

Saif glared back impatiently. "No, I knew something like this would happen. He's a white supremacist and he's targeting Muslims now. I have to do something about this. I'm a cop for God's sake!"

"What would you do?" Elias said.

"I have to find this psycho Hoffmeyer, and put an end to his terror."

The radio crackled back to life. "All officers, return to local precincts."

Saif and Elias jumped into their cruiser at once. Outside the precinct doors, they saw Jessica, Emmanuel, and the other rookies waiting for Captain Mancini.

"It's Hoffmeyer," Saif said, scanning their faces for a challenge to his assertion.

"I agree," Jessica said. "How likely is it that there's multiple bombers in the same week?"

"We have to do something," Saif urged. "How can we just sit around patrolling empty streets while he kills innocent people?"

"Broadway was empty?" Emmanuel asked, surprised. "Steinway was quiet too. I think people are afraid."

"Of course they are," Saif huffed. "Everyone knows Hoffmeyer's targeting minority communities, and Astoria is one of the most diverse neighborhoods in the whole city. But THINK guys, where would someone like him be hiding in New York City?"

"If he hates minorities, he's probably hiding somewhere without many of them," Emmanuel said. "What are some neighborhoods with no diversity?"

"His last confirmed attack was in Brooklyn," Jessica added. "Could he be somewhere like Williamsburg?"

"I don't think it matters where his attacks are," Elias argued. "He is never at the scene of the crime. He just orchestrates it."

"That's true," Saif said. "Maybe he's on Staten Island?"

"No, it's too hard to get in and out of there. We've had cops stationed at the Verrazzano since the fugitives escaped," Emmanuel pointed out. "There's no way he got over it unnoticed."

"He couldn't have taken the ferry?" Elias said. They all smiled at the preposterous idea of Hoffmeyer stuck on the crowded, rundown Staten Island ferry.

"Where else…" Saif thought aloud. "Manhattan? The Bronx? Anyone have a crazy idea?"

"Maybe…" Jessica said. "What if he's based somewhere like the Upper East Side?"

Everyone tried to think of why that would be impossible, but no immediate objections arose.

"That would be pretty crazy," Elias said finally. "The Upper East Side is super white and super wealthy. Imagine, he's just chilling in a penthouse somewhere on Park Avenue."

"That would be insane," Jessica laughed.

Saif didn't want to imagine. He wanted to catch Hoffmeyer. The latest attack at a mosque had lit a fire under him. He was determined to do something about it.

Captain Mancini finally arrived and the rookies followed him inside the precinct.

"You all have heard by now of the recent explosion that went off at an East Village mosque earlier today. The

FBI has confirmed to me that it was in fact a bomb and not a gas explosion."

"I knew it!" Saif hissed.

"The FBI have also informed us that the bomb used today was less sophisticated than the one used in the Brooklyn Bombing," Captain Mancini continued. "Nonetheless, they have not ruled out Hoffmeyer and his associates as being responsible. Due to the FBI now handling his case, I am not able to share more details than that. I commend you all for the important work you are doing, and stress the importance of staying alert, being communicative, and following instructions. To stop this reign of terror in our city, we must work together and rely on each other. These are dark times…"

Though the details and sentiments being shared by Captain Mancini were important, Saif's mind raced with other thoughts. The idea of catching Hoffmeyer engulfed him. Jessica's suggestion of the Upper East Side kept coming up. It was a paper-thin lead, not even a real lead, but he felt compelled to take action. The newfound trust his community had put in him would not go to waste.

After Captain Mancini's briefing concluded, Elias and Saif cruised back to Broadway and re-assumed their positions. It was still as empty as before, and that was driving Saif insane.

"Elias, I feel like I need to do something. I can't just sit here motionless. Hoffmeyer could be planning his next attack right now."

Elias put a hand on his shoulder. "I know brother, but what can we do?"

"Stop asking me that," Saif snapped. He thought in silence for a moment. He wanted to say his plan, but he was afraid of how Elias would react. "I want to go scope out the Upper East Side," he finally said.

Elias searched Saif's face and saw there was no changing his mind. "Go for it. I'll hold it down."

"Really?"

"Of course," Elias replied. "Back in the academy I always knew I could trust you. I know you're afraid for your community. And nothing is happening here. Now it's your turn to trust me."

"You're a legend," Saif said. "Please don't let Captain find out I left."

"I won't."

"All right…" Saif said, uncertain on what to do next. "I guess I'll go home and change first. I have to be undercover."

"Good luck man," Elias said. "I'll be here. Text me if you find anything, or if you need backup."

"Will do," Saif said, and he turned to walk towards home, feeling adrenaline rocket through him like electricity.

Saif knocked lightly before entering his apartment. He didn't want his mother to know he was back, because she might send him off for errands if she thought his shift had ended early. Hearing nothing from inside, he unlocked the door with his key and darted into his room. His heart was pounding as he switched into khaki cargo pants and a baggy white t-shirt. He kept his gun hidden in the small of his back under his waistband. Despite the weather, he tossed on a loose windbreaker to further hide the gun's bump. Lastly, he hid his badge in one of the cargo pockets in case he needed to show it. *Anything else…? Handcuffs!* He tossed a pair into another cargo pocket. Now, he was ready to go.

Chapter 15: Yasin

As he made away from the scene of the bombing, Yasin nearly tripped on a gap in the sidewalk. He dove behind a row of bushes to compose himself. His eyes tried to focus on his hands while he opened and closed them slowly. He couldn't feel any pain yet. Once the adrenaline died down, he knew he would.

He was about to crawl out of the bushes when he saw six police officers sprinting to the bombsite. He leaned back and watched them fight through the crowd that had built up around the mosque. A firetruck pulled in front, blaring its siren so people would move. He heard his own loud, labored breathing, and tried to make sense of what had caused the explosion. Was it a targeted attack?

He sat and watched firefighters run up the ladder attached to their truck and climb into a second floor window, disappearing behind a cloud of black smoke. Moments later, they started to come down, carrying residents two at a time. Their clothes were covered in dust and their bodies convulsed with hacking coughs.

While he watched, his vision became steady, and he knew it was time to go. He looked the other way and saw the street was empty. He slowly got to his feet and felt a sudden pain in his shoulder and back but forced his legs to carry him forward. At the next avenue, he saw the downward steps leading to the L train. He hid his face in his hat and shot down the steps.

On the platform, he was relieved to find no police. He jumped on the first train that arrived. While the doors closed in front of him, he saw police running down the steps in a hurry. The last thing he saw as the train pulled away were the cops sealing off the stairs with yellow caution tape.

Yasin sank into a bench and caught his breath. He thought people were looking at him strangely. But he also wasn't sure if it was just paranoia. He tilted his head forward and adjusted the cap to obscure most of his face, just to be safe.

A couple stops later, he exited the train and pushed through the throng of people trying to get on. He didn't know where he was or where he wanted to go. He just wanted to get away, far away. He went up a staircase, down a hall, following the movement of the crowd, doing everything to fit in and not stand out. Then, a sign caught his eye: *NW to Astoria-Ditmars Blvd.* Yasin's mind flashed back to the job listing he had seen. *Maybe it's a sign.* He didn't know exactly where in Astoria the Al Iman mosque was, but if he could find his way there, he could have a job and a safe place to stay, at least temporarily.

He floated over to the side of the platform where the N train sat open, drawing him in. It was not very full, and he walked all the way to a seat tucked away in a corner. He moved the cap over his face and let his head hang back, as if he was asleep. But his ears were perked up and actively listening.

"Stand clear of the closing doors, please."

The doors attempted to close, then slammed open again. *Oh no. They're coming to get me.*

"Stand clear."

The doors slowly tried to close again. *Please let it close, ya Allah.*

The doors locked in shut and the train began to move. *Alhamdulillah.*

"Stops are being skipped on south bound N,Q,R,W trains from Herald Square to Canal Street," the conductor's voice rattled through the speaker. "NYPD are investigating suspicious activity in the East Village."

Anxious voices broke out in the subway car as the riders learned about the attack from their phones. Yasin fiddled with his hands, not daring to look up at anyone.

"You chose the worst time to plan this trip!" Yasin's ears perked up, hearing the female voice shouting in French. The way she spoke was very formal to his ears, not like the French they spoke in Guinea. It must have been a tourist from France.

"But how was I supposed to know this would be happening," the man's voice argued back. "We planned this trip months ago."

"We should be relaxing in a five-star Tunisian resort right now," she huffed. "Instead we're in a hot stuffy train and there's a maniac killer on the loose. I told you the States were dangerous." She said the word 'States' in English with a mocking tone.

The train continued to make its stops: Herald Square, Times Square, 57th Street, and 5th Avenue. After the conductor announced each stop, he would say "Astoria-bound N train." Every time he said it, Yasin's heartbeat quickened with anticipation and hope. Finally, after Lexington-59th Street, the train clanked toward Queens.

They soon entered the dark tunnel separating Manhattan and Queens. It seemed like safety was waiting for him on the other side. His body rocked as the train picked up speed, hurtling through the darkness faster than between any stop before. It screeched and squealed as it turned through corners and around bends. Then, distant light from the Queens side started to filter into the tunnel.

Suddenly, there was a loud *bang!* and the roaring train grounded to a whisper. The speakers inside the subway car crackled to life.

"We apologize, there is an obstruction on the tracks. Please be patient while we investigate the issue."

Yasin didn't dare to lift the hat off his face, but he heard groans around him. His heart raced even faster now and sweat collected under his arms. Time even seemed to stand still. Then the speakers crackled again.

"Once again, there's an obstruction on the tracks. We apologize for the inconvenience. We should be moving shortly."

The occupants of the car started to talk to each other again. They were starting to get impatient. Yasin was beyond impatience. *Allah, please, let me get off this train!*

"Folks, we'll get moving momentarily. It looks like a bird or a small animal was on the tracks. It's being cleared now."

"Perfect, a freak accident right when I'm going to an interview," he heard a young voice very close to him say. Other voices around him grumbled with similar sentiments.

"Folks, NYPD are now on the scene," the conductor blurted suddenly, and Yasin's blood ran cold. "We are being diverted onto a different track. Please evacuate the car at the next station. Thank you for riding with the MTA."

Hushed whispers now filled the car. "What's going on?" a young woman near him cried. Yasin squirmed in his seat. He would have to make a run for it when the train opened.

The subway car crept forward very slowly. It was just a hundred feet shy of the next station. Everyone rose and lined up by the doors, anxious to get out. Yasin peeked from under the hat. The station platform was crawling with cops. They were funneling people off of the platform and up a single flight of stairs.

When Yasin's train car finally opened, he jumped up and forced his way into the middle of the desperate crowd. He heard whispers of the name Hoffmeyer. *Was it him that bombed the masjid I was in?* Mayhem ensued on the platform as people shoved and pushed their way up the stairs. Yasin felt like a pinball in the crowd, bouncing off the shoulders of everyone around him.

On the next level, everyone made a run for the final flight of stairs that led to the street. At the last moment, Yasin stole a look back at the cops on the lower level and saw a sight that shoved his heart into his throat.

From the tracks under the subway car they were just in, the police dragged out Whisper's viciously mangled dead body, his bloodied gray mane unmistakable.

Chapter 16: Saif

In the early evening Saif arrived at the 96th street stop on the 6 train. His plan was to scope out the Upper East Side starting at the top, where it bordered on Harlem, then work his way all the way down to the area known as Lenox Hill, bordering Midtown East. Within this enclosed area were some of the highest net worth individuals and most expensive real estate in all of New York City.

As soon as he got phone reception again underground in the 96th street station, a text from Elias came through.

they just caught fugitive #3, luis almanzar

Saif paused in front of the staircase that led to the exit, momentarily distracted from his mission. *Where was he hiding?* He texted back.

he was apparently living in a tunnel between manhattan and queens. earlier today the n train smashed into him while he was on the track and the cops found him dead on arrival.

Saif grimaced. Getting crushed by four hundred tons of steel was a brutal way to die. *That's rough.* He replied. *Wonder how he survived so long down there anyway, without food or water.*

he was probably scrounging on scraps like a rat. based on how he looked in his mugshot he seems used to that lifestyle.

That's messed up. Saif texted back quickly.

hey, don't forget what he did. he sexually assaulted multiple women in public.

Saif couldn't think of any rebuttal to that. He turned his screen off and zipped up his phone away in his cargo pocket. The station was hot. It was two levels underground but felt like seven. The shirt under his flashy windbreaker was already slick with sweat, but he couldn't take it off or the imprint of his hidden gun might show. He bounded up one staircase, and then another, skipping two stairs at a time. On the street, the evening sun was hidden by residential skyscrapers that towered around him, providing ample shade. *Now, where to begin?*

He slowly walked across the street on Lexington Avenue, passing a park filled with kids squealing in excitement while running through a water sprinkler. All seemed normal. He took a left on 96th street, going eastwards. Though the streets were full of speeding cars, the sidewalks were eerily empty. At Third Avenue, an unexpected sight caught his eye. On his left, a beige, marble minaret rose into the sky, standing beside a massive pastel green dome. A sign outside read: *The Islamic Cultural Center of New York.* Saif was taken aback by its size. He had heard of this mosque, referred to as the 96th Street Mosque, but he had never made it out here during all his years of living in New York City. He couldn't believe such a large and prominent mosque like this existed in Manhattan.

He shook his head and reminded himself of his mission. He was here to look for suspicious people or activity that could potentially point him to Hoffmeyer. He looked up at the gleaming condos high above him. *Could Hoffmeyer be hiding in any one of these?*

After strolling a few blocks down Second Avenue, he approached another city park. It was square-shaped and had a ring of benches surrounding a playground in the middle. He quickly scanned the park for anything suspicious. As he watched, he noticed the park was quite filthy. Trash piled high in garbage bins and rats scurried around, just as the sun began to set.

"Um, 'scuse me," said a voice behind him. Saif was standing right in front of the entrance of the park, and a man wearing baggy, torn clothing was trying to get in. The man was clutching a pizza box in his grimy hands, and had spots of dirt on his face. He had a large smudge of red pizza sauce over one eyebrow. Saif knew it wasn't blood because he could see dark green specks of oregano and basil in it.

"Sorry, go ahead," Saif said, trying to hide the expression of disgust on his face. He moved out of the way and drifted off down Second Avenue, but something in the man's eyes was somehow familiar. He walked around the corner and turned right on 90th Street to another side of the park. There, he stood behind a bush and watched the man quietly.

The man sat in a far corner of the park and opened his pizza box. He watched the spot where Saif had stood for a solid minute before picking out a slice and starting to eat.

Between each bite, he sat still, looking around him nervously.

Very suspicious, Saif thought. *But why does his face seem so familiar?* Saif continued to watch him, thinking hard. Something about his eyes, or the area around them, reminded him of someone. Then he realized it reminded him of himself. Something in his mind clicked. He whipped out his phone to text Elias.

I found hik, he typed quickly, not taking his eyes off the man. *For real this tine.*

who?? don't tell me its malik clark again.

It is! It's him!! Saif insisted.

alright, if it's really him, send a picture. the real malik has a tattoo above his right eyebrow.

Saif opened his camera app and tried to zoom in on the man eating pizza. He kept looking in different directions and it was hard to get a still photo. When he finally got one, he remembered something. *He's got pizza sauce on his face. You can't see it clearly.* He sent Elias the photo he took.

are you telling me that homeless man is malik clark? i could maaaaybe see it, but you need to make sure he has the tattoo. its supposed to say 'krooked'.

Saif anxiously bit his fingernails in thought. How could he get a clearer view of the man's forehead? He stepped back quietly, then ran over to a halal cart parked on the sidewalk on Third Avenue.

"One chicken over rice, please. I'm in a hurry," he ordered, anxious to get back to the park and the man.

"Sure brother, no problem," the friendly man replied. He got to work immediately, searing and chopping up marinated chicken thighs on his grill, scooping fragrant rice into a plastic container, and adding a simple salad on the side. "Whitesaucehotsauce?" he asked all at once.

"Both, please," Saif said. He watched his food get drenched in that sweet mystery sauce that he could never get enough of. The smells were mouthwatering, but he had to stay focused. The man neatly placed the food container in a bag, added a plastic fork and a heap of napkins on top, and handed it to Saif.

Saif took out a ten-dollar bill and paid the man. He grabbed his bag and hurried back to the park with his food. Rats scurried out of his way as he walked over to a bench close to the man eating his pizza. A few other people had taken up residence in the park.

Saif casually opened his box of food and took a few bites in silence. Through his peripheral vision, he could tell the man with the pizza was staring at him. He took a few more bites of his food, stuffing his face with forkfuls of sauced chicken. As he ate, the man started to relax.

Then, Saif made his move.

"Oh," he said, dropping a bunch of napkins on the floor between him and the man. He leaned down to pick them up, getting a closer look at the man's face as he went down. On the man's tan skin, under the pizza sauce, he thought he saw a tinge of blue writing.

"Need some?" Saif asked as he gathered his scattered napkins. The man stared at him with deep suspicion. Then he stirred weakly, attempting to get up.

"Here," Saif said, handing him a fistful of napkins. Before the man could turn away, Saif raised his arm and forcefully brushed the man's forehead with the bunched napkins. The man shouted in fright, but with the light of a nearby lamp, Saif clearly read the word "krooked" above his right eyebrow. Malik Clark jumped out of the bench, throwing a half-eaten slice of pizza at Saif's face, narrowly missing him.

Saif leaped after Malik, chasing him around the circle of benches surrounding the playground and outside the park. Malik tried throwing anything within reach at Saif: parked bicycles, store signs, and even people, but Saif continued to close the gap. Malik took a sharp turn into traffic, dodging cabs and delivery trucks hurtling down Lexington Avenue. At 83rd street, he turned again, sprinting past outdoor dining arrangements and throwing chairs in his wake. They ran several blocks until Park Avenue, where a doorman shouted.

"Officers! They're over there!"

Two patrol officers stationed on Park Avenue joined the chase, pausing traffic and calling in other units to block off the area. A woman shrieked in terror when Malik and Saif whizzed by her.

Saif was getting tired, but he knew the man must be getting tired too. Then he saw two officers cutting off Malik ahead.

"Stop him!" Saif cried, pointing at Malik. "He's one of the Steinway Seven!" Malik then took a sharp turn towards Central Park, but the two officers coming the opposite way didn't change direction.

"He's headed to the park!" Saif shouted, but the two officers kept sprinting towards him instead. Saif stopped in his tracks. An officer barreled into Saif's stationary body, sending him flying several feet backwards and hitting his head on the concrete.

A few seconds later, Saif regained consciousness, finding his hands cuffed to a lamppost.

"What the hell are you doing?!" Saif shouted immediately. "You're letting him get away!"

"We need to see some ID," one of the cops said.

"I'm a freaking police officer you idiots!" Saif shouted. "I literally found one of the fugitives and you let him escape again!"

The two officers looked at each other skeptically.

"As I said, we need to see some ID," the same cop repeated. Saif groaned in frustration. "I seriously can't believe you guys arrested a cop and let an escaped convict get away. My name is Saif Belkacem. My badge is in my right pant pocket. Great job guys. Fantastic police work."

The officer reached down into Saif's pant pocket and took out his badge. He stared at it for a moment, then looked up at his partner.

"I think he's a cop," he said with a tone of surprise.

"Of course I'm a cop, now let me go and go find the guy for God's sake!" Saif bellowed.

The two cops shifted into high gear, letting Saif loose from his handcuffs and speaking rapidly into their radios to shut down Central Park. The officers then ran off into the darkness, leaving Saif alone on the concrete without so much as an apology. He picked himself up, dusted himself off, and took the subway home in utter humiliation.

Chapter 17: Yasin

Yasin slipped away into the crowd fleeing from the scene surrounding Whisper and walked briskly towards Steinway Street. An hour later, he arrived at the unmistakable Al Iman Mosque, towering over its neighboring shops with a distinctive pink minaret. It was just around iftar time. People streamed towards the mosque's wide-open doors, clogging the entrance as they took their shoes off and fitted them into small shoe-sized shelves.

The men inside were already lined up for prayer. Yasin followed hand-written Arabic signs to the basement, where he purified himself for prayer using the huge oval sinks made for that purpose. He heard a beautiful voice upstairs start reciting the Quran. He went back up and joined the prayer.

The imam was gifted with a powerful voice, but he used its strength sparingly. At points, he read light and soft, and at others, with a deep and solemn tone. But when his voice reached its highest pitch, imbued with emotion and passion, Yasin felt his heart stir so strong it felt like something had moved within his chest.

At the end of prayer, Yasin emerged from a peaceful dream and re-entered an unpleasant reality. There was a commotion as people around him stirred and volunteers started to unfurl long floor mats for eating on. Other volunteers entered from a back door, carrying tall stacks of plastic food containers. They spoke in rapid Egyptian Arabic, directing each other in a system of controlled chaos.

"Please take a seat brother, over there," a young man instructed Yasin. Another group of volunteers entered from the main entrance, all heaving one massive pot of soup. They lugged it onto a table and it fell in a low thud that threatened the table's legs. A man with a gray-speckled beard wielding a huge ladle started pouring the soup into small plastic cups.

Yasin went to stand in line for the soup and was soon handed a warm cup and a piece of bread. He wandered over to a seating area and plopped down. There were no spoons available, so he sipped the soup straight from the cup. It was far tastier than he had expected. Chickpeas, lentils, and tiny chunks of meat swam in a delicate tomato broth. The bread, however, was quite stale.

Before he finished the soup, a volunteer rolled over a cart loaded with food containers and handed one to Yasin. He opened it and found a roasted chicken quarter on a bed of rice. Another man then dropped off a small container of salad to go with it. Now surrounded by a veritable feast, Yasin felt deeply grateful. Ramadan was a time of sacrifice and togetherness, and it felt like the spirit of that was alive in the building. He couldn't tell if people around him were wealthy or impoverished, but everyone there prayed standing shoulder to shoulder and ate on the floor sitting side by side. However, Yasin couldn't help but remember that this heartwarming scene was only a fleeting escape from his cruel reality.

"So, how's your first Ramadan going?" he heard a young voice across from him. It was an Arab teenager, and he was speaking to someone who looked like they could be African American.

"It was pretty hard at first, not gonna lie," the African American teenager laughed, "but I think I'm starting to get the hang of it."

"It's already the last ten days, so you're doing great!" the Arab teenager said. "Even if you've been doing it all your life, it's still tough."

"Really?" his friend said. "I thought it would be easy for you by now."

"Nahh." The Arab kid laughed. "If it was easy to fast people would do it every day. You get a lot of rewards for it."

"I feel like for my next Ramadan, I could optimize things a bit better. Like maybe prepare my suhoor the night before and have more protein. The water part isn't as bad as I thought, but I get super hungry by like, five."

"Yeah, usually I'm trying to get everything important done early in the day, so I can rest later. But sometimes, you just have to learn to sit with the hunger and do what you need to do."

"Mm, I like that, sit with the hunger," the African American kid echoed. "I really feel like the discipline aspect of Ramadan is huge for me. If I can hold myself back from eating and drinking, I can definitely avoid things like smoking. I used to be addicted to my vape but I quit for Ramadan."

"Maybe for good!" the Arab kid smiled.

Yasin was touched by their earnestness. When he first left Guinea six years ago, his son Taha was only nine. Taha would now be around the age of these young teens, and he thought that if Taha was spending his Ramadan in Guinea like these boys were, he would be a proud father.

Yasin collected the last grains of rice in his bowl and cleaned up his surroundings. The mosque was beginning to clear out now that people had finished their food. He sighed. The past few weeks had been exhausting. He lived in permanent anxiety, knowing his freedom could be cut short at any time. And he was now reminded that he wasn't able to reach out to his wife and son, who used to depend on his earnings to survive. All he could do was pray that their community back home stepped up in his absence, and try to find a way to support them again.

Outside the mosque, Yasin looked for the restaurant he had seen an ad for. The Arabic note said to find a man named Ali outside his store next to the Al Iman Mosque. He walked along Steinway Street, but there was only a hotel and a laundromat. Then, the third door down, he saw a small grocery store and meat market. He went inside.

"Salam, I'm looking for Ali," he said. The man behind the counter replied to his salam, but stared blankly afterwards. Then he mumbled something in Arabic and tried to gesture with his hands that Ali had left and would be coming back. Yasin nodded, getting the idea, and started wandering around the small store. He walked the narrow aisles, surrounded by shelves loaded with Arab products from pastas to condiments to cans of ful and hummus. He approached the back of the store, where meat was displayed in large glass coolers. Behind the counter, there was a skinned and gutted goat hanging from a hook in the ceiling. To the side there was a small fridge stocked with neatly stacked trays of bright red sausages.

"That's my famous merguez," a man said, coming up behind him. "Would you like to try some?"

"Are you Ali?" Yasin asked, turning around. "I am here to ask about the job."

"Oh good, just in time," Ali replied. "My restaurant next door is opening tomorrow."

"So you didn't hire anyone yet?"

"No, I'm having a hard time finding anyone right now," Ali frowned. "Even Steinway is not as busy as it usually is during Ramadan. Probably because of all those killers on the loose. You're not one of them, are you?" He laughed and clapped Yasin on the shoulder. "Just messing with you."

Yasin laughed nervously, trying to think of something to say.

"Yes, it's really scary what Psycho—I mean Hoffmeyer—is doing."

"A psycho he is, and I hope he is caught soon. His last attack at Madina Masjid really shocked me. I was just there the day before putting up the job listing." Ali shook his head in sorrow. "I remember when I first came to America thirty years ago, that was the first masjid I went to. That's why I put the job listing there. I wanted to give an opportunity to someone just trying to survive like I once was."

"By the way, I was also interested in the room that you mentioned," Yasin remembered suddenly.

"Ah, yes! So, that will actually be right inside the restaurant. Let me take you there."

Ali led Yasin to a storefront next door. Inside, everything looked clean and ready, staged like a TV set. Ali led him to a locked door in the back and took out a ring full of keys and tried some of them, until one finally turned.

"Okay, this one would be yours," he said, handing Yasin the key that worked. "I have another copy somewhere, but keep this one safe." Behind the door was a windowless room with a thin mattress on the floor, a plastic chair and table, and a tiny bathroom hidden behind a curtain. "It is quite small," Ali said apologetically.

"It's perfect." Yasin smiled.

"So do you still want to try that merguez?"

They walked back to the gleaming kitchen and Ali ran his hand over the stainless steel countertop. "Not too bad, eh? I was lucky to get a great deal on the kitchen equipment. The guys planning to open a restaurant here split up and abandoned the project, so I bought everything half-price." Ali beamed as he looked around, stars twinkling in his dark pupils. "Seeing it all come together is like witnessing the birth of your child." He went around the counter and busied himself in the kitchen, throwing a few red sausages onto the spotless grill. They started to sizzle, filling the restaurant with a tantalizing meaty aroma. "I don't get my fresh baguettes in until the morning," Ali said, "so I'll have to just give you the sausages by themselves."

"No problem," Yasin waved his hand. He was still surprised Ali had agreed to hire him without so much as an interview. He guessed Ali was out of options with opening day coming so soon.

"So, this is going to be you," Ali said, pointing to the sink behind him. "I will have a friend run the grocery store while I get the restaurant kicked off. For now it'll just be me and you here." Ali took the sausages off the grill and put them on a plate. "The seats inside the restaurant were all folded up on the tables, but there were some outdoor seats set up. Should we take a seat outside?" he suggested. Ali went to quickly wipe the grill clean while Yasin settled on a wicker chair.

"So you own the grocery store and now you're opening a restaurant too?" Yasin asked.

"Correct," Ali said. "You know, I have been thinking about doing this for a long, long time. In fact, it's been years in the making. I was just scared to take the risk. I knew that running two businesses at the same time would be a lot of work."

"So what made you finally do it?"

"It's funny…" he smiled wryly, recounting what had happened. "There's this kid I've known for a long time, almost his entire life—frankly a very arrogant kid. I know his mother well too. A couple weeks ago, he stopped by to buy some groceries, and we had a little chat, as usual. Let's just say…he lit a fire under me, you understand? He made me realize that, even though I've had success, alhamdulillah, if I have the ability to do more, then why not?"

"May Allah grant you more success," Yasin said. "And this sausage is delicious!" It was the perfect level of spice and bursting with flavor. "What else is on the menu?" he asked.

"During Ramadan, we'll have a special menu with traditional entrees. But the normal menu will include sandwiches with that merguez you're eating, we're gonna have garantita, which is a typical Algerian sandwich using chickpeas, we're gonna do frites omelette, another classic, and then of course loubia, which is a bean dish."

"Oh, is that where the name of the restaurant comes from?"

"Yes, exactly. There's a famous restaurant I used to go to growing up, near the Casbah of Algiers—that is what we call the old part of the city. The French destroyed most of it when they colonized us, but part of the old city survived. Me and my friends would go there to explore. After a long day there was one place that we ate at often, because it was cheap and had all the good sodas." Ali's eyes went distant as he recalled his youth.

"It's a simple hole in the wall spot called 'Le Roi De La Loubia', or 'Malik Al Loubia' in Arabic. I think it's become even more famous since I was younger, but I haven't been back to Algeria in many years. I doubt you'll ever go there, but if you ever happen to be in Algiers, it's a wonderful place full of good memories."

"Maybe I will go someday," Yasin said, staring up at the gleaming storefront sign above them that read 'King of Beans'.

Chapter 18: Saif

The day after his arrest, Saif clocked in at work and tried to keep his head down. He was still furious about what happened the day before, but he knew telling the captain about it would be a bad idea. He found Elias sitting in front of his computer in the break room. He cleared his throat, and Elias looked up at him in surprise, shutting his laptop screen.

"What happened yesterday?" Elias whispered. "You didn't answer my texts after you said you found Malik."

Saif looked around for listeners and lowered himself into a chair. "You won't believe it," he said bitterly. "But first, did anything happen after I left? Did the Captain hear that I left my post?"

"No, nothing happened. I just continued like normal, I checked IDs, managed traffic, kept an eye out. But as far as I can tell he doesn't know. I don't see how he could have found out—"

Just then, they heard a voice ring across the precinct. "BELKACEM!"

Saif jumped in his chair and scrambled to his feet. Elias opened his laptop screen again and slid down his chair out of view. Saif gingerly stepped out of the break room and into the common area of the station. Captain Mancini's face was red in anger, from his sharp jaw all the way up to his bald head.

"You directly disobeyed orders yesterday. You were stationed on Broadway. You abandoned your post and almost cost us the capture of a dangerous fugitive."

"But I was the one who—"

"Silence! In my office, now."

Saif hung his head in shame while multiple officers of various ranks stared in confusion and secondhand embarrassment. He trudged into the captain's office and took a seat. Captain Mancini looked around at the others in the precinct, his anger rising instead of dissipating. "This does not concern any of you. Back to work!" he barked, his beady eyes nearly bursting from their sockets.

Sounds of shuffling papers and heavy booted footsteps filled the air while Captain Mancini watched, breathing heavily. When he felt satisfied, he went into his office and slammed the door shut after him. The glass in the door rattled ominously. Elias watched the back of Saif's curly head in worry.

"Now, tell me everything that happened, and do not even try to lie, because I have heard from officers on the scene already. From the beginning."

Saif squirmed in his seat while the captain spoke. He had a foreboding feeling that his cop career was destined for a short life. Then, as he started to recall what had happened, his own anger began to build, and shame morphed into indignation. "Fine, I'll start from the beginning," he said. "I was on Broadway, doing my job, and not a single thing was happening. Meanwhile, there's a mass murderer on the loose who's now bombing mosques and apparently nobody can find him. So I left my post, on my own volition," he added, remembering not to implicate Elias, "and nobody else told me to do this. I left my position, changed into some street clothes, and went to find Hoffmeyer myself. My first thought was to go to the Upper East Side--"

"Hoffmeyer, hiding in the Upper East Side? Why in hell would he be over there?" Captain Mancini interrupted.

Saif sat in embarrassment for a moment, his eyes glazing over while he thought of a comeback. *Screw him, I'll just keep going.* "I got off at 96th Street and started to search for clues. That's when I found Malik Clark. He was posing as a homeless person, or maybe he was homeless, and he was about to eat a pizza. I first made sure it was him and then I tried to grab him, but he made a run for it. I pursued him down several blocks, and then he got cut off by a few other cops who were in the area, but to my surprise, instead of going after Malik, which I was literally yelling at them to do, they went after me. They tackled me, arrested me, tied me to a pole, and let Malik get away."

"Malik didn't get away after all. Local officers from the 23rd Precinct, who were doing their jobs, were able to locate him in Central Park soon after."

"Well, I did most of the work anyway," Saif shrugged.

"Those officers cleaning up your mess is the only reason you aren't being terminated today," Captain Mancini glowered. "If you had cost us catching one of the fugitives, I'd be asking for your badge right now. And besides that, your meddling could have led to something far worse. You are damn lucky nobody was hurt."

"But I was the one who found him. Nobody would have found him without me," Saif insisted.

"Alright, that's enough arrogance out of you. You are not the only cop that can do this job."

"Clearly I was, because those two cops from the 23rd are blind," Saif said, raising his voice. "Or maybe…"

"Maybe what?"

"Nothing."

"Spit it!" Captain Mancini demanded.

"Maybe those cops racially profiled me. I was in street clothes. And they didn't believe me when I said I was also a cop." Saif instantly regretted sharing his true feelings.

"So you think you were racially profiled? Because two cops were doing their job? What's next, are you going to sue the NYPD?" Captain Mancini sighed, rubbing his temple with one hand.

"Umm, no—" Saif stammered. "But I was mistreated. It was humiliating. I'm sure you'll be disciplining those two officers, right?"

"Those two officers did nothing wrong," the Captain doubled down in a slow, stern voice. "They identified a threat and they dealt with it."

"So I'm a threat now? I was literally protecting our city by getting a dangerous fugitive convict off the streets."

"I don't care. You weren't supposed to be there. You defied direct orders and that's why you're suspended for one week, effective immediately. That badge," the captain snapped, "is what distinguishes you from regular people on the street. When you decide to take it off, I can't guarantee what will happen to you."

"A week?" Saif protested. "And what do those officers get? At least a day suspension, right?"

"I don't have time for this nonsense. Your discipline could have been far worse. You're lucky that those officers who arrested you were willing to defend you to their captain, since they're getting the credit for the capture of Malik Clark."

"What?" Saif cried. He was the one who deserved the recognition for catching a fugitive in one of the biggest outbreaks in city history. It was his name that should be mentioned in the commissioner's next briefing. It was him who should be celebrated in the neighborhood. He made an immense effort to compose himself in the face of the captain.

"A week, rookie. And that's me being lenient."

Saif took a deep breath and got up to leave.

"I'm going to need your gun, Saif." the captain said gravely.

Saif took his gun out of its holster and placed it gently on the desk. Then he unclipped his badge from his uniform and placed it beside the gun. It felt heavier than he remembered.

"See you next week, Captain." Saif left for the exit wordlessly without looking back at Elias. He walked directly home.

"Saif, you're home early?"

Saif wasn't in the mood to explain to his mother what had happened, but he did want to get it off his chest, at least a little bit. He floated behind her while she was washing dishes, waiting for an opening amid the clanking of cups and plates.

"Mama, I'm sorry. I have bad news."

"What happened?" She turned the water off and dried her hands.

"I made a mistake and got suspended. But the captain isn't being fair."

"Suspended?" she asked, rubbing her eyelids. She was still in her pajamas. "What does suspended mean? Do you still get paid?"

"Umm, I think so, I'm not sure." He was starting to regret bringing it up. "I'm super tired. I'm going to take a nap. Can we talk about it later?"

"Sure, go take a rest." She swiveled back to the sink and added some soap to her sponge.

Saif started unbuttoning his uniform while walking to his room and then crashed into his bed face first. He lay there for several minutes, while his anger dissolved into an all-consuming depression. Then drowsiness overtook him, and he fell into a dreamful sleep.

Saif never dreamed of his father. Since he was two, it had always just been him and his mother. The only way he knew of his father was through a few grainy photos they had in a photobook, and stories from his mother, but even his mother didn't like to talk much about him. About her deceased brother, she spoke often, and Saif knew him pretty well. But of her husband, his mother could only manage to speak for a few minutes before falling silent and teary-eyed.

In his dream, Saif was looking up at his dad from the height of a small child. His father stood tall and broad shouldered, wearing camouflage military fatigues. His face was freshly shaven, revealing his strong jaw, which Saif could see in clear view from beneath him.

As he watched, his father took a seat at a wooden dining table in the middle of the kitchen. His mother came into view and went to the stove to cook something. She turned around and brought a still sizzling pan over to his father's plate. Her face looked young and wrinkle free; her eyes bright with life.

It looked like she spoke to his father, but the words were fuzzy and undecipherable. His father sat straight backed, as if a ruler was inside his uniform. He ate with impeccable table manners, cutting into the meat with a fork and knife, not a single morsel of food falling when it was raised to his mouth. Saif noticed on his head a black beret, slightly off center, but perfectly placed to be that way.

Saif looked at his father and felt joy in his heart. He knew, watching him, that this was the man he wanted to become all his life. This is how he wanted to look and to carry himself. This was the confidence he'd always needed. He wished that his father had been there to nudge him in the right direction through all of life's battles.

As he watched his father chew his food, awards for his service manifested. First, a pin appeared on his collar, then a green and red ribboned medal on his chest. The medal split into a row of medals. His father was gaining distinction. He was also aging. His hair started graying, and then, suddenly, he fell face first into his plate. Saif tried to shout, to cry, but all he could do was watch.

The dream shifted into the scene of a funeral. He watched as military officers carried a coffin with an Algerian flag draped on it. They solemnly marched through a grassy field. It was a cemetery. The marching men stopped before a deep hole dug into the dirt. They lowered the coffin into the ground. Muffled voices were heard around Saif, like people talking underwater. Then, he watched the men shovel piles of dirt back into the hole. A few more sounds of voices were heard and then it was all silent. Saif was alone in front of his freshly buried father.

For the first time in the dream, Saif began to speak. Though he couldn't hear himself say the words, he felt thoughts leave his mind.

Baba. I miss you.

Baba, can you hear me?

Baba, I need your help.

Nothing happened. Then, he heard a voice, or rather, an alien thought entered his head.

I hear you, my son.

Saif's heartbeat quickened. *Baba, I don't know what to do. It's not fair. I completed the academy, I became a cop. I just wanted to take care of Mama, and be brave like you. But they're suspending me. It's not fair. It's humiliating. Is it really because I'm brown that they treated me that way? Am I always going to be treated like a criminal? Am I overthinking it? I just don't know anymore. I just want to keep people safe. I want to protect my community. Like you did.*

Saif didn't hear anything back. He worried that he had imagined his father's earlier answer. *Should I quit the force? Should I stick with it? What should I do?* Saif asked.

Then, he heard the foreign voice again. It sounded different to his own inner voice, more gruff and masculine. *Listen to your heart, my son. It will guide you as long as you keep it clean from illness. Protect your heart, and it will tell you where to go. And pray for me, Saif. Not everything I did was heroic. I've made mistakes. I've done things I'm ashamed of. If you care about me, pray for me.*

Saif woke up, still hearing his father's voice in his head. *Pray for me…*

He put his hands together, open like a cup. "Oh Allah, please have mercy on my father and grant him a place in heaven." Then he sat in his dark room and thought hard to remember the exact words his father had said to him.

Listen to your heart…

Saif closed his eyes and listened, but he heard nothing back.

Chapter 19: Yasin

It was opening day at the King of Beans, or rather opening night, because Ali expected most of their customers to be fasting during the day. Ali told Yasin to arrive around five in the afternoon to begin preparation, but also because he planned to host a watch party for a soccer game that was scheduled for 5:30.

It was the World Cup qualifiers, and Algeria was playing in a heavyweight matchup against Egypt. The vibe on Steinway was tense. Much of the community comprised of Egyptian immigrants, just as most of the restaurants and businesses on Steinway were owned by Egyptians. However, in recent years, Algerians had started immigrating to New York City in larger numbers. The rivalry between the two national soccer teams had also migrated to New York.

On the street, people announced their allegiances on their chests with brightly colored jerseys, and businesses proved their loyalties through national flags decorating store entrances and windows. At King of Beans, the Algerian flag was draped in the back of the restaurant, but it was clearly visible from the street through the front door window. When Yasin arrived, there was already a group of men on the outdoor chairs chatting with Ali. They were speaking Arabic, but in a dialect that Yasin couldn't quite understand.

When Ali noticed his presence, he got up. "Ready for our first day?" he said, rubbing his hands together in excitement. He led Yasin inside and closed the door. "By the way, I'm embarrassed to ask, but what was your name again?"

"Hussein," Yasin blurted out. He didn't know any Husseins, but maybe that's why the name felt stronger as an alias. Since Ali was aware of the prisoner breakout, he couldn't afford to use his real name.

"We still have a few hours before iftar service begins," Ali said, "but the game starts in about twenty minutes. Could you help me arrange the tables and set up the TV? It just came in this morning. It's still wrapped in the back."

"Of course," Yasin replied, and he got to work. He went around to the back of the store behind the counter and found a massive box. On one side of the box was a printed image of a TV that advertised a 65 inch screen. Though he wasn't good with technology, he thought he could at least open it and set the TV on a table for Ali to configure.

Meanwhile, Ali reviewed his menu for the day. He had arrived earlier that morning to prep ingredients so he didn't have to start cooking until a couple hours before iftar. He had about an hour to watch the game with his friends before he had to begin the soup.

Once he had the TV out and plugged in, Yasin called Ali. "I'm not sure exactly how to set it up," he confessed.

"No problem, I got it from here," Ali said. "Can you set up the chairs so they're all facing the TV?"

Yasin nodded and went back to the front of the restaurant, moving tables to the side and arranging chairs facing Ali. It was nearing game time and the men outside were peering in through the window. Ali managed to get the TV on and was flipping through the channels.

When Yasin finished, Ali instructed him to open the doors, and the crowd collecting outside started to spill in. They were dressed in jerseys of green and white; some wore retro jerseys from an earlier time, and some wore brand new styles with intricate designs. Though it was near the end of the day, when fasting people were usually very tired, the energy in the building was palpable. Much of the audience, Yasin observed, were middle-aged Algerian men.

The more Yasin listened to their unique dialect, the more he could piece together some of what they were saying. He had always loved learning languages, and he even spent a year studying Quranic Arabic as a teenager in Guinea, but that was traditional Arabic. This version of Arabic was different—it had shorter vowel sounds and words he had never heard before. But Yasin also heard French words mixed in, and so as he listened, his knowledge of the two languages started to click, and he was suddenly able to grasp the gist of what people were saying.

Ali finally found the game and turned up the volume, drowning out the voices that filled the restaurant with the pregame commentary that had already begun. Instantly, the eyes of everyone in the room were glued to the screen.

The players of the Algerian national team were introduced first. They stood in a solemn row while the camera panned across each player's face and the Algerian national anthem filled the stadium. The restaurant fell silent. The powerful words of the anthem spoke of the bloody revolution and the fight to be a nation free from colonialism. It lionized the martyrs who died for the cause and called for a unified national spirit.

After it concluded, the Egyptian national team were introduced, and like a flip of a switch, chatter filled the restaurant again.

People continued to stream inside, some seemingly on a whim after noticing the game was on. Yasin left the seating area to leave space for customers and went to stand in the kitchen. He couldn't see the TV clearly anymore so he just watched the crowd. Although he didn't have a horse in the race, his heart was pumping in anticipation for the match. He had absorbed the contagious energy of the room and wanted to see Algeria win.

He was also surprised by the diversity in the faces before him. Though the majority of people had tan skin, there were a few men with pale skin and red hair and broad shoulders, and a couple with darker complexions than himself, slim-framed and sporting afros. It seemed the whole range of Africa was captured in this one country. On the screen, the Algerian team mirrored the diversity.

Then the players took their positions on the field. The game was being played at the brand new Nelson Mandela stadium in Algiers. Because both teams were fasting, they scheduled the start for ten at night, so the players would have a chance to eat before the game started.

Action erupted as soon as the whistle was blown. The Algerian team started the match at a blistering pace, and in a quick succession of passes, they had come within shooting distance of Egypt's goal. Under a minute into the game, Algerian star winger Riyad Mahrez took a shot, and the ball curled into the top left corner of the goal.

"Allllahhhh!" the announcer roared. "Shnuwa hadha?! Shnuwa hadha ya Mahrez!"

"Bah bah bah bah bah!" one man near the TV exclaimed, wringing his hand in admiration while watching the slow motion replay.

The rest of the half was not as eventful. The players went into the tunnel at halftime with Algeria still up one-nothing. Yasin busied himself in organizing the kitchen while the men chatted in Arabic.

At the start of the second half, the Egyptian side entered with renewed energy. It seemed like a fire had been lit under them during the break. They attacked the Algerian goal like a pack of wolves. Every time an Algerian defender deflected the ball, clearing it out of the way, the Egyptians gathered the ball and continued their attack. Sighs of relief filled the air when one shot was narrowly cleared by the Algerian goalie, the ball brushing his fingertips and then hitting the goalpost.

The crowd in the restaurant was still as they watched the final minutes. Even their breathing was hardly perceptible. Then, as the clock hit ninety minutes, the unspeakable happened. Egyptian star Mohamed Salah was fouled within the box, and he was awarded a penalty.

The men in the restaurant erupted in anger at the call. Some shouted at the referee on the screen as if he could hear them, pleading for him to change his mind. Others covered their faces with their hands, unwilling to watch. Ali stopped stirring his bubbling soup and made a silent prayer. Yasin came around the counter, angling his face to see the TV screen.

Mohamed Salah approached the penalty box and arranged the ball in its place on the white circle. He stepped a few paces back, ran forward slowly, then passed the ball easily in the center of the goal while the Algerian goalie leaped toward the left side.

Loud groans filled the room. Some people got up and left. Others stayed and complained. Despite the soured mood, Yasin had to stifle a laugh when someone swore that the game was rigged.

"Hey, at least we got a draw and not a loss," Ali said to the patrons, trying to salvage something out of the game. "The iftar is almost ready. Go pray next door at Al Iman and come back to eat."

While the group filed out slowly Ali approached Yasin with more urgency. "I need you to re-arrange the seats and tables for dinner. Then, put out those new bowls, plates, and utensils. Once you're done setting the tables, we will pray here in the store quickly and then start serving soup and appetizers."

"Got it," Yasin said. He got to work returning the tables and chairs to their prior arrangement. Ali turned the heat off of his soup and put the freshly fried bourek in the oven to stay warm. The rest of the meal was ready to be served. There were three choices of entree: Ali's loubia, a recreation of the bean dish that gave his restaurant its name, couscous with chicken and vegetables, or a noodle dish peculiar to Northern Algeria called rechta, also served with chicken and vegetables.

Once the tables were set and the food was ready, Ali pulled out a prayer mat and they prayed together in the back of the restaurant. Ali read short passages from the Quran so they could be ready for the influx of customers right after. Yasin could tell he was stressed, and he resolved to be as helpful as he could for Ali's big opening night.

Then people started to come in. Yasin recognized the first customers as those men who were sitting with Ali outside before the game started. They took two large tables in the center and moved some chairs to all fit together. Ali served soup and bourek to his table of friends and took their orders. Yasin quietly served cups of water and set full pitchers on each table.

While the group dug into their appetizers, Ali's eyes watched the door. Nobody else had come in yet.

"Can you go outside the door and encourage people to come in?" he looked at Yasin hopefully. Yasin really didn't want to go. He wanted to stay hidden in the back of the restaurant. But seeing Ali's anxious face made him feel bad.

"Okay—" he started. Then Ali changed his mind suddenly.

"Actually, I'll go, can you watch the guys here and help them if they need anything?"

"Yes, I can do that," Yasin said, relieved.

Ali took his rubber gloves off and went outside. He stood in the middle of the sidewalk ushering people in. Yasin had once been too shy to do that kind of thing. He had to quickly shed any timidness when he arrived in New York, and especially when he started his job selling handbags and sunglasses to tourists. The only way to get people to pay attention in New York City was to be bold. But now was not the time to bring attention to himself.

A young couple walked in, the doorbell announcing their arrival. Yasin came around and showed them to a seat.

"We have a Ramadan special today: soup, bourek, and choice of one of three entrees," Yasin announced, displaying a printout of the menu and prices. He made eye contact with Ali through the window, who gave him a thumbs up. "Should I start you off with the appetizers?"

"Sure, that would be great, thank you," the young man said. Yasin nodded and fetched the couple their soup and bourek.

While the couple decided on their entrees, Yasin went to refill the water pitchers for the first group. It was his first time ever working in a restaurant, and it was actually kind of fun.

"I think I'll go with the rechta," the young woman said when Yasin returned to check on them.

"And I'll have the loubia," the young man said. He said the word *loubia* confidently. Yasin guessed the young man was Algerian, or at least North African. "That's what you guys are named after, right?" he asked.

"Exactly." Yasin smiled. He gathered the menus and then looked up outside at Ali. He tried to make a face that read, come help!

Ali walked in a moment later, two couples entering ahead of him. He came around the counter and met Yasin.

"The young couple there ordered one rechta and one loubia," Yasin informed him.

"All right, good. Can you take the orders of these people while I get that ready?"

"Yes," Yasin said.

A bit over half an hour later, the patrons of King of Beans had mostly wrapped up their meals. All but Ali's original friend group had paid their bills and left.

"Not a bad day," Ali said, clapping Yasin's shoulder appreciatively. "Thanks for all your help, Hussein."

"Of course," Yasin said. "Should I start cleaning the tables?"

"That would be great," Ali smiled. He wiped his hands with a towel on the counter and went to take a seat with his friends. Ali had served them mint tea earlier and now poured himself a cup.

Though there were moments of stress during the day's operations, Yasin felt a sense of accomplishment. Ali was a kind man, and Yasin was glad to be doing work that benefited a small business owner, rather than a greedy food delivery app. He then felt sad, because he knew he was doing this job temporarily, and would be leaving as soon as his first paycheck came in. If he wasn't on the run from the police, he would have loved this job.

Ali's friends soon took their leave. Ali forced them to take some of the food that was leftover, sending everyone home with bags of to-go boxes. Yasin then washed the last of the pots and pans. When everyone had left, the restaurant fell silent for the first time in hours. Ali took a seat on a stool by the counter and started counting up the day's revenue.

"How did we do?" Yasin asked.

Ali thought for a moment. "I had higher hopes, but it wasn't a bad day, alhamdulillah."

"It's only our first day," Yasin said hopefully. "I'm sure it will pick up."

"I know it will. I rushed to get everything running, you know, trying to get it open during Ramadan, but people haven't had the chance to find out about us yet. But tomorrow might be a great opportunity to raise some awareness."

"What's happening tomorrow?" Yasin asked curiously.

"I just found out about it from one of the customers," Ali said. "She told me there's something called Suhoor Fest happening on Steinway. The street will be blocked off for vendors from ten o'clock to two in the morning. A lot of people are going to be coming here, she said."

"What exactly is a suhoor fest?" Yasin asked. "Isn't suhoor later in the night?"

"Honestly I don't know," Ali laughed. "All I know is we need to be prepared. We need some type of easy quick food to serve. Maybe mini merguez sandwiches?"

"Sounds delicious." Yasin smiled, but the prospect of big crowds sounded more than unsettling.

Chapter 20: Saif

The day after his suspension, Saif slept in until noon. Even then, he still felt tired when he woke up. He lay in bed unmoving, staring at the cracks in the tiled ceiling of his room. He had no idea what he was going to do for the next week. And he wouldn't be getting paid either, which stressed him out even more. He had promised his mother he could take care of the rent this month.

Finally, around two in the afternoon, he rolled out of bed onto the floor. He didn't want to face his mother because he still hadn't explained why he was suspended. Then, she walked in.

"Saif, wake up, you've been asleep all day," she fussed. "It's not good for you."

"Fine, help me up," Saif said, raising his arms from the floor. She bent over and reached for his hands, but Saif felt ashamed at the last moment and got himself up.

"I know you're depressed from whatever happened at work, but you can't hide in your room," she said gently. "Come sit with me in the salon and watch a movie or read something." She tugged his arm towards the door and he followed her into the living room. The sunlight shining through the windows felt like a floodlight.

Saif plopped down on the couch and pulled his phone out. There were missed calls and text messages, including from Elias, and dozens of other notifications. He tossed his phone on the other side of the couch, away from arms reach, unwilling to engage with anything or anyone.

He eyed his laptop beside him on the coffee table. He hadn't logged into his personal laptop since he started working as an officer. He decided to open it and surf the news. When he opened the screen, a Facebook tab was still open, and there was an unanswered message from his cousin in Algeria on the screen. The only reason he ever opened Facebook was to chat with him. As he typed out a reply to his cousin's greeting, he noticed, strangely, that there were tons of other unread messages. Skimming through the names, they were coming from people he hadn't spoken to since high school. He clicked on one of them.

Yoo Saif how you been man?

Another said, *Saif we need to catch up, been too long!*

Still another said, *Bro I was just thinking of you, we gotta chill sometime!*

He was confused. Why were all these people he hadn't spoken to in years suddenly reaching out? Then, a message from somebody he distinctly remembered disliking, added more context. His name was Eric, and he had bullied Saif way back in middle school, but they became more or less friendly by high school.

Yo, you're a cop now right? Do you guys have any leads on the seven guys who escaped?

Saif was surprised that Eric was so interested in the case that he decided to reach out to him. He started typing out a reply. *Yeah, I'm with the NYPD. We've caught four guys so far. I just caught one of them myself.*

A moment later, Eric started typing again.

No way that's dope man. Yeah I've been following the news. Who do you think will be caught next?

Saif was confused again. It seemed like Eric thought this was a game.

I hope we catch Hoffmeyer, he's the most dangerous for sure, he typed back.

The text bubble appeared again in their chat. *But do you think he'll be caught? I think he's the smartest one from the three left, he probably will survive the longest.*

Saif doubled down. *I don't really care if he's smart, or how long he survives. All I know is we're doing our best to capture him and send him back to prison, where he belongs.*

Eric started typing, then stopped. Then he continued typing. *So does that mean the NYPD isn't focusing on the other two guys then?*

Saif was frustrated. What was Eric digging for?

I guess, he finally typed.

Do you have any hunch on who's going to be harder to find between Yasin and Terrence?

Annoyed, Saif closed the chat window. He wondered if everyone else who had messaged him was also digging for information about the case. As he scrolled through the names, he scrolled down too far to see a message three years earlier from Rayan, his best friend from high school.

Congrats on getting into QC! My parents decided to move back to Astoria next year so I'll still be around. Right now my plan is to do one year of community college here and then transfer to Baruch.

He remembered that Rayan's family moved to Boston after eleventh grade, for Rayan's dad's job, and they had hosted a big going away party that summer. During the following year, Saif's whole friend circle slowly fell apart, because Rayan was the glue that kept everyone together. Instead of finishing school off with a bang, senior year ended in a whisper. When he received that message from Rayan after graduation, he was too bitter to reply.

Now, three years later, Rayan would just be wrapping up his junior year at Baruch. Saif felt guilty for never answering his message. He wondered if Rayan was still in Astoria, and what else had transpired since they last spoke. *I might as well see if he's free this week while I'm suspended…*

Hey Rayan, hope you've been well. He erased the message back to *Hey Rayan*, and started again.

Hey Rayan, my bad I never saw this

He erased everything and took a deep breath.

Sorry I never replied, Rayan. It's been a while. Would you be down to catch up sometime? His finger hesitated over the enter key, then he closed his eyes and pushed down. He shut his laptop and went to see what his mom was doing. She was sewing a new button onto one of his pants.

"Oh, thanks, Mama," he said. "That button has been loose for a while."

"No problem." She smiled, but Saif could tell she was smiling just to cheer him up.

Saif stood there awkwardly for a moment while she fixed his pants. "By the way, I found out I will still get paid while I'm suspended."

His mom nodded, acting like she didn't care whether he was being paid or not, but he knew the money mattered to her. When he first started working, he had promised her his salary would help pay back some of their overdue bills.

"Do you remember Rayan?" he asked out of the blue.

"Your friend? Yes, what happened to him? He moved to Boston right?"

"Yeah, he did, but apparently his family moved back," Saif explained.

His mom looked up at him and smiled again. "That's good news, right?"

"Yeah, I guess so."

"Why don't you go out for tea or coffee with him to-night? You should get outside and do something."

"Maybe," Saif hesitated. "I haven't seen him in years though. I wonder if he's changed."

"Everyone changes," his mom shrugged. "But good memories last forever."

Saif wondered what she meant for a moment but didn't ask. He didn't know if she was quoting an Arabic proverb or just making something up. Either way, he did have good memories with Rayan. He couldn't help but grin as he remembered how funny Rayan used to be, always coming up with the funniest roasts.

Saif went back to his laptop and opened the screen. He saw he had already received a message back from Rayan. *Yoo Saif I missed you bro. I'm glad you're still alive. I'm down. Are you still in Astoria?*

Yeah I'm still here, Saif typed back.

Have you been to the new Qahwah House? I heard they have a nice backyard patio at this one.

No I haven't. I've only been to the OG Brooklyn one.

Let's hit it up then. Tonight after iftar?

Bet, see you then bro!

Saif closed his laptop and went to choose what he would wear. His mind raced with memories of Rayan and their old friend group. Random names and faces and places popped into his head, causing his lips to spread in a wistful smile. He never realized how much losing his old friend group had left a hole in his life. Maybe he and Rayan could bring the old gang back together.

After iftar, Qahwah House was packed. There was a line out the door for people to order, but it felt good to be outside. The air had cooled into a perfect summer night. Saif wound his way around the people in line and walked inside, looking for Rayan's familiar face. When he didn't find it, he remembered that it had been years since he had last seen him, and he might look different now. Saif continued into the store and walked to the back of the cafe looking for the backyard patio Rayan had mentioned. There, sitting at a table engrossed in a book, was Rayan.

"Salam, Rayan," he said. He glanced at the cover of the book. "You, reading? What's that all about?"

Rayan slowly looked up from his book and then his mouth spread wide in a grin. "Wa alaikum assalam, big man! How you been? Nah, this book is amazing, bro. It's called A Dying Colonialism by Frantz Fanon." He looked at the cover while he said the name. "We're studying it in my political theory class. It's a must-read."

"If you say so," Saif said. "I'll see if the library has it. I don't buy books."

"I'm sure they have it. It's famous. Oh, I went ahead and ordered for us if you don't mind," Rayan waved a beeper. "Adeni shay pot for two."

"Sure, yeah that sounds great," Saif said, taking the seat opposite Rayan. "Man, how long has it been since we last saw each other?"

Rayan looked different. He was wearing contacts now, instead of the glasses Saif remembered, and he had a curly beard that obscured most of his face, making him look much older than when they were in high school.

"I think since that summer after junior year," Rayan said. "We've changed so much since then."

Saif didn't know if he fully agreed. "I miss those days though," Saif reminisced. "Remember that time in French class when you splashed a mouthful of water on Monsieur Fournier and he had to go home and change?"

"I did?" Rayan scratched his head, his ears turning red.

"Yeah, it was the funniest thing ever. We were all trying to hold as much water in our mouths as we could without laughing and then Monsieur Fournier snuck up behind you and—"

"I know, I know, it all sprayed on Monsieur Fournier," Rayan finished. "What grade was that again?"

"Eighth grade," Saif answered, his punchline deflated.

"You know, that was one of the good things about my move to Boston," Rayan reflected. "I was able to reinvent myself. It's kinda funny actually—people there thought I was a nerdy introvert."

Saif's smile faded completely. It was clear that the Rayan sitting before him wasn't the same Rayan he had preserved in his memory.

"So you're at Baruch now?" Saif asked flatly, changing the topic.

"Yeah, it's been great so far," Rayan said, his energy returning. "I started out as a business major but I switched into international relations now. I want to work at the UN when I graduate, in sha Allah. What about you? You still at Queens College?"

Saif shook his head. "No, I'm taking a little break from school," he lied. "Actually, I just started a new job as a police officer."

Rayan's eyebrows went up. "Oh, with the NYPD? How's that been?"

"Pretty crazy to be honest. Have you heard about the big jailbreak?"

"Of course, who hasn't? I was just reading a fascinating article actually," he said. "There's a billionaire offering 100K of his own money to anyone who finds one of the last three fugitives."

"100K?" Saif's eyes grew large. "I wish I was making that kind of money. I literally just found one of them the other day."

"Yeah, well if you find out why he's doing so you'll be surprised." Rayan's tone started to sound different to Saif.

"Why?"

"Because his employees haven't been going into the office ever since the jailbreak. He's so bent on employees being in office he's willing to spend his own money on public safety. In a way, it makes perfect sense, if you research the history of why the police were first created."

"And why's that?" Saif asked, his eyes narrowing.

"The first police force in America was founded by the government to help catch escaped slaves," Rayan explained. "The police system was never about public safety. It was about protecting profits and corporations."

"Just because it started that way, which I'd still have to research and confirm, doesn't mean it's been the same since all those years ago," Saif retorted. "If we weren't here keeping the streets safe, criminals would take over."

"But how much of that crime wouldn't even happen if poor people were taken care of?" Rayan rebutted. "If you really dig deep, the police have always been used by the elite as a weapon to enforce the status quo, and disproportionately target black and brown people."

"Bro, I didn't come here for a lecture. I just wanted to see you. Apparently you had other ideas," Saif snapped. "I still remember the old you, the one who put mayo packets under people's chairs, who hacked the school website and changed the principal's headshot to a photo of yourself. You move away for a couple years and read a few books and now you think you're better than me?"

"I'm only telling you all this cause I care about you," Rayan said, keeping his composure. "I don't want to see you waste your potential." Just then, the buzzer on the table started to shake, signaling that their tea was ready for pick-up at the counter.

"I'll get it," Saif said, rising quickly. He grabbed the buzzer in a clenched fist and marched away. *It pisses me off when people talk about my life as if they know everything I've been through. If I had so much 'potential', I'd be at an Ivy League right now, not suspended from my job.*

The chatter was deafening inside the main part of the cafe. Saif approached the Yemeni man at the counter and handed him the vibrating buzzer. The man turned it off and then handed him a tray with two small round cups and a glass pitcher full of golden-brown milk tea. "Enjoy," he said with a smile. Saif carefully picked up the tray of tea and returned to the backyard deck, all the while wondering how he was going to shift the conversation with Rayan. He had come in so excited, but now felt deeply disappointed.

Saif set the tray down and sat silently. Rayan picked up the pitcher without looking at him and poured two cups of tea; he handed the first to Saif and then poured one for himself. Saif broke the silence before taking a sip. "Listen, I don't wanna argue today. I understand you have your opinions on the police system and it's totally fine. I agree, there's always room for improvement. But in our world today, there are a lot of bad people, and there's also good people. And when there's a criminal trying to break into your front door, you need someone to call, don't you?"

Rayan seemed unwilling to compromise. "Saif, I know you're a good person at heart, but being part of an evil system over time will make part of that evil rub off on you. And that's what I don't want. If you want to educate yourself, I have some excellent book recommendations."

"Why do you get all your ideas from books? What about real life? What about the history of our home country, Algeria? My dad gave up his life fighting evil people trying to rip their country apart. Have you ever spoken to your parents about it? People in their generation don't even bring up the civil war. The nineties are called the Black Decade. Wanna talk about history? My father lived it. My dad was a hero, while you just sit here reaping the rewards of his sacrifices."

Rayan fell silent for a few moments in contemplation. Then he made an expression that looked like he decided to say what was on his mind, no matter how it would be received. "Yeah, I've studied the civil war," Rayan said firmly. "I've even written a whole paper on it for school. And you know what really happened? The Algerian military, which unfortunately your dad was a part of, crushed a popular movement that won the presidential election fair and square. The old guard didn't want to let go of power and that's what led to all the bloodshed. People like your father fought for old corrupt men who destroyed the lives of countless people."

"Y-you don't know what you're talking about!" Saif cried. The backyard deck fell silent as everyone turned their heads to stare at Saif. Then he got up and ran out of the building before Rayan could see his tears.

Chapter 21: Yasin

After the second day of iftar service at King of Beans, Yasin and Ali started to prepare for the Suhoor Fest that night. More than a thousand people were expected to descend on Steinway Street from all over the five boroughs. They had just over half an hour before the first people would arrive.

Outside on Steinway, vendors were actively setting up their stalls on the street, which the police had blocked off from traffic for the night. They ranged from food stalls of various cuisines to dessert and coffee stands to clothing popups and Islamic art displays. The festival was planned by the Malikah Center, an organization created by Egyptian women who had grown up on Steinway. Volunteers from Malikah milled about, checking in with vendors and setting up welcome tables at entry points bookending the festival. There was a heavy security presence this year; both NYPD officers and private security guards were at the scene.

"Do you have any extra masks?" Yasin asked Ali while putting on rubber gloves. "I want to take extra health precautions since we'll be serving so many people."

Ali gave him a curious look but went and found a few in a cabinet. "Do you think I should wear one too?"

"It's up to you," Yasin said, taking a mask and fitting it over his mouth and nose. "But it might be a good idea."

Ali put an extra mask in his pocket and then went to the front door and pulled it open all the way, keeping it stuck open with a portable door stopper. "By the way, I called my son to help us tonight," he told Yasin from afar. "We'll need someone by the door guiding people in."

"Good idea," Yasin called back, lugging a box of fresh baguettes from the storage closet and placing it on the counter. "Are we doing dine-in services?"

"I was thinking we could have a few chairs out front, on the sidewalk," Ali said, pointing with his hands. "And maybe a couple tables inside by the window to attract people."

"Got it," Yasin said, "And are we serving any dishes from the iftar menu or just the merguez sandwiches?"

"We have French fries, a few other sides. Oh, and we have some soup leftover from iftar." Ali scratched his chin. "Maybe I can offer soup for free with a purchase?" He looked at Yasin for feedback.

"That's good," Yasin pursed his lips. "But do we have to-go bowls?"

"Good point," Ali frowned. "Can you go grab some from my store next door? I have to start cooking. The key is hanging right over the aprons."

Yasin grabbed the keys and went outside. The vendors were all ready and set up, and their owners watched in anticipation for people. The smells of the various foods melted together into one tantalizing aroma. In just one area around King of Beans, Yasin saw a Jamaican food truck, an abaya and thobe shop, a natural perfume stall, and a chai cart.

Next to the restaurant, he unlocked the door with Ali's key and turned on the lights to search for to-go bowls. The store was a bit messy. Ali had been focusing on the restaurant while his friend ran the shop, but it didn't seem like he was running it well. After several minutes of digging in the back of the store, Yasin uncovered a stack of paper plates, cups and bowls. He grabbed the bowls and turned back, shutting off the lights again.

Now, Steinway Street was buzzing with activity. Hundreds of people had entered the few blocks between 30th Avenue and Astoria Boulevard. He rushed back to the store, where he found Ali and his son already serving customers.

Yasin wound his way to Ali, who had his hands full with trays laden with sandwiches. "Switch places with Ayoub," he said breathlessly. "He doesn't know what he's doing."

Ali's son Ayoub was about nineteen, wearing a two-toned tracksuit and foam slides on his feet. He sported a taper faded mullet and had a luxury brand crossbody bag over his chest. One look at the stitching on the bag and Yasin knew it was fake. He had sold hundreds just like it in his old life.

"Thank God," Ayoub said, handing Yasin the paper and pen he was using to take orders. "I was supposed to be out there talking to girls, not doing this."

"Ayoub, watch your mouth," Ali growled. "You're supposed to be bringing customers in, not wasting time."

After Ayoub went to stand outside the open doorway, Yasin looked at the paper. He could barely read what Ayoub had written. Even his own English handwriting was better, and he had never formally learned it.

Ali noticed his confusion and came around to help. He had another tray of sandwiches in one hand. "I have no idea what it's saying. Ayoub!"

Ayoub came back impatiently. "What Baba?"

"What name is this here? The one that ordered three sandwiches and two fries?"

"Umm…Mun..Murl…"

"How can you not read your own handwriting? I send you to school for what? Forget it, just go back to whatever you were doing." Ali went outside to the people waiting on chairs. "Someone ordered three sandwiches and two fries?"

A teenage girl wearing a purple hijab raised her hand tentatively. "For Muniba?"

"Yes, Muniba, that's who it is," Ali said, looking back at his son in displeasure, who rolled his eyes.

"And for the soup and two sandwiches?" a young man sitting with a young woman asked hopefully.

"Coming right up," Ali smiled.

Yasin already began pouring the bowls of soup inside. Ali grabbed two toasted baguettes, added a few sizzling merguez sausages, then slathered homemade harissa mayo on the other side. He handed the sandwiches to Yasin, who added them to a tray already loaded with the soup and then served them to the young couple.

"I can't deal with him today," Ali said to Yasin, glowering across the store at his son outside, who was chatting with two young women. "Thank God I have you here."

"Alhamdulillah. At least we're getting good business from this Suhoor Fest," Yasin said. He brought down his mask for a moment to speak. It was sweltering near the grill.

"Yes, this is amazing for business," Ali's mood flipped. "I wish they did this festival every night in Ramadan!"

Business continued to pick up through the night. Ali had priced his menu cheaply, hoping to make a lot of quick sales, and his strategy had worked perfectly. It turned out that many of the vendors that night were quite expensive, and word of mouth about Ali's store had led many price-conscious people over. Ayoub had gotten serious about his role too, and he convinced many young people to stop in and grab a bite. By midnight, Ali had topped sales from the previous two nights of iftar service combined.

Once the crowd grew smaller, Ali took a much-needed break from the hot grill. He stepped out to get some fresh air, and Yasin took over. They were running low on bread, and a new batch of harissa mayo had to be mixed up. Yasin took the mayo out of the fridge and looked over the simple handwritten recipe from Ali.

1 cup mayonnaise
2 tablespoons harissa paste
1 teaspoon garlic powder
½ teaspoon cumin
½ teaspoon salt

Yasin fished a new can of Tunisian-imported harissa out of a storage cabinet, then mixed all the ingredients in a large bowl until it was a thick orange sauce. He set it aside and started grilling a fresh batch of merguez. Then, Ali returned, holding a bag.

"Hussein, you should take a walk around and explore," he said, setting aside his shopping. "Don't worry, I can handle the store for a bit," he said, seeing Yasin's sudden look of trepidation. At the same time Ali had entered, two police officers walked up to Ayoub outside.

"Sure, I'll take a look," Yasin answered. He bent down quickly to tie his shoes when the officers walked into the store. Ali went out and took their orders. While Ali kept the officers occupied, Yasin slid smoothly around them and went outside.

Yasin now took in the festive atmosphere without thinking about work. He noticed a string of lights hanging between two lamp posts, with lit up words in the middle that read Ramadan Mubarak. It was past midnight now, but the crowd was more animated than ever, people cradling cups of Yemeni tea and coffee in their palms, talking and laughing loudly.

Yasin was reminded of Ramadan nights in Guinea, when people stayed up all night, eating and drinking and visiting family. One year as a child, his parents took him to the capital, Conakry, to visit the newly built Grand Mosque. He remembered being stunned by its gigantic size and by its beautiful white and gold pillars painted with turquoise accents. In Conakry, he remembered the wondrous feeling of being surrounded by so many different ethnic groups and hearing so many languages. He had heard stories about the diversity of the holy cities, Makkah and Madina, but had not yet had the opportunity to go. But here in New York, he could imagine what it might feel like to be around Muslims from all over the world.

The Muslim community here, in one of the most diverse cities in the world, was like a melting pot within a melting pot. There were South Asian Muslims from India, Pakistan and Bangladesh; there were African Muslims from Senegal to Somalia and Morocco to South Africa. There were Muslims from Indonesia and Malaysia. There were Turkish and Albanian and Bosnian Muslims. In Makkah all these different nationalities would be there, but they would have spoken different languages and come from distinctly different cultures. Here in New York, everyone brought a piece of their heritage, but they also shared an American identity.

As Yasin observed the various cuisines and styles of clothing around him, he wanted to sit down and learn the stories of all these different people. He wondered if the people walking around realized how much of a miracle this was. The only thing that could come to mind was the verse from the Quran where Allah says:

> *O humanity! Indeed, We created you from a male and a female, and made you into peoples and tribes so that you may ⸢get to⸣ know one another. Surely the most noble of you in the sight of Allah is the most righteous among you. Allah is truly All-Knowing, All-Aware.*

If only I could stay here and bring my family to join me, he thought, *I could have a beautiful life here.*

After reaching the end Yasin doubled back for King of Beans. When he returned, he saw Ali still in the kitchen. He went to see if Ali needed any help.

"We're out of bread, soup and almost out of merguez, so I think this will be the last order. Why don't you go sit for a bit with those brothers over there?"

Ayoub was sitting with three young men at a table by the window. Yasin approached them and pulled up a chair.

"This is Hussein. He's working for my dad," Ayoub introduced Yasin to the others. He looked at Yasin. "This is Juan, Alberto, and Ilyes. I was just asking them what they thought of the merguez."

"It's amazing, bro," Juan said. "It reminds me of Mexican chorizo. The one we have in Colombia is more firm, like the Spanish kind."

"Yeah, it tastes similar to our Mexican chorizo," Alberto said. "When mi Mama hears about this, she'll be so happy. She's been eating halal with me ever since I converted, but nobody makes halal chorizo."

"That's nice of her," Ayoub said. "How long ago did you convert?"

"Two years ago, for me," Alberto said. Juan said two and a half, and Ilyes smiled and said, "I'm Moroccan. I was born and raised Muslim."

"How did you guys all meet?" Ayoub asked.

"We were on a tour of the Alhambra in Granada three years ago," Ilyes said. "I was visiting Spain from Morocco, and they were coming from the US," he pointed at his two friends.

"Wow, and you all just happened to meet again here in New York?"

"Well, after the tour ended we followed each other on social media. When I moved here a few months ago, I reached out to them and we reconnected. The funny part is when they came to Spain they weren't Muslim yet, so it was a big but nice surprise to find out they accepted Islam since we met!"

"Yeah, that trip really started the journey for me," Alberto said. "It was my first time learning about the history of Andalusia. I never knew about how Islam was in Spain for 800 years. They never taught it to us in school. Even my parents didn't know much about it."

"Same here," Juan said. "When I came home I kept researching about Andalusia and that led me to research Islam and then I converted soon after."

Yasin was burning with questions. He himself had barely learned about Andalusia in school, and found it fascinating. "If you don't mind me asking, what about Andalusia made you curious about Islam?" he finally asked.

Juan answered first. "I think because it made me wonder, what if my ancestors were Muslim? In Latinoamérica, they fill our heads with tales about Islam being a scary foreign religion, but when I learned about Andalusia, I realized Islam was baked into my own ancestry and culture. Did you know like 4,000 words in Spanish come from Arabic? Words like arroz, aceite—"

"Even barrio!" Alberto chimed in.

Ilyes smiled and nodded. "The culture they created in Al Andalus was extremely unique. It was not just Arab, or just Spanish. And though it wasn't a utopia, Muslims in Spain brought in a golden age while the rest of Europe was still in darkness."

"And now we've got Moroccan, Mexican, and Colombian Muslims in New York City all eating Algerian chorizo at a suhoor fest," Ayoub grinned.

"Hussein, can you give the customer this order?" Ali's voice interrupted their discussion. Yasin got up and took over the wrapped and bagged to-go order to a woman waiting outside.

"Need help cleaning up?" Yasin asked Ali when he returned.

"Sure, thanks," Ali said, setting down the towel in his hand.

"By the way, your son—he's a good kid." Yasin spoke to Ali in a low voice so Ayoub couldn't overhear them. "The way he's speaking with those young men shows he has good character."

"Really?" Ali asked, sounding surprised, watching Ayoub. "That's good to hear. You know, we don't get time to talk too much. He has his friends and his car and he lives his own life."

"If I have any advice for you," Yasin said seriously, "it's to make the time to spend with him. Wallahi, it's a blessing to see your son grow up before you. I wish I had my son here with me."

Ali swallowed a lump in his throat. "Thank you for the reminder, my brother. I will make a stronger effort to, in sha Allah."

After a moment, Ali went and sat down on the chair Yasin had left behind. He put an arm around his son's shoulder, while Yasin wiped a tear behind the counter.

Chapter 22: Saif

Saif stormed out of the backyard patio, hot tears welling in the corners of his eyes. He hoped and prayed that nobody in the cafe recognized him or noticed he was crying. It was near midnight, but the line outside had grown even longer. He sidestepped the line and turned towards 23rd Avenue, where thankfully far less people were walking and the street was darker.

Now, he walked slower and took a moment to think. *Was Baba actually a bad person?* He had always taken his mother's word, that his father was a hero, that the civil war was fought because terrorists tried to take over the country. *Is Rayan right? Or is he just making it up?* His hand moved to his pocket to do a quick online search, but he feared what he might find.

During his walk home, his ears caught the Quran being recited from afar. Soon he pinpointed the source—a building that looked like an old church had its front door wide open and men in thobes were walking up the stairs to go pray. He paused by the steps, looking up at the warm light pouring from the entryway, hearing the imam's voice flow out of the open doors and onto the street, like a pure flowing river. His heart shuddered, and his feet felt stuck to the floor. Then he thought of his mother at home. *How could she lie to me all these years?*

He stormed off again towards home. He was going to confront his mother and find out what the truth was, from her own mouth.

As he neared Steinway Street, heavy traffic slowed him down. Cars were circling around, backing into street parking, and their honks filled the night air. He saw masses of people walking towards Steinway and wondered what was happening. The street was blocked off from cars for what looked like a food festival. But the crowds were getting in his way, and he refused to be distracted from the anger he wanted to carry.

Saif pushed through the masses of people and fought his way onto the sidewalk where less of them were walking. His nose was picking up delightful smells: sizzling chicken satay, grilling lamb chops, and stewing birria tacos; but he held his breath, the hole in his chest demanding full attention.

"Merguez sandwiches, only five dollars!" he heard a voice ahead of him. It was Ayoub, Ammu Ali's annoying son.

"Yo, Saif, cop a quick sandwich for me, my dad—"

"Shut up," Saif growled, staring straight ahead without looking.

"Screw you too bro!" Ayoub's voice faded behind him.

When he finally reached his building, Saif marched up the stairs. He waited in front of the door and rehearsed what he would say. *I'm gonna tell her I know the truth. I know she lied to me all my life. And if she doesn't come clean and tell the real full truth of who Baba is…I will never forgive her.*

When he swung the door open, he saw his mother's face, smiling and happy that her son had reconnected with an old friend, and Saif forgot everything he wanted to say. He began to sob.

His mother pulled him in and hugged him without a word. He rested his head on her shoulder, and his tears soaked the scarf wrapped loosely around her. After what felt like several minutes, he lifted his head and walked with her to the sofa.

"What happened with Rayan?" she asked softly.

Saif took a deep breath. He looked at his mother with red eyes full of sincerity.

"Mama, please tell me the truth."

Her eyes became worried about what he might say.

"Mama, I know Baba wasn't a hero. Rayan told me about how the civil war first started. It was the military that started everything by coup-ing the new leader that was elected. All along, Baba was working for the oppressors. Why did you keep this away from me all these years?"

His mother sighed and closed her eyes.

"Saif…"

"Mama, I need to hear the truth. What really happened that year when everything started?"

"Fine, I will tell you everything," she said, switching to Arabic, as she often did when she talked about his father. "I promise."

Saif adjusted his body on the couch and straightened his back. He was ready to hear what she had to say, no matter how much the truth hurt.

"Your father," she began, "Najmeddine, was not a bad man. He was someone who aspired to a career in the military to be like his father, who was a martyr from the revolution. He had grown up without his father, just like you, but he had more relatives around him: uncles, aunts, and grandparents too. But you have to remember, at that time getting into the military was extremely tough. It was the highest achievement to make it into the armed forces. It represented carrying the torch of the shuhada that defeated the French and freed our people from colonialism. And though your grandfather was a distinguished fighter in the revolution, in reality he had left little for your grandmother, and your father grew up in poverty. So your dad worked against all odds to be selected as a young soldier. He sacrificed his education, his social life, and everything else to be like his father."

"But is it true that he was part of the coup?" Saif asked.

"There were a lot of factors that went into it. Before we judge something, we have to know all the factors, right?"

"Right," Saif said.

"In the eighties, many Algerians traveled to Afghanistan to fight with their people against the Soviets. Your father was still a teenager at that time, so he never went, but many young men from our city had gone. When they came back, not only were they adapted to brutal warfare, they also gained an intense hatred of the Soviets, and the communism which they represented. At that time, our government had a socialist system that was friendly with the Soviet Union. When the Algerian government was pressured to open elections to multiple parties, many of those young men who fought communism seized the chance to elect a party that replaced the socialist government, which they viewed as a hostile ideology."

"That makes sense," Saif said. "So the Algerian government was under threat from these men?"

"Kind of," his mother replied. "But it wasn't just those fighters who wanted change in Algeria. A broad coalition was brought together under one movement that opposed the ruling party, which had controlled Algeria since independence. Anti-communist Afghan war veterans, people who wanted a larger role for Islam in politics, European-oriented Algerians who wanted liberal capitalism; all these groups united against the ruling party, the Front de Liberation Nationale, in the name of democracy. When the election concluded, the Front Islamic du Salut, a party advocating for Islamic values, won by a large margin and dealt a heavy blow to the establishment."

"I see," Saif said. "And the government just couldn't let go of power, like Rayan said," Saif said gloomily.

"I won't try to tell you otherwise," she said. "Since Algeria was founded to this day, it's been run by the same generation of men who fought in the revolutionary war, and they've become arrogant about it. They think they're the only ones who deserve to run the country as long as they're alive, and that's not right."

"Definitely not," Saif said.

"But at this time your father was just a young fresh officer in the military, and he wanted to prove himself. When the leaders of the military ordered the coup, your father took his instructions and did not complain. When the army replaced the country's leadership with army-aligned people, they jailed the leadership of the new party that had won as well as thousands of activists. It was then that things went from chaotic to truly violent."

"But who started the killing?"

"It's very hard to tell. Some say the military, some say radical supporters of the opposition party, but with all the misinformation that was going around, nobody knew what was the truth. People who opposed the military fled into the mountains and established army camps there like the Algerian revolutionary fighters did against the French. They planned attacks against military leaders and military-aligned politicians, journalists, academics, and eventually, even anyone who spoke French; they said using the language of the colonizer was equal to treason.

"The military fought back. They battled guerilla forces fiercely, taking back towns and major cities from the rebels. They also infiltrated their ranks, discovering their plots before they could take place. Our streets turned into war zones, and people were afraid to go outside. Businesses struggled, and the economy was on the brink of collapse.

But the military still had control of the oil fields and were able to sustain themselves through them."

"This is way worse than I imagined," Saif said. "Where was Baba in all this?"

"Your father was stuck in the middle of all this bloodshed. He was just a young man. Just trying to do his best to be like his father and to protect the people around him. But he was in over his head, and every night he would come home shaking and unable to speak." Saif's mother took a deep breath. "I still remember seeing corpses rotting on the streets. People were so scared to go outside that they didn't retrieve the bodies of family members who were killed. We would hear of massacres happening on the radio. In a village near us, your father was sent to rescue survivors after reports of an attack by extremists. There were no survivors." Her eyes were cast downward, her fingers plucking at each other. "Years later, he told me what he saw: pregnant women with their bellies sliced open, children hacked into pieces—" Saif's mother's voice cracked. He put an arm around her while she wiped her tears with her scarf.

"During the war there were moments of peace. They tried negotiating a ceasefire, with the help of the European Union. But it was impossible to come to an agreement. The war broke the country into many groups, and even within the military there were disagreements. Some wanted to sign a ceasefire, others said there was no peace until the rebels were permanently crushed. It was after the ceasefire fell through that your father was gunned down right on our street. I ran over to him while holding you. I showed the killers that you were in my hands so they wouldn't attack me. I begged for their mercy. In your father's final moments I spoke to him. He told me to take you and go far away, to leave Algeria and to never return."

By now, Saif was crying again. He had never heard these details about his father's death.

"Your father was a good man," Saif's mother insisted, staring at him with red puffy eyes. "He was just a young man, born into a bloody war, and he never had a chance to decide who he wanted to be."

Saif put his hand on her trembling one and her wrinkled skin felt tender and fragile. He sat there, unable to produce words that could match the depth of emotion she was experiencing. Then she suddenly got up and went to her room. A few moments later, she returned with a bag in her hands.

"It's your father's old djellaba," she said, handing the bag gently to him. "I haven't washed it since he last wore it. It's the last thing that I have of him."

Saif slid the long robe out of the bag and ran his fingers over its brown wool. He closed his eyes and tried to imagine his father wearing it. It smelled faintly musky, as if the last perfume he had worn had clung to it all these years. As he held it, he felt various powerful emotions fighting for his mind, creating such a storm that he felt dizzy. But one feeling was certain: acceptance. He finally knew who his father really was, and he understood the forces that had governed his life and his eventual death.

"Thank you, Mama," he said, smiling at her. He found a red fuzzy cap still in the bag. "Can I keep his chechia too?"

"Of course," she said. She reached out for it and Saif handed it to her. After a moment she placed it snugly on his head with both hands. "It looks good on you. You just need a haircut."

Saif laughed and stood up, and kissing his mother on her forehead. He put his new possessions back in the bag and took it to his room, stowing it safely in his closet. Feeling tired, he went to lie in bed, but the thoughts in his head refused to let him sleep. He stared into the darkness of the room for several minutes, listening to the sounds of the wind rustling the trees outside.

I just wish Baba didn't have to die for these power hungry people. So many innocent people died in this war, and for what? Why does so much blood need to be spilled for the sake of the rich and powerful? Why do we always have to go through so much pain to discover our humanity? And…what am I willing to die for, or not die for?

Chapter 23: Yasin

Once their final customers had left and Ayoub had gone home, Ali came back to find Yasin wrapping up cleaning the kitchen. It was nearly two in the morning, and the vendors of the Suhoor Fest were shutting down.

"You can go to bed, I'll close up." Ali said, still wide awake.

"It's okay, I was thinking of just staying up anyway until suhoor," Yasin replied. "I don't want to go to sleep and accidentally miss Fajr."

"I figured the same," Ali said. "Do you want to have some tea?"

"Sure, that sounds great." Yasin went to take a seat by the window where the young men were seated earlier. Ali put a kettle on the stove. The smell of fresh mint filled the air while it boiled with green tea leaves and sugar.

Yasin watched the quiet street, vendors disassembling their stalls and loading their things into truck beds, and felt like the amazing energy he had experienced earlier that night was suddenly gone. It seemed to him like a metaphor for Ramadan; in the blink of an eye, the blessed last ten nights of the month had begun, and soon, Ramadan would be over.

Ali arrived at the table with a tray holding two elegant tea glasses and a traditional tea pitcher. Yasin had seen the same tea set being sold at Ali's other store. Ali set the tray down on the table and poured tea from the pitcher while standing. It fell into the cups in a long stream of minty green liquid. As the cups filled, the pressure of the tea hitting the cup slowly built up into a thick layer of foam at the top.

"Merci," Yasin said, taking the glass nearest him.

Ali took a seat and sipped his tea, facing the window as Yasin was. They both looked on in silence. Then Ali spoke. "You know, I've been here almost thirty years now," he reflected. "When I came here, there were not more than a handful of Algerians in the whole neighborhood, maybe even the city."

"How did you decide to come to New York, instead of Paris or Marseille?" Yasin asked.

"That is a long story." He paused and took another sip of tea. "Are you sure you want to hear it?"

"I have nothing else to do now," Yasin said cheerfully.

Ali took another slow sip of tea, savoring the sweet minty flavor for a few seconds. He started to speak, still looking outside the window, but in his mind, memories danced on the glass. "I was about twenty, twenty-one years old and studying in university at the time. I was accepted into the engineering program, which was very prestigious, but my true passion was writing. Some of my friends and I started a newspaper at our university. Mainly we wrote in support of the youth movement at that time to establish a new political party. We wanted to replace the corrupt ruling party that controlled the country since our independence. My friends and our generation were born after independence and we had no memory of colonialism. So when the old fighters spoke about their heroism in the great war, we would be silent out of respect, but in reality, we felt that many of these men were not pushing the country forward, rather they were living in the past.

"Our newspaper, which we wrote using false names, was very popular, especially on campus. We covered the anti-apartheid movement in South Africa, where the Afrikaner nationalist government was suppressing Mandela's party. We covered the revolutions of Latin America, the collapse of the Soviet Union, and so many other events of that era, and slowly we began to feel that it was time for our own change.

"On the day the government decided to allow new parties to sign up, we celebrated in the streets. It seemed that finally, our voices would be heard, and our talents would be valued in the effort to bring prosperity to Algeria. In the months before the first election, my friends and I had become big supporters of the Islamic Salvation Front. They were a new party who, to put it simply, advocated for establishing Islamic law as the foundation of our country's laws. Algeria is a deeply religious country, and these ideas were popular and exciting. At our local mosque, we used to gather every week and discuss how to achieve the perfect Islamic vision for our country. In our view, the revolutionary fighters who were in control of our nation had done the first job of expelling the French, but my generation wanted more. We wanted to replace the system inherited from the French with one guided by the same Islam that the French fought so hard to crush and erase. I assume the French were similarly aggressive in Guinea?"

"Absolutely," Yasin said. "We were in fact the first country south of the Sahara to achieve independence from France. But right away, the French colonialists who were still in Guinea tried to sabotage our new country. On their way out of Guinea, they destroyed everything they could. They burned hospitals and medicine, destroyed sewage pipelines—they even took the light bulbs out of streetlamps. My grandfather told me they thought everything belonged to them, and if they couldn't stay they would take it home."

"Subhan Allah. May Allah's curse be on those thieves and criminals." Ali's face bore unrestrained disgust.

"But I understand what you're saying," Yasin added. "The revolutionaries in Guinea held on to power for many years. They didn't give the next generation a chance to become leaders."

"Unfortunately, that seems to be a universal problem. Even in the mosques here, the elders shut out the youth from getting involved." Ali shook his head. "How can we protect our kids' futures without their involvement?"

"Slowly they will drift away, just like we left our own countries," Yasin said sadly.

"Exactly. Back in those early years, my friends and I were still naïve and hopeful. We campaigned. We wrote. We gathered. We debated ideas from morning to night. We studied other countries and successful popular movements. When it came time to vote, we rallied everyone we knew and showed up to the polls. We really believed that there was no way a movement as powerful as ours could fail. And when the results showed our party had won, everyone celebrated in the streets. Our party had won by a landslide in all the major cities.

"Then, the small fear that we had been ignoring all along came true. The military elite who ran the country refused to hand over power to the winning party. They arrested the leaders of the party and rounded up thousands of activists across the country. Me and my friends barely escaped because we were young and still in school. But we refused to stay silent. We kept writing in our newspaper, criticizing the moral failure of the ruling party who had promised free and fair elections. We appealed to the UN, the EU, the Americans, and the rest of the world to step in and enforce the will of the people. But nobody listened, or cared.

"In our newspaper, we advocated day and night for nonviolent demonstration. We truly believed that we could pressure the government to accept the results. Others were not so patient. One of them was our deputy editor, Zakariya. He was very hot-headed, and he argued that just like during colonialism, the only way to achieve regime change was by picking up arms. No matter how much we tried to convince him, he was adamant and listened to nobody.

"A few weeks after the military coup, Zakariya joined a group of men who had smuggled in weapons from Mali through the Sahara. Zakariya was the youngest member of their militia. In '94, Zakariya's group took over our city violently, expelling all government affiliated personnel and declaring our city a government-free zone. My family and I hid in our home, but Zakariya had informed his bosses about our newspaper, and their commander, a scary man by the name of Abdulwahab, came knocking on our door. My parents were terrified. They didn't know that I was part of the newspaper.

"For the next several months, Abdulwahab forced me to continue publishing anti-government articles. The one thing I refused to do was to praise him and his followers. Along with my team, I continued to write pieces pressuring the government to allow the peaceful transition of power. Those months were the scariest moments of my life."

"Did he make you advocate for violent revolution?"

"He ordered us to, but we found ways around it. He was barely a literate man himself, and he would tell Zakariya to read it to him. But the threats of Abdulwahab became the least of our worries as the war raged on. I remember sometimes I would go out to buy bread and I would have to walk over dead bodies on the streets. The smell was something I will never forget. The image of cats and dogs eating human flesh still haunts me.

"Then in late 1995, I believe, there was a referendum to sign a ceasefire between the various groups and the military. I wrote in support of the ceasefire for the newspaper, even though Abdulwahab was against it. Then, while the negotiations were still happening, the military suddenly stormed our city and took control back from the forces of Abdulwahab. We all cheered for them, and we finally felt safe in our own neighborhood, but for me, the safety was short-lived.

"A few weeks after Abdulwahab and his men were expelled, I was outside buying groceries when I saw a man in military clothes talking to my parents at the front door. I waited around the corner for him to leave before returning home. I asked my father what he was asking about, and he told me they were looking for me. I had not written for the newspaper for several weeks at that time, but I was suspicious of the military. I didn't trust them. There were stories going around about massacres in local towns by the extremists while military forces stood by and let it happen, so that the public would turn against the rebels. There were also conspiracies that people within the rebel ranks were double agents for the military. I later found out this was true in at least one case.

"After the military came to at my parents' home, I contacted one of the other editors of our newspaper, another good friend, and we met clandestinely for a coffee. He confirmed that the military had come asking about him too, and he was currently living with his uncle. When I reached out to the others, I realized that Zakariya became an informant for the military, and he gave the addresses of everyone who had written for our newspaper to them."

"The betrayal always comes from those closest to you," Yasin muttered. "And those hurt the most."

"Wallahi, they do. By then I knew I had to escape. I packed a small bag and traveled to the capital, where my cousin studied and lived. I cut off contact with all the people from the newspaper and stayed with him for a month, but somehow, the military found out I was there too. They came to the door one day and I hid inside while my cousin told them I had left. Again, I had to escape."

While Yasin listened to Ali's story, he found more resonance than Ali would know. The constant lack of safety, hiding from authorities, and having to escape. Though Ali had done nothing wrong, he was subjected to these horrors, like Yasin now was. "Were you able to leave the country?" Yasin asked.

"Alhamdulillah, I was. Despite my distaste for France, it seemed to be the only option left. A trusted friend of my cousin filled out asylum paperwork for me, and I was able to board a ship to Marseille, about one day's travel. But in all of France, I only knew one person, my aunt in Paris. My plan was to take the train there, and hopefully she would let me live with her, at least for a short time. Everything went smoothly. I arrived in Paris and surprised her when I knocked on her door. But when I got there, it was not the safe haven that I imagined. On the third night of staying there, I witnessed something that caused me to leave my aunt's house for good."

"Not again!" Yasin groaned.

"Again! It was my aunt's husband. He came home late one night extremely drunk. I was shocked. I had never seen someone drunk before in my life. He stumbled through the door, growling and cursing at his wife. From the expression of my aunt, it seemed that this wasn't the first time she had experienced this, but she was also embarrassed for me to see it. She told me to go to my room, but when I saw how unstable he was, I worried about her safety. She tried to calm him down, and tried to send me away, but I stood in between them. That night, I wrestled him to the ground and choked him until he passed out. Then, I packed my belongings and I left.

"I had nowhere to stay that night. I wandered around the streets of Paris, watching couples stroll by holding hand in hand and families have dinner at outdoor cafes. I walked and walked and walked until suddenly, I found the Eiffel Tower above me. For a moment it captured my wonder; despite my pitiful situation, I remember thinking it was more beautiful than in the pictures. I sat on the lawn in front of the tower, entranced for some time, until I fell asleep.

"For a few months, I lived on that Eiffel Tower lawn. I was lucky enough to run into some enterprising Algerians who were selling fake Lacoste polos on the street. Since I hadn't had food in days, I asked them if they could help me find work. They said their factory was always hiring. That night they took me to their boss, a French man, who was running a fake Lacoste empire. He was doing millions in sales, both in France and in exports to North Africa.

"I got started working in his factory doing twelve hour shifts every day, sewing little alligator logos on plain polos. The pay was terrible—not nearly enough to afford food and a place to sleep. When winter came around, I resorted to sleeping in a homeless shelter, which turned out to be more dangerous than the streets. Every day there were turf wars between the West Africans and North Africans, and anything you owned could get stolen."

"That's surprising," Yasin commented. "Here, don't we West Africans get along with you North Africans pretty well?"

"There's not many of us Africans here, so we have to stick together," Ali said. "But trust me, in Paris we are everywhere." He laughed. "Anyway, when I refused to pledge loyalty to the North African gang, they kicked me out of the homeless shelter, and I went back to sleeping in front of the Eiffel Tower. I nearly froze that winter. The only thing keeping me going was following the news in Algeria. The war was getting worse still. Hundreds of thousands were dead. I tried sending messages back to my family through contacts, but I couldn't find a way to get through."

"Then, in the spring, I got my chance to move to America. One of the newspaper writers, the oldest of us who had graduated university and was already a brilliant engineer, received a visa to live and work in the US. I received a note from him, and he told me he could get me to America too. He had married and was planning to stay in

America for good. I told him that I was interested in joining him. He filled out the paperwork for me to be an asylum-seeker. A few months later I flew from Paris to New York. This time, I made it my goal to build a dignified life for myself here."

"And ma sha Allah, you did so," Yasin said. "I never would have guessed that you lived through all of that. I've only known you for a few days, but you're always happy and positive, and you've found success here from nothing, Allahuma barik."

"Wallahi, it wasn't easy to start over. Sometimes, I feel like I've lived two entirely different lives. In my first life, I used to be grounded in my country's soil, filled with excitement for my nation's future. I fully expected life to play out the way I had planned it in my grand teenage visions. Then, abruptly, like the early death of a family member, that me died. I had to build a brand new life here. I'm a businessman now, not a journalist. I've learned a third language, started a family, and built a new social circle. But every now and then, I get stabbed with memories. Faces of people I knew and loved haunt me, joyful moments from my youth torment me. When that happens, I mourn the death of that version of me all over again."

"I know what you mean," Yasin said. "But for me, I feel like I'm neither here nor there."

"That feeling fades away," Ali said. "You'll see over time. I hope you can bring your family here to live with you soon."

Yasin nodded, but he turned to look away, because he couldn't meet Ali's eyes and tell him the truth.

Chapter 24: Saif

It was the last day of Saif's suspension, and he still wasn't sure about what he wanted to do. Going back to work after his arrest felt like accepting humiliation. Rayan's words played through his mind, about the police being an immoral system, and how he was going to get corrupted by it. He thought of the story of his father, who joined the military with good intentions, then got sucked into a violent civil war that took his life. He thought about God, and what God would want him to do. But he felt that it was his life, and he had to figure it out alone. Like he had always done.

He sat in his bedroom on his laptop, mindlessly scrolling through social media. On the side panel, #Hoffmeyer was trending. He clicked on the hashtag. Images and videos flooded the screen. *Hoffmeyer was killed.*

Saif's eyes grew large as he pieced together scraps of information from various posts. He searched Hoffmeyer in a separate tab to see if it had hit the news. ABC had a brief digital article up.

Stephen Hoffmeyer, notorious criminal convicted of several bombings, finally caught, killed

Late last night, Stephen Hoffmeyer was killed in a dramatic shootout with FBI operatives at the long-abandoned Kings Park Psychiatric Center in Kings Park, Long Island.

FBI spokespeople say Hoffmeyer had been using the psychiatric center as a headquarters for operations ever since his escape from custody. Several other members of his criminal organization were killed in the shootout.

Officers from the Suffolk County Police Department have shut down the area surrounding the former psychiatric center, which has been out of use for nearly three decades, and was locally popular as a destination for urban explorers. The entire hospital complex includes over a hundred buildings, many of which are condemned and in extreme levels of decay.

Join us tonight at six for a full broadcast, with live reporting from the scene.

Saif ran out to the living room with his laptop. He dug between the couch cushions for the remote. "They found him!" he called out to his mother in the kitchen. "They found Hoffmeyer!"

He set his computer down and flipped to the right channel. They were just beginning the live broadcast. A Black man with a serious expression was speaking. Saif turned up the volume.

"Late last night, FBI special agents discovered Stephen Hoffmeyer's lair at the Kings Park Psychiatric Center in Long Island, where they joined forces with the Suffolk County police department to storm the crumbling thirteen-story structure known as building ninety-three. Hoffmeyer and twelve of his associates were killed in the subsequent shootout. Two local police officers were also killed, and three were critically injured. The FBI is still unraveling details about Hoffmeyer's shadowy organization, which perpetrated at least two high profile bombings in the city, and is still being investigated for other attacks."

While the TV anchor spoke, video of the FBI raid played in a loop, taken from an aerial view. SWAT teams wearing black vests emblazoned with 'FBI' in large block yellow letters slowly surrounded a tall, rundown building. They inched forward, and then all at once, they rushed the building, smashing through cracked windows, kicking down thick doors, and some even airdropping from helicopters to enter through the rooftop access hatch. It was a nighttime raid, and many agents were outfitted with heat vision goggles or thermal scopes on their rifles. Saif was relieved that Hoffmeyer was caught, but the spectacle of his capture gripped him as if he was watching an action movie.

As he rewatched the same clip again and again, and the anchor ran out of ways to repeat the few facts he knew of the case, Saif noticed other small things. Nature had reclaimed the land the building stood on, and it was wild with trees and brush. The building was also covered in graffiti, hard to see in the dark video but seemingly all over the front side of the building. The roof had wide holes in it, exposing wooden beams beneath it. Saif had shivers from imagining how it must have looked inside. If he had received orders to storm that building, he didn't know if he'd be brave enough to do it. Then, the news channel shifted cameras to a young woman in their studio.

"Now we'd like to bring on Julia Nowicki, ABC senior crime correspondent, who has more information about the Kings Park Psychiatric Center."

"Thank you for having me on," Julia said with a practiced smile. "I've been able to gather some new information about building ninety-three, the structure that Hoffmeyer took over when he escaped custody. Building ninety-three is part of a massive psychiatric hospital campus. The first buildings were established in 1885. Building ninety-three is the largest building of about a hundred in total, standing thirteen stories high, and was the main patient housing building. Others were designed for specific purposes, from housing geriatric patients to violent, mentally insane patients. It turns out that Hoffmeyer's own father was once held in maximum security building number fifteen, also known as the Wisteria House. This may be part of the reason he chose this location to be the headquarters of his terror organization."

"Thank you, Julia, for that analysis," the news anchor said as the camera moved back to him. "We now turn towards FBI spokesperson Matt D'Andrea, who has more details on the raid that has captured who could be the most high-profile fugitive in New York City history."

A man in a crisp suit appeared on the right side of the screen, with the anchor's face being shifted to the left. The man was wearing sunglasses and had a wired microphone around one of his ears.

"Matt, thank you for joining us today. Tell us more about how this operation unfolded."

"FBI Special Teams and the NYPD have been collaborating on this case for weeks," he said. His face barely seemed to move when he spoke, and the dark sunglasses obscuring his eyes made him seem even more reticent. "We currently believe that the escape of the seven convicts was orchestrated purely for Hoffmeyer's benefit. While the other fugitives are still considered dangerous, they are far less likely to pose a threat to the public."

While Matt spoke, new footage began to play on the screen, replacing the space where the anchor was previously. It seemed to Saif like bodycam footage, probably from a Suffolk County cop. It showed a man's arms outstretched with a pistol clutched in both hands. The camera was outfitted with night vision, lending the footage a green hue.

As the officer swiveled left and right, looking for Hoffmeyer in different rooms, more of the interior of the building was viewable. It was in horrid condition. The walls were damaged with holes larger than basketballs, revealing fragile beams holding them up. The parts of the walls that were still standing were smothered in graffiti, words that were too obscure to read. The floor was littered with bricks, wooden pallets, medical equipment, rusted pipes, dirty mattresses, syringes, and piles and piles of unidentifiable junk.

Then, a flash of motion caused Saif to jump while he was watching on his couch. It was a man in an all-white outfit, running out from behind an downturned bathtub. The officer fired his gun and the screen blurred instantly.

"Frightening scenes we're seeing there," the anchor said after a pause from the FBI agent. "We sure are glad Hoffmeyer is no longer around. Thank you for your service, Agent D'Andrea. We turn back to Julia Nowicki with details about the final two escapees of the Steinway Seven."

While Julia began to speak, seven photos appeared on the screen. Over five of the mugshots, big red X's covered the men's faces, which were also faded in black and white. Two men remained in full color: Terrence Howard and Yasin Bamba. Terrence looked angrily at the camera in his photo. He had a patch of reddish-blond hair on his afro, and on his neck, a tattoo of two playing cards were barely visible. In the other mugshot, Yasin Bamba seemed to stare through the TV, his eyes tinged with sadness and confusion.

Saif pulled his computer over his lap to research each remaining man. First, he looked up Terrence Howard. It was a fairly common name with varying search results, so he switched over to the News tab. Here, articles populated the screen about fugitive Terrence Howard. He skimmed over some headlines.

Terrence Howard, 33, convicted of first-degree murder and handed life sentence

What's that floating in the canal? Gowanus residents recount horror of finding murder victim Rachel White

Who is Terrence Howard, TikTok's latest celebrity crush?

Saif rolled his eyes at the last headline. After skimming some articles, it seemed Terrence's case was pretty straightforward. He killed his girlfriend, dumped her body in a canal, and got caught. Yawn. As soon as they found him, he would rot in his cell for life.

Yasin's case, however, seemed more interesting. During the police briefing, Saif recalled that little was shared about Yasin. Even online, nothing seemed to come up under Yasin Bamba. He scrolled past random LinkedIn profiles, Instagram results, and Wikipedia pages about African leaders. Then, an article from a Harlem newspaper caught his eye.

Harlem Residents Demand Justice For 'Innocent'
Steinway Seven Fugitive

The small photo next to the headline showed a young African man speaking on the street into a wireless microphone. Intrigued, Saif clicked on the article.

As the NYPD's search for the Steinway Seven continues, some Harlem residents are speaking out. Amadou, who wasn't comfortable sharing his last name, says he is an old friend of convict Yasin Bamba, who is still at large since his escape from custody. Yasin is one of two fugitives who still haven't been caught, along with Terrence Howard. The NYPD is offering $25,000 to anyone who provides a tip that leads to either capture.

Though Yasin was convicted of drug trafficking last month, and sentenced to twenty years at the Sing Sing Correctional Facility upstate, Amadou insists Yasin is innocent. Amadou, a fellow undocumented immigrant who has known Yasin since they arrived together in New York nearly five years ago, says Yasin is a devoutly religious man who would never have sold drugs.

"Yasin is like a big brother to me," Amadou said to the Harlem Advocate, standing near 145th street in Harlem. "He is a pious Muslim man who would never get involved with these things."

Local residents of the Guinean community, and more broadly the West African community in Harlem, have echoed Amadou's concerns. Many have called for a retrial, hoping for a chance to testify on Yasin's behalf. There are concerns that Yasin's undocumented status may have contributed to a bias against him in the case.

When asked why he decided to speak out now, over two weeks after the escape, Amadou was tight-lipped. "I'm worried about his safety," Amadou said. "He doesn't deserve to be hunted down like this. If he is caught, at least give him the dignity of a safe flight back home to Guinea."

The NYPD has refused to add comment on whether they would accept new information in Yasin's case that could potentially lead to a retrial. "We demand justice," Amadou said. "I don't believe justice has been served."

Saif's head spun as he read the article. He wanted to believe Amadou's powerful testimony. He knew how brave it was for an undocumented immigrant to speak to the media. However, it would be an uphill battle for anyone trying to prove Yasin's innocence. *How do you explain having five whole pounds of fentanyl in your possession?* Even if he was somehow absolved of his drug trafficking charge, Yasin had escaped custody. In the best-case scenario, after Yasin was caught, he could inform the NYPD of who supplied him the drugs and maybe secure a protection deal.

Saif lay back on the couch and remembered he had work early tomorrow. If he was lucky, he might be able to convince Captain Mancini to place him on Yasin's case. Then he could dig deeper into exactly what had happened. *Who gave him the drugs? And what was he planning to do with it?*

It was time to do some real police work.

Chapter 25: Yasin

A few days after the Suhoor Fest, Yasin arrived at King of Beans, where Ali was waiting for him with a smile.

"Your first paycheck," he said, handing Yasin a crisp white envelope.

"It's been a week already?" Yasin asked in genuine surprise. He opened it to find a short stack of crisp twenty-dollar bills.

"Time flies, right?" Ali clapped him on the shoulder. "Ramadan's already almost over."

Business had picked up the last few nights. The night before, they had a full house for iftar service for the first time. Yasin had gone to sleep late after washing all the dishes and was still tired now. "Thank you so much," Yasin said, still staring at the cash.

"No need to thank me, you earned it." Ali said. "Go ahead and put it away, and then let's get started on today's menu. I'm thinking of doing a dish called berkoukes today. I'm not sure how to describe it—it's like couscous, but bigger. Anyway, you'll see how it looks in a moment."

Yasin went to his tiny room in the back of the restaurant and kneeled on his mattress on the floor. He took the money out of the envelope and counted it. It was two hundred, as expected. He folded it under his pillow, adding it with all the money he had earned from doing deliveries. He now had $445 in total. That should be more than enough to pay for the taxi ride to Philadelphia.

He sat, counting the money again just to be sure, even though he knew he had it right the first time. He had yet to spend a single dollar from Guillermo, patiently waiting for this moment. But now, he had second guesses about his original plan. He was enjoying his new job. He wished he could start over with a new identity and stay here, in Astoria, working for Ali. But he didn't let his mind linger too long on that impossibility.

Even with his original plan, things would be extremely risky. He was going to have to sneak his way over to the East Village and find the exact same taxi driver he spoke to. Otherwise, he would have to find a new taxi driver in Astoria willing to take him out of the city, but there was always the risk of someone informing the police. Suddenly, he remembered the bombing that he had barely survived at Madina Masjid and realized that his whole plan fell apart. With the masjid nearly destroyed, there was no way the same taxi driver would still be going there to pray.

Yasin decided he would need to convince a local taxi driver to help him escape the city. Hopefully the price wouldn't dramatically rise with a new driver. On the bright side of all this, he wouldn't have to leave Ali immediately.

He packed the money back under his pillow and went out to help Ali prepare.

Ali was rolling little balls of dough on the counter. "Everything good over there?" he asked.

"Yes, I was just putting it away safely with the rest of my money."

"Oh okay, good. Thanks for taking care of the dishes last night," Ali said. "I think that's the most customers we've had yet. Can you believe we fit twenty-two people in here? Maybe we can do two more!"

"Oh, earlier when you mentioned Ramadan ending soon, that reminded me," Yasin said, "what will the work hours be after Eid?"

"Good question. I think we'll open around eleven for lunch service, probably close for a couple of hours and then reopen for dinner service. Maybe if I can hire more help we can stay open longer. What do you think?"

"I think that would be a good idea. People love your food. I'm sure you can make the money back by staying open and hiring more people."

"That's very nice of you," Ali smiled. "I just need to find a way to get my food in front of more people than just Algerians. Maybe I should hire my son to make some tickytacks or whatever."

"What's that?"

"I don't know, but I heard it's how all the kids are finding out about restaurants nowadays."

"I see," Yasin said, watching Ali continue to hand roll the round berkoukes pasta. "Do you need any help?"

"Not yet, I'll be doing this for a while. Why don't you go pray Asr next door and come back?"

"Good idea," Yasin said. He needed to find a new taxi driver anyway.

Yasin went next door to Al Iman mosque. There was still fifteen minutes until Asr prayer began. He grabbed a Quran from a shelf nearby, took a seat on the floor with his back against the wall, and started to read silently. He had a view of the window to his right, which allowed him to see people coming in.

After reading for a while, a man went up and made the call to prayer. Yasin returned the Quran to the shelf and lined up next to everybody. Then, while looking out the window, he saw a taxi pull in, park, and a man come out. He looked at the man and quickly committed his face to memory. Prayer began.

Once they were done praying, Yasin immediately looked back to see if the man was there. The taxi driver was making up part of the prayer since he had started late. His face was still dripping wet from making wudu. Yasin turned back to the front and waited patiently. Soon, people around him started to leave. When Yasin looked back again a moment later, the man was gone.

Yasin jumped up and ran over to the shoe racks by the exit to find the man putting on his second shoe and getting up to go. "Wait!" he called.

The man turned back impatiently.

"Brother," Yasin said breathlessly. "Can I ask you a question? You're a taxi driver, right?"

"Aywa," the man nodded.

"How much would you charge to take me to Philadelphia, one way?"

"Philadelphia?" the man snorted. "Too far."

"Please, brother." Yasin begged.

"Five hundred dollars."

"But another taxi driver told me four hundred—"

"Then go with the other guy. I don't want to go to Philadelphia."

"No, no, please. Listen, I have four hundred and forty-five dollars right now."

"Okay, so get the rest and come back." He turned to leave and Yasin watched him jump into his taxi and drive off. He would have to work for another week with Ali before he could afford the trip.

When he got back to King of Beans, Ali had gotten started on the sauce for the berkoukes main dish. Yasin started setting up for the night: arranging tables and chairs, setting plates and cutlery, and getting the appetizers ready. They both worked with patient urgency, Ali a whirlwind in the kitchen, and Yasin a whirlwind outside of it, and then at eight on the dot, everything was ready.

The restaurant was still and silent. Yasin looked at Ali in excited anticipation of another busy night. They both relished the peace of the moment, before the first group of customers would begin the chaos.

Despite fitting in another table and two extra chairs that night, King of Beans was at full capacity again. Ali was ecstatic. He floated around, humming a melodic tune, while Yasin stacked dirty plates and cups and brought them over to the dishwasher.

"I knew opening in Ramadan was a good idea," Ali beamed in the kitchen. "We work for half a day and make a full day's income!"

"Are you saying there's room for a Ramadan bonus?" Yasin suggested wryly.

Ali laughed, then looked at him seriously. "You know what, good idea. Make it to Eid, and I'll give you that bonus." He winked.

"I'll get the plates outside," Yasin said. *A nice Ramadan bonus could help me get started with a new life in Philly. I hope there's a lot of Muslims there. Maybe I can find a job like this one.*

As he approached the exit, he saw a man in a full camouflage outfit sitting on their outdoor seating. He was reading a newspaper and smoking.

"Sorry brother, I need to clean up here. This is a private business."

The man looked up at him with red puffy eyes. Yasin looked and noticed the blunt in his hands.

"Arright, fine," the man said, getting up. He walked off and Yasin followed him with his eyes, seeing the man go into a hookah bar. Then, he started to stack the plates outside, but his eyes fell on the newspaper the man left behind. It said "Arab Astoria" in English and Arabic on the front page, but the text of the articles were all in Arabic.

Yasin sat on a chair for a moment and tried to read it. The front-page article had a full color picture of Donald

Trump shouting angrily, his hair blowing wildly in the wind. Yasin tried to test his Arabic by reading the headline.

President Trump Announces
Expansion To Muslim Travel Ban

The article itself went into more detail, and it took Yasin a long time to get through it.

Last week, US President Donald Trump announced new severe restrictions on all travel from many countries with Muslim citizens, including Afghanistan, Burma, Chad, Eritrea, Guinea, Iran, Libya, Somalia, Sudan, and Yemen, among others. The ban includes all types of visas, such as immigrant, tourist, and student visas.

Anyone with a current green card or previously issued visa will not be included in the ban. The new ban is expected to force refugees from war-torn countries, many where the US military has been involved, to seek alternative places to take refuge.

The Council on American-Islamic Relations, also known as CAIR, has called Trump's latest ban 'unnecessary, broad, and ideologically motivated'. For those who are in New York, the legal rights

Yasin was proud of how much he was able to understand from the article, but once the meaning sat in his mind,
he felt hurt. The ban would affect so many innocent people,
including people he cared about. When he was in Guinea,
people spoke about America like it was a place for anyone,
a country built by immigrants, which was so unique and
attractive to people in the old world, where ethnic groups
and tribes had lived for centuries on the same land. He
used to think, if only I could get to America, I could build
a life for myself, as long as I worked hard. But since he had
arrived, he had not found that to be the reality. He wondered if it ever had been.

Looking for a new topic, he turned a wide page over
to see what else had made the news. What he saw made his
heart jump into his throat. There, on the next page, staring
at him was himself.

Yasin looked up and around him wildly, wondering if
the man who had left the newspaper had seen him and
made the connection. He looked back and saw Ali still in
the kitchen using his phone. Nobody around him on the
street had seen the newspaper in his hands. He snuck another peek at what the article said about him.

*Two Fugitives Still At-Large
Following the Capture of Hoffmeyer*

Under his mugshot photo, Yasin's name and nationality were written. He recognized the man in the photo next to him as Red. It said his real name was Terrence Howard.

Yasin shut the newspaper and rolled it up tightly. He stood up and turned to face Ali through the window. Ali still hadn't moved. He stuffed the rolled-up newspaper into his pants from behind and pulled his shirt over it. Suddenly, he heard an intense whistle by his ear. Then, a second shot whizzed by. He felt something hot slowly dribble down his neck. Shrieks filled the air around him. The man working the halal cart nearby shouted in terror and fell to the ground.

Yasin felt dazed. He staggered over to the door of the restaurant. His ear was ringing. His legs felt heavy. He saw Ali open the door and usher him inside, and he staggered over to his room and fell onto his mattress.

Chapter 26: Saif

Saif woke up early for his first day back to work at the 114th precinct. His game plan was to pretend that nothing happened, keep his head down, and try to find a way onto Yasin's case. He arrived twenty minutes early and was surprised to see Elias, Jessica, and an older female detective already there, chatting in the break room. They all fell silent and looked up at him when he walked in.

"Saif, we've missed you, man," Elias said first. "It wasn't right for them to suspend you for that."

Saif smiled sheepishly, scratching the back of his head in embarrassment. "Forget it. It was a dumb idea anyway."

"I can't believe you actually went to the Upper East Side just because I mentioned it," Jessica said. "I was just spitballing—it wasn't even a real lead!"

"I did find someone hiding out there, so it wasn't a total failure," Saif replied.

"True, we heard about that," Elias said.

"Did you have any other guesses on where the last two guys could be?" Saif asked Jessica sarcastically. "Cause I could go investigate it."

They all laughed, and then the older detective reached out a hand to shake Saif's. "I'm Detective Kaminski, by the way. You can call me Bea."

"I'm Saif. Great to meet you."

"Detective Kaminski was just telling us about one of the last two fugitives, Terrence Howard," Jessica said. "Do you mind starting over for Saif?"

Detective Kaminski nodded. "Sure, I was just getting started anyway. A few days ago, we got a tip that was quite disturbing. Jessica was working the tip line and she was the first person to bring it to me. Do you want to describe it, Jessica?"

"Sure," she said. "I got a call from an older-sounding person with a funny accent who said they saw a man matching Terrence Howard's description being kidnapped by a group of men wearing suits in Hudson Yards. The man on the phone said he was just a tourist, but he insisted he had seen the kidnapping happen and was sure it was our fugitive. He said they put Howard in a black car and drove off."

"Seems like a promising lead," Saif said. "Did you get the exact location?"

"Yeah, over the phone, I had the man walk around and read street signs. I gathered that he was at the overpass on thirty-seventh street between ninth and tenth avenue. I remember the whole time he kept complaining that the area was so unwalkable compared to Amsterdam, and that New York wasn't as nice as people said, and the weather was way hotter than he had expected. Once I had the location down I had to hang up on him because he started asking for recommendations on things to do indoors."

"Summer tourist season is brutal," Elias complained. "I try to avoid midtown so I don't have to run into those people."

"So we drove by to check out the area," Detective Kaminski picked up, "and found nothing. If it was as the man had said, they picked Howard up and disappeared faster than we could get there. And the area is so windy that anything left behind would have been swept up." She paused to swig her coffee. "I kept that lead on the back burner while we checked out other leads, but two days ago, I drove by again, and found something. I stood there for a while, the area that Jessica had identified, and watched where the wind swept trash to. I realized there was a patch of grass where trash was collecting, like fast food wrappers and plastic cups and stuff, and I dug through there for a bit. There was tons of junk, but one thing I noticed was half of a hundred dollar bill. I took it back to the lab and we ran some tests on it."

"What did you find?" Elias asked. "Coke?"

"Traces of cocaine are on like eighty percent of bills," Detective Kaminski said. "So yeah, we found that, but it wasn't out of the ordinary. What was more interesting was a few drops of blood on it. It seemed like someone had bled on it while doing a line of coke. I sent the bill to forensics to do a DNA test on the blood and they found a match. Some twenty-eight-year-old guy named Mike Whitman. He was arrested ten years ago in Ohio at a frat party gone wrong, but never faced jail time. Now, he's working in Hudson Yards for a Hedge Fund as an 'Investor Relations Specialist'."

"That's a fancy way to say sales," Elias said. When he saw the look of confusion on everyone's faces, he shrugged. "My cousin does it, and I thought he was a big deal, until I figured out what his job actually was—schmoozing with rich people so they invest with the fund he works for."

"So did you find this Mike guy?" Saif turned back to Detective Kaminski.

"We did. Last night, I brought Jessica along to an address we had on file. I know those finance guys work long hours, so we went pretty late, around eleven o'clock. It was a sixty-story high rise, and his apartment was on the forty-ninth floor. Super bougie place. When we arrived the front desk tried to stop us, until we threatened to call in a SWAT team. Then they backed off."

"It's like they think their tenants should be above the law," Jessica piped in.

"We got there and as soon as we got out of the elevator, we heard techno music blasting. We followed the noise and it led us to Mike's apartment. I put my ear by the door and it sounded like a circus. We knocked, and then a guy opened the door with white powder all over his nose and wild eyes. He slammed the door shut. I kicked it down and saw one of the most insane parties I've ever seen in thirty years of being a cop. The room was thick with smoke, everyone was doing drugs, and one guy was chugging a bottle of Henny while jumping on a marble dining table. When the guy turned around, he threw up all over a man in a suit passed out on the ground, who I recognized as our guy, Mike."

"It was genuinely crazy," Jessica said. "I remember not knowing where to look because everything was so disturbing, and then I looked up outside the window and noticed the amazing view of the skyline. Then I looked back down and nearly threw up myself."

"That isn't even the most surprising part," Detective Kaminski continued. "I had Jessica guard the door while I went to get Mike, when I discovered our fugitive, Terrence Howard, tied up on the floor next to Mike, face down. I flipped him over and tried to shake him up, but he was unresponsive. Jessica called EMS and they rushed over. They said he was barely alive and if we hadn't called an ambulance over, he could've died."

"They also said he had a ton of drugs in his system," Jessica added. "Amphetamines, Cocaine, LSD, you name it."

"That's horrible," Saif said. "Why in the world was Howard there? Why did they kidnap him?"

"That's what we just pieced together. Once we found Terrence, the guy who was jumping on the table tried to escape, but Jessica knocked him down and arrested him. We took him and Mike and Howard to the Midtown South Precinct while we called in backup to deal with the situation in the apartment. Mike's friend ended up being his colleague Lucas, but Lucas was tight-lipped about why Howard was there. Mike was still knocked out, so we put him in a different questioning room. When he finally woke up, we told him we had Lucas. He asked what Lucas had told us and we said we heard all about how they had kidnapped Terrence Howard. Once he heard Terrence's name he admitted to everything."

"So what was the reason?" Saif asked. "Did they just kidnap him out of some drug-fueled insanity?"

"It was related to a bet," Jessica explained.

"A bet?" Elias asked, confused.

"Yeah," Jessica said. "There's a few betting apps that have taken over the city recently. People have been betting on things as random as the weather on a particular day to who's gonna be the next coach for the Knicks. There's been a big market for betting on which fugitive is going to be the last to get caught."

"At the precinct early that morning, Mike explained that they were driving by one day when they recognized Howard living by the bridge," Detective Kaminski carried on. "When the Steinway Seven first escaped, Mike and Lucas had made a bet on Howard through one of these so-called prediction apps. The other fugitives started getting caught one by one, and their small investment of twenty-five-thousand grew to over a *quarter million* in value. And Howard was still an underdog to the other fugitive, Yasin Bamba. That means if Howard made it to the end, their bet could have paid out a million dollars."

"A million dollars?!," Saif gasped. "So they tried to kidnap Howard until Yasin was eventually caught, and then they would release him to us to get their payout?"

"I guess so," Detective Kaminski said. "A stupid plan, but it may have worked."

"Glad you caught them," Elias snorted. "Gambling is rotting people's brains these days."

"Don't you bet on basketball?" Saif said.

"Yo, please don't remind me, I've lost way too much money on that crap. I quit."

"That's what they all say." Saif smirked. "If I see you doing it again, I have permission to punch you."

"Don't get your hopes up," Elias said. "But for real, all this stuff makes me feel disgusted. What's going on with the hedge fund guys now?"

"They're on their way to Rikers right now," Detective Kaminski said.

"Hey, maybe one of them'll be cellmates with Howard in prison," Saif joked.

Detective Kaminski shook her head, laughing. "Anyway, the job isn't done yet. We still have one man on the loose."

"I may have a lead on that," Saif said, remembering the article he read interviewing Amadou. "There's a guy who claims to know Yasin in Harlem. He was interviewed in a local paper there. I'm thinking he might know something we don't."

"It's possible. Bamba's last residence is in Harlem," Detective Kaminski said. "Send me the article, I'll check it out."

"Will do," Saif said. "Um—would it be possible for me to officially join the investigation on Yasin?"

"Can I join too?" Elias requested.

Detective Kaminski smirked at Jessica. "What do you think? Should we let them tag along?"

Jessica laughed. "Sure, as long as Saif doesn't go running off somewhere undercover."

"Fine, I'll talk to the cap about it," Detective Kaminski said. "First, I need to sleep. I've been up for more than eighteen hours. But later tonight, we can go check out that lead you mentioned. Let's meet back here tonight at nine?"

"Perfect," Elias said immediately.

Saif hesitated. He had promised his mother to eat iftar with her around eight-thirty that evening. But he couldn't miss the chance to be part of the case.

"See you all then," he said.

Chapter 27: Yasin

Yasin wanted to yell in pain, but settled for deep breaths instead. He dabbed his ear with his hand and smudges of dark red stained his fingertips. In the tiny room, Ali was hunched over his phone, dialing for an ambulance.

"No!" Yasin cried. "You can't call the police."

"But you're bleeding!" Ali argued.

"I know, but no matter what, the police can't see me. Please, if they come, don't mention me."

Ali knelt and wiped Yasin's neck with a paper towel. His ear seemed to have stopped bleeding, but he winced when Ali dabbed it gently. Ali left the room and closed the door. The police would likely arrive any moment to investigate the scene.

Yasin prepared his things in case he needed to escape. He grabbed the cash from under his bed and stuffed it into his pants pocket. Was someone trying to kill him? Or was it a random shooting? He took off his shirt splattered with a few drops of blood and gently patted his ear with it, breathing heavy through the sharp pain. He carefully put on a clean shirt, and then looked for a hat he could wear over his head. He found the baseball cap he'd worn before and tenderly put it on, having to balance it sideways to fit over the top of the ear where the bullet had lightly grazed him. Now ready, he peeked outside the door and saw Ali talking to two police officers.

Yasin quickly stepped back and shut the door. *Did they see him?* He stood against the door with his body, blocking it from opening. He controlled his breathing to be as silent as possible, closing his eyes and trying to calm his beating heart down. He thought of where he could go to hide. The only place that came to mind was Al Iman masjid next door. The building was large and there would be many places to hide. After what seemed like an eternity, he carefully peeked out again through a tiny crack. The police officers were gone, and Ali was walking straight towards him. Ali noticed the door was slightly ajar. He mouthed, *come!* and beckoned Yasin with his hands. Yasin slowly opened the door and went out to meet him.

"The police said they've caught the guy who shot his gun and they might come back and ask further questions once they figure out his motive. I told them I didn't know who he was, even though they said he was sitting on my outdoor chair earlier. Did you see him?"

"I didn't get a good look, but I did tell someone to leave a moment before I heard the gunshot." Yasin's mind flashed back to the man's face. *So he did notice me from the paper! Or was he just crazy?*

"At least he was found and caught. Please, take care of yourself. The police have shut down the entire area. If you have somewhere else you want to go, go now. I can manage the restaurant. My son can help. Prioritize yourself."

"Thank you, Ali. I think I'll go to the masjid next door, if that's okay."

"Please do. And stay safe."

Yasin crept forward towards the exit and looked both ways multiple times. It was late in the night and people had all scattered after the shooting. The entire area was blocked off with yellow tape. On the floor, he noticed two spent shell casings, with white circles drawn in chalk around them. Seeing no police, he darted for the masjid entrance next door and rushed inside.

The lights were dimmed inside the masjid, but there were people sitting in different corners of the prayer hall, leaning against walls. A low hum of the different voices, some low, some high, reading various passages from the Quran, vibrated through the still air.

Yasin walked slowly towards the back of the mosque where it was darker and emptier. He saw a short staircase that led downstairs. At the bottom of the staircase, he found himself in a large basement, where on one side there was a set of bathroom stalls, and on the other side, there were three separate doors. He went one by one, trying to open each door, hoping to find an empty closet he could hide in for the night, but they were all locked. Then, the last door opened, and he was face to face with the imam of the mosque in his office.

Yasin stood stiff like a statue. He wasn't expecting to see anyone, let alone the imam.

"Can I help you, brother?" On the imam's face, Yasin saw only concern.

Yasin stood there, unable to speak, staring desperately.

"Come inside my office," the imam said, turning sideways to make space. When Yasin didn't move, the imam took him by the elbow and gently brought him forward.

Yasin finally gathered enough energy to walk himself in. The office seemed like it would be large if it wasn't for all the things packed inside. There were bookshelves on all four walls—tall dark wooden shelves laden with hardcover books, Arabic lettering on their spines. Some of them looked new and smelled of leather, others looked well-worn, with cracked edges. There were several warm lamps to make up for the lack of windows in the basement; a small table with a half empty bag of peanuts on it; a desk with a large leather chair behind it; a tripod with a camera attached to it, and a dusty fabric armchair facing the desk. The musky scent of bukhoor filled the room.

"Sit down," the imam gestured to the armchair, taking a seat on the leather chair behind the desk. He seemed slightly younger than Yasin, maybe in his mid-thirties, with a short black beard and wire-rimmed glasses. The imam closed the open Quran that he had been reading from before Yasin knocked.

"You seem distressed," he said to Yasin, peering carefully above his glasses. "What's troubling you?"

Yasin paused for a minute, then finally found something to say. "I need your help, shaykh." When he said those words, tears began to flow down his face, thick salty tears that danced around his lips and finally slipped between them onto his tongue. Yasin wanted to keep speaking, but his chest shuddered, and his back twitched, and his gut quivered. All of the emotion of the past few weeks that he had bottled up now clawed its way out of his heart. Anxiety, fear, sadness, regret, worthlessness, longing for a time when he felt safe and at peace. He just wanted to melt into his wife's arms, and to soak in his son's carefree smile. The imam simply sat and watched him with kind eyes, patiently waiting for him to continue speaking.

"Wallahi shaykh, if I open this bottle that is my heart, it may not be able to close again."

The imam took off his glasses and closed his eyes. "My dear brother," he said, looking up to watch how Yasin received his words. "I want you to know that any pain you are going through now is not unrewarded. Our Prophet, peace be upon him, said that no pain, not even a small prick of a thorn is experienced, without some of the victim's sins becoming forgiven. And if you go through so much pain that all your sins have been forgiven, then your pain turns into rewards. Your rank in heaven is raised instead." He waited for Yasin to understand the depth of his message. "Now, tell me what's going on? Is your life in danger?"

Yasin was no longer crying. He glanced at a small mirror on the imam's desk and saw grayish-white trails of dried salt beneath his eyes. He rubbed his face with both knuckles and looked back at the imam. "Shaykh, I admit I am not perfect. I have made some decisions in the past that I regret. But what's happening now is just too much for me to bear.

Yes, my life is in danger, and I have nowhere to go and nowhere to hide. I feel lightning striking me from above and the earth shaking beneath my feet and the wind lashing out at me from every side. I just want peace."

"My dear brother, Allah tests his beloved people more than anyone else. What did the Prophets go through? Remember Prophet Yusuf? He was betrayed by his own brothers who plotted against him and abandoned him in a well. Then, he was found by travelers and sold into slavery. And still his struggle had not ended. He was framed by the wife of his new master and put in prison for many years, with nobody to remember him and advocate for him. And through all that, Allah took care of him and made a way out for him. He made Yusuf the most powerful man in Egypt and reunited him with his father. After all that struggle, what did Yusuf say? He said, 'My Lord has ever been gracious to me.'"

Yasin reflected on the story of Prophet Yusuf. It was one he had heard many times, but now it resonated with him more than ever. *He was wrongly imprisoned just like me*, he thought. *As long as I'm still alive, there's still hope.*

Seeing Yasin's body language relax, the imam offered more advice. "On this day of distress, Allah has led you to His house, the masjid, and there is no better place to be for the one in need of Him, right? You are here, in the final nights of Ramadan, the blessed last ten nights. And tomorrow night is the twenty-seventh night, which is likely to be Laylatul Qadr. What better time to be here in the masjid?"

Yasin nodded and smiled, feeling humbled by the idea that God was guiding him here all along.

"My brother, the perspective you have now, of recognizing your powerlessness before your Creator, is a gift. He is guiding you to reach the sincerest level of trust in Him that is possible on earth. I want you to repeat this phrase constantly until tomorrow night, the twenty-seventh night of Ramadan, is over. It is the night that many of our scholars have said is the Night of Power; a night when all prayers and requests are accepted by God."

"Okay shaykh, I will," Yasin said. "What dua is it?"

"It is: Hasbi Allahu la ilaha illa Huwa, Alayhi tawakkaltu wa Huwa Rabbul arshil adheem. In English, it means: 'Sufficient for me is Allah; there is nothing worthy of worship except Him, I place my trust in Him and He is the Lord of the mighty throne.'"

Yasin repeated the phrase a few times in Arabic until his tongue had memorized its movements. "Thank you so much, shaykh," Yasin said. He wiped his face with both hands again, squeezing the edges of his eyes. He now felt intensely sleepy.

"You are welcome to stay in my office," the imam said, putting his glasses back on.

"No I don't want to bother you—"

"I insist, my brother," the imam said, rising. He rummaged in a cabinet and pulled out a small pillow. "Please, sleep here for the rest of the night. I will come get you for Fajr prayer in a few hours."

Yasin couldn't resist the offer. He was exhausted—physically, mentally and emotionally. He took the pillow graciously with both hands and got as comfortable as he could on the thick carpet on the floor. The imam turned off the lamps in the room and left quietly. Yasin closed his eyes and instantly fell asleep.

As his consciousness descended slowly into darkness, a vivid set of dreams emerged to replace it. Yasin's mind started to see the events that had unfolded over the past few months in a different light. Previously jumbled memories played out in a logical sequence, and faces of people he knew were projected in high definition under his eyelids. The more he slept, the more raw memories boiled down to reveal a clearer story of events. Then he woke up with a few blinks of his eyes.

He was angry. Very angry.

Chapter 28: Saif

Saif managed to scarf down iftar with his mother in ten minutes. Then he got dressed and rushed back to the precinct. The others were all there when he arrived, fifteen minutes after nine.

"There he is," Elias said anxiously.

Detective Kaminski looked clearly annoyed by his tardiness, but she didn't say anything beyond what her expression implied.

"Let's get in the car," she said shortly. The precinct was mostly deserted, but the night shift was starting to arrive. One night shift detective shot a dirty look at Detective Kaminski, who returned it back to him.

"What's that about?" Jessica whispered to Detective Kaminski once they were out of earshot.

"I used to work with him, when he was on the morning shift. He's as dirty a cop as they come."

Jessica looked back at the other detective. He was short and round and wore thick plastic glasses. "Really? Him?"

"Don't put anything past anyone," Detective Kaminski said. "First thing you should learn as an officer."

They jumped into a SUV parked outside the station, Detective Kaminski at the wheel. "Saif, do you have an address?" she asked him.

Saif suddenly realized he didn't. *How could I have said I had a lead with no address?*

"I'm guessing you don't," Detective Kaminski gathered. "Do you at least have an idea on where to go?"

"Yes," Saif answered quickly. "The article says Amadou was interviewed at 145th Street in Harlem."

"All right, let's head there and see if we can get anyone on the ground to lead us to him," Detective Kaminski muttered. She reversed quickly and then changed gears and hit the gas, speeding southbound towards the RFK Bridge.

Is she mad at me for being late? Saif mouthed to Elias across the back seat. Elias simply shrugged. Saif thought about earlier in the day, when she seemed happier. *Maybe that was because she had just cracked Terrence Howard's case. Now she's back in work mode.*

Thankfully, Jessica changed the subject. She was always good at conversation. "What makes cops go dirty?" she asked curiously.

Detective Kaminski exhaled slowly and her shoulders fell. She seemed like she'd been waiting for the chance to share her perspective on this topic with young, inexperienced cops like them. "Unfortunately, one thing you all will learn is not everyone joins this job for the right reasons," she began, pressing the brakes gently as she spoke. "When

I was a rookie back in the nineties, there was a case that rocked the NYPD, and the whole city. It was a PR nightmare."

"What happened?" Elias asked.

"Before I tell you what happened, let what I'm about to say be a lesson to never become complacent about why you do what you do. There were a lot of good cops who became implicated in this scandal." Detective Kaminski looked at Elias for a moment in the back seat. "We're here to protect and serve the community. Don't ever forget that."

"Understood." Elias gulped and looked at Saif when she turned back, but Saif saw her still looking at them in the rearview mirror.

"They were called the Dirty Thirty, based out of the thirtieth precinct," she started. "In the eighties and nineties, as ashamed as I am to admit it, corruption was widespread within the NYPD. And the thirtieth precinct was at the center of it all. Funny enough, we're headed to their territory right now." She looked over her shoulder and merged onto the bridge, speeding towards Manhattan. "During those years, Harlem was known as the cocaine capital of the country, maybe even the world. There was so much coke running through Harlem that even the cops had to get in on it."

They hit some traffic over Randall's Island and Detective Kaminski flipped on the siren to get through.

"So, the chief architect of this operation was Sergeant Kevin Nannery. His crew at the thirtieth were called

Nannery's Raiders. They took control of Harlem's coke business and became the biggest drug lords in the city."

"Where did they get the drugs from?" Saif asked.

"They stole them. That's what I'm talking about when I say corruption isn't always planned. It sneaks up on you. You do a few drug busts, take down some suppliers, and then suddenly you have millions of dollars worth of pure cocaine in the evidence lockers, and your mind starts thinking of possibilities. Nannery's Raiders took control of the entire market. It was like introducing a new apex predator in an ecosystem. They raided—" she made air quotes with the fingers of one hand— "the hideouts and trap houses of drug dealers, gathered their drugs and cash, and instead of logging it, they sold the drugs to other dealers out of the thirtieth precinct for half the price. Within a year, they had the whole coke business under their thumbs."

"They sold drugs out of a police precinct?" Jessica was dumbfounded. "How long did they get away with this?"

"For a few years," Detective Kaminski nodded slowly, her lip curling. "Until they were infiltrated by Barry Brown."

"Who's Barry Brown?" Saif asked.

"He was a cop sent to investigate their precinct from the inside. He worked with them for more than two years, diligently rising through the ranks and tracking everything he saw. Transactions, crooked officers, drug dealers, safe houses, everything. When all was said and done, more than thirty officers were arrested, fifteen faced jail time, and two of them even committed suicide."

"Damn," Saif exhaled.

"How come only fifteen faced jail time? It sounds like it was a huge operation," Jessica asked.

Detective Kaminski bit her lip silently for a moment. "It's called the blue wall of silence. Where officers defend each other and refuse to talk. When Barry concluded his investigation, it was really tough for him to prove everything in court, without cooperation from the people that were involved."

They all fell silent for the rest of the drive. Detective Kaminski slowed down and then parallel parked on 145th Street.

"But things are better now?" Jessica asked before they exited the car.

"Yes, they are," Detective Kaminski said resolutely, without looking at her.

She doesn't believe that, Saif thought. He looked at Elias to see if he caught her body language, but he hadn't seemed to notice. Then, a worrisome thought popped into his head. *I wonder if Elias would ever become corrupt.* Saif didn't want to imagine it was possible. Elias had been a stand-up guy since the academy. But Detective Kaminski's story rattled his trust. *I know I would never do what those cops did.*

They all got out of the SUV and walked along 145th Street for a few blocks, approaching a busy intersection where the street crossed Frederick Douglass Boulevard. Saif looked around, hoping to magically recognize Amadou's face from the article he had read. He pulled it up again on his phone and looked at the photo to remind himself how Amadou looked.

"Let's split up into two groups and ask people around," Detective Kaminski said.

"I'll go with Saif," Jessica said. Detective Kaminski and Elias turned left on 145th, while Saif and Jessica went right.

"It's hard to believe someone would sign up to fight crime and then end up being a drug kingpin themself," Jessica said.

"Really? I believe it," Saif said. "We're not always the good guys, you know."

"What do you mean?"

"Didn't you hear the detective's story? And at the end, didn't you notice she didn't look at you when she said things have gotten better?"

Jessica looked at him sharply, but she nodded. "I did notice that," she said. "But I think your attitude is unhealthy. Back at the academy, when I was thinking about giving up, you were the one who motivated me to keep going. Now you're the one having second thoughts?"

"Listen, Jessica, I know you've always been a super positive person, but even you can't be this naive. Study the history of policing and get real. The system has a lot of flaws. And if you don't understand that, you could fall into exactly what Detective Kaminski was talking about."

Jessica's face didn't change but her eyes fixated on him indignantly. Finally, she looked away and approached a passerby.

"Hi, can I ask you a quick question? Have you met this man before?" She yanked Saif's phone out of his hand and showed the middle-aged woman the photo of Amadou.

"Hey—" Saif objected, but then he looked at the woman to see if she did know Amadou.

"No, never." The woman gave them a suspicious face and walked away.

Jessica went to another man and asked him the same question, still holding Saif's phone.

"No hablo ingles." The man looked away from the screen and waved them off with his hand.

"Conoces a este hombre?" Jessica asked.

"No, lo siento." The man looked at her in surprise, but still didn't look at the phone. They walked away.

"You know Spanish?" Saif asked, but Jessica didn't answer. "Come on," Saif said, trying to get his phone back. Jessica still ignored him, approaching another woman on the street holding several grocery bags. "Fine, I'm sorry, you're not naive," Saif said, catching up. Jessica finally gave him his phone and waited for Saif to question the woman in front of them.

"Hello ma'am, have you seen this man before?" The woman was wearing a traditional African dress and looked very stylish.

"Amadou," she said simply.

"Yes!" Saif said, "His name is Amadou. Do you know him?"

"It says there Amadou," the woman said, pointing at the screen.

"Oh, so you don't know him?" Saif sighed.

"What is this about?" the woman asked.

"We need to speak with him about Yasin, one of the Steinway Seven suspects. Amadou says he knows him."

She shook her head. "Ask him over there. That man selling beads and perfumes on the table. He knows almost everyone in the neighborhood." Then she walked away towards the bus stop lugging all her bags.

Saif and Jessica approached the man with long locs at the table she pointed out. "Do you know this man? His name is Amadou. He's not in trouble, we just need his help for a case we're working on," Saif explained.

"Oh, he's one of them Africans," the man said, eyeing the photo carefully. "I don't know how they're making a profit. I sell each of these prayer beads for ten bucks, and I buy them for three. They're out here selling them for five. How can I compete with that?"

"Do you know him sir, or not?" Jessica asked.

"Oh, I know him. He has a table down by Seventh Avenue not far from here. Just keep going down and you'll see him."

They walked off together using his directions. "Look, if there wasn't a Barry Brown, then Sergeant Nannery would never have been caught," Jessica argued. "There have to be good cops, or else the corrupt ones rule. Right?"

Now, it was Saif's turn not to answer. They walked in silence until they came upon a dark-skinned man re-arranging his wares on a table at the corner of 145th Street and Seventh Avenue. He was selling traditional African clothes and trinkets rather than luxury bag ripoffs. His face shifted when he saw Saif and Jessica approaching him. "Hello officers, can I help you?" he asked uneasily.

"Maybe you can," Saif said. "We're looking for Amadou."

Amadou swallowed nervously. "That's me. What is this about?"

"It's about Yasin Bamba," Jessica said. "Do you know him?"

"I do," Amadou said. "He was a good friend of mine, and he is innocent."

"I've read the paper that quoted you," Saif said. "I just want to know more information. When have you last seen him?"

"You don't believe me, do you?" Amadou said. "You think I'm lying."

Saif and Jessica looked at each other, wordlessly agreeing to play along with Amadou until he decided to open up.

"So he's innocent, you say," Jessica said. "What makes you so sure of that?"

Amadou sat down and put the wooden bracelet in his hand on the table. Foot traffic was starting to die down as the neighborhood prepared to go to sleep. "When Yasin was arrested, we thought it was just for selling counterfeit goods, or maybe due to his undocumented status. None of us feared it was something worse. When he—when I found out weeks later, I was shocked. Yasin as a drug dealer? That is impossible."

"Why is it impossible?" Saif asked. He saw the uncertain look on Amadou's face. "Listen, I'm only here to talk about Yasin. The more you tell me about him, the more I can make sure justice is served in his case. Nothing you say will be used against you."

Amadou nodded and took a deep breath. "You have to know Yasin to understand. I met him almost five years ago, on my way to the United States through Mexico to seek asylum. I made an arrangement with a group from Colombia to transport me to the US border safely, but in southern Mexico, something terrible happened. My Colombian guides were shot and killed by a cartel in Chiapas. All fourteen of us who were packed in the back of the van were kidnapped for ransom. We were held in a small mountain village. That's when I met Yasin."

"He was part of the cartel?" Jessica questioned.

"No, of course not," Amadou said. "He had been kidnapped also, a few days earlier. Anyway, as people reached out to their families and had their ransoms paid off, our group of hostages became smaller and smaller. I became close with Yasin, because neither of us had any family that could be reached. After a few weeks the cartel got tired of feeding and housing us for no pay and decided we were useless as hostages. They sent some of us—mostly the Africans and Asians who were from far away—to a huge farm and made us work. There were a few older local farmers who told us what to do, even though most of us didn't speak their native language. We dug holes, planted seeds, and harvested leaves from full grown plants."

"Were these marijuana plants?" Saif asked.

"Coca plants. I realized it because I noticed the local farmers chewing the leaves to get energy. Some days they wouldn't eat anything all day but had more energy than the rest of us. Soon, we started to chew them too, because we were barely given anything to eat more than a meatless stew once a day. And if we didn't work, the cartel would whip us with leather cattle whips. One day after a terrible beating I started to chew the leaves, and it was like a magic potion. I suddenly began working three times faster."

"Why are you telling us all this?" Jessica asked impatiently.

"Wait, let him finish," Saif said. He found Amadou's story fascinating.

"I tell you this because through all of this forced labor and lack of food, Yasin refused to chew the coca leaves with the rest of us. I asked him why, and he said because it was haram."

"What's haram mean?" Jessica interrupted.

"It means not allowed in Islam," Saif answered quickly. "Go on."

"So I told Yasin that I was Muslim too, but this was an extreme circumstance, and Allah would forgive us. But he refused. He would get beat and whipped for not being as productive as us, but still he refused to chew the leaves."

"So that's why you think he wouldn't be a drug dealer," Saif concluded. "Because he didn't take any drugs himself. But how do you know he wouldn't sell them?"

"I don't know for sure, but I know he is a principled man, and he wouldn't do something haram," Amadou said.

"Wait, how did you guys escape?" Jessica asked Amadou.

"After a few weeks of working for the cartel, they cut us loose. The coca plant farm wasn't working as well as they thought. It was supposed to compete with Colombian cocaine, but the Mexican cartel found it was still cheaper to buy the drugs from the Colombians than trying to grow it themselves. So Yasin and I walked all the way up to Texas and sought asylum, and then the governor sent us here."

"That must've been a long walk," Jessica said.

"Yes, it took us about fifteen days."

"Listen Amadou, even if Yasin is innocent somehow, we need to bring him in for questioning, and we need to know more about how the drugs were found in his merchandise," Saif said. "Is there anyone you know of who might know more about Yasin's whereabouts?"

Amadou looked sad, as if he hoped his story would have convinced them to let Yasin go. "You can try speaking to Suleyman, he also knows Yasin well."

"Where can we find Suleyman?" Jessica followed up.

"He just moved out of our apartment to live with his new wife. They're staying around the corner from here."

"Can you write an address here?" Saif asked, handing him a notepad and pen.

Amadou took the pen and quickly scribbled an address on the paper.

"Thank you Amadou. We'll be in touch."

"You know, my grandma is from Oaxaca, which is close to Chiapas," Jessica said as they walked back to meet Elias and Detective Kaminski. "A lot of my family has been hurt by the cartel."

"I'm sorry to hear that," Saif replied, but his mind was preoccupied by what Amadou had shared about Yasin. If Yasin was as pious as the story suggested, he felt a deep sense of admiration for him. Privately, Saif really wanted Yasin to actually be innocent.

A few blocks later they caught up with the other two. "Hey, find anything?" Elias asked.

"We have an address," Saif said, wagging his notepad.

"For Yasin Bamba?" Detective Kaminski perked her head up from her notepad.

"No, but someone who knows him well apparently."

"Alright, let's go," the detective said. It was now getting quite dark out, and street-lamps were sparse.

The group of four approached the address Amadou had given them. It belonged to a nice brownstone building. They walked up the widely spaced stairs to the front door. Detective Kaminski rapped the door three times hard. The door opened slowly.

"Hello? I didn't call the police," a man's voice said.

"Are you…Suleyman?" Detective Kaminski asked, reading the name from Saif's notepad.

"Yes, and what is this about?"

"We'd like to speak to you about Yasin Bamba."

Suleyman was silent for a few moments. "Give me one moment," he said, closing the door. They waited outside in the cool night air for him to return. Then, the door opened wide this time. The four officers stepped forward into the home.

Inside, Suleyman led them to a small but comfortable living room and took a seat on the sofa. His eyes were watery. "Yasin Bamba. I knew him well," he said, wiping away tears.

Saif looked around at the others to speak, but they all stayed silent, hoping Suleyman would open up more.

"You know I called in to your tip line a few weeks ago," Suleyman continued. "I heard from a mutual friend that Yasin was doing delivery work in the East Village."

"That was you?" Jessica raised an eyebrow at Saif. Saif remembered how Jessica had told him about the tip while they were working outside the youth event at the mosque.

"Yes, I was afraid he was in danger," Suleyman said, sniffling. They all sat watching Suleyman while his chest heaved in poorly stifled cries. "And then—and then he was killed." Suleyman began to wail loudly, holding his face in his hands.

"Yasin Bamba was killed? Are you sure?" Saif asked in shock.

"Yes, unfortunately I have confirmation from someone who was there that Yasin died in that horrible bombing at the Madina Mosque. A trusted friend of mine told me he was inside when it happened. Hoffmeyer killed my best friend," Suleyman howled.

Saif, Jessica, and Elias looked at each other wide-eyed, their first time hearing this. Then, all three of them looked at Detective Kaminski, who was avoiding their gaze.

"Suleyman," Detective Kaminski said, rising from the sofa and reaching into her back pocket. "You're under arrest for the attempted murder of Yasin Bamba."

Chapter 29: Yasin

The imam knocked softly and entered his office to find Yasin sitting on the armchair, reading from a Quran.

"Surah Yusuf?" he asked.

"Yeah," Yasin said, looking up.

"I brought you something to eat for suhoor. We have about twenty minutes left to eat." He handed Yasin a paper plate laden with watermelon slices, dates, half of a banana, and a cup of yogurt with a plastic spoon. Yasin closed the Quran carefully and set it on the desk, then took the plate with both hands and started to eat.

"You aren't the one who shot a gun earlier, are you?" The imam suddenly asked, eyeing him warily. "I just heard about that."

"No, that was not me shaykh," Yasin said as he pitted a date. "They already caught the man who did that. I would never do something like that."

"I see, that's good." The imam's face flooded with relief. "We will be praying Fajr soon. Afterwards, I would like to have my office back, so I can complete my revision for Taraweeh. We're finishing the Quran tonight, in sha Allah."

"Of course, shaykh. Thank you for your kindness and hospitality."

"No need to thank me, brother." The imam turned to leave, but he left the door slightly ajar this time.

Yasin slowly ate his food and thought about his next move. He had a solid theory of how the drugs ended up in his merchandise that fateful night, but there was nothing he could do about it now. He was still in danger, and he still needed to leave the city immediately. But he didn't have enough money yet for the taxi ride. He needed Ali to pay him early for the last two days of work. That meant coming clean to Ali about everything. It was the only way.

Once he was done eating, he left the imam's office and went to wash up for prayer. On the other side of the basement, men were already washing their hands, faces, arms, and feet at the sinks made for that purpose. Yasin joined them.

In the mirror, Yasin assessed the state of his ear. It was mostly healed. He tried to clean it as much as possible in the sink. Little dark flakes of blood fell off and rehydrated as they touched the running water, turning the sink below him pink. Once he cleaned his ear, he rubbed down the sink with soap using his hand, ignoring the curious looks from the other men, and went upstairs to join the rest of the congregation.

The men who were gathered near him for early morning prayer were still sleepy, likely to be going straight back to bed afterward. They wore pajamas under their thobes and stifled yawns as they lined up. The imam was wide awake, however. It seemed as if he didn't need sleep in Ramadan. He looked at Yasin right before he turned to lead the prayer, giving him a supportive nod and smile.

After prayer, most people quickly rose and left the mosque to get a couple more hours of sleep before the workday began. Yasin lifted himself to his feet and dragged himself over to a dark corner of the prayer hall, feeling sleepy again. He curled up facing the wall and fell into a dreamless slumber.

It was Ali who woke him up this time. He gently tapped Yasin's shoulder until he rolled over onto his back and his vision cleared up. "Ali?"

"I need to speak with you."

"I need to speak with you too."

"You can go first then."

"No it's okay, I'll go after you."

"No, really," Ali insisted. "I guess what I want to say depends on what you want to say."

"Fine," Yasin said. He sat himself up against the wall and rubbed his face. "What time is it?"

Ali checked his watch. "It's almost one in the afternoon."

Yasin took a deep breath, rubbing his eyes. "Ali, I'm not who you think I am. I'm sorry, I haven't been telling you the truth."

Ali looked concerned but not surprised. "Who are you, then?"

"My name is Yasin Bamba, and I'm one of the Steinway Seven."

Ali sighed. "I know."

"You knew?"

"Not until the shooting last night. But then I started to piece things together. I found that article in the Arabic newspaper in your room. I vowed to never read that rag, ever since the editor rejected my application to write for them, but I discovered it in your room, and when I flipped through it and saw your picture I realized why you were so afraid of the police."

"But I didn't do what the police have accused me of," Yasin said. "I don't want you to think I'm a criminal."

"I've seen the way you speak with people, the way you work hard, I've witnessed your honesty and your eagerness to help others. I know that you're a good man," Ali said. "But why were you arrested in the first place?"

Yasin sighed. "I'll tell you the whole story, but you have to believe that I'm telling the truth." Yasin looked Ali in the eyes earnestly.

"All right," Ali said. "Let's hear it."

"When I first arrived in the US, I knew nobody but Amadou, a man I met during the journey here. Amadou's cousin Suleyman had already been here for years. Suleyman knew everyone in Harlem. He knew the street language, he mastered the street fashion. He was the perfect contact to have. Suleyman set me and Amadou up with the first job most people from our country get —selling fake merchandise on the street. I was given Gucci sunglasses, Louis Vuitton Bags, Prada purses, and other fake things to sell near the subway station on 125th and Lexington. Amadou was up on 145th and Seventh Avenue. We both moved in with Suleyman, who shared an apartment with a few other Guineans by 145th Street, but Suleyman was rarely there anyway.

"I was grateful for Suleyman's help getting us set up, but I was not very impressed with his lifestyle. He frequently smoked marijuana, and sometimes came home clearly drunk. His cousin, Amadou, spoke to him and gave him advice many times, and Suleyman always listened to him like he was going to change, but the next day I would see him smoking again shamelessly. Anyway, I don't want to linger on his bad habits as much as the company that he started to keep.

"I realized he was messing with bad people when he came home at four in the morning one night, slamming the door and shouting. We all woke up right away, wondering what was going on, and Suleyman pulled a gun out of his pants and told us to be quiet. We all became scared, even Amadou, who didn't know about the gun. We took shelter in the bathroom and then after many hours Suleyman came and told us it was safe."

"That's very strange behavior," Ali said. "Maybe he owed money to someone? Did you all move out?"

"I wanted to leave that next day, but Suleyman was still our boss, and I couldn't leave until I found something else to do for work. As our boss, he would go around and warn us when police were doing sweeps of our merchandise. That's what happened the day I was arrested. That day, I heard Suleyman's whistle, and I knew what to do. I rolled everything up into a bag and took it over my shoulder and ran. Suleyman caught up with me, and he said the police were right behind us. He told me to go down into the subway and jump on the first train, then he went in the other direction.

"I did as he said. I ran down the subway steps, but there was an officer down there. I couldn't turn back because there were two already chasing me. So I just laid my stuff down and put my hands up, like I was taught to do if I get caught. I thought they would just take it all away as usual. How foolish I was! The cops gathered around my merchandise and started searching it carefully, looking for something. And that's when they found the drugs."

As he recounted the story, Yasin remembered Suleyman with visceral anger. *That wretched man ruined my life! How stupid I was to trust him!*

"So Suleyman planted the drugs on you," Ali concluded. "And he's still free now?"

"I guess so. He let me get arrested for his problems and he's somewhere out there enjoying his freedom."

Yasin's hand began to shake with anger at the thought of Suleyman sitting in their old apartment as if nothing had happened. *Everything I've gone through... it should have been him. The horrible, overcrowded, and filthy Rikers Island jail, the constant running from the police. And now I have to leave everything here behind and start all over again somewhere else.* "I'm sorry, Ali," he said. "If I could, I would stay and work with you. I feel bad that you will be understaffed now for the final days of Ramadan."

"Well, now I have to work with my son for a little longer until I can find more help, but someone reminded me that spending time with my son was a privilege, not a burden." Ali winked. "Wallahi, I am sorry that you have to deal with all this. If there's any way I can help you, I am at your service."

"Oh, by the way, did the police come back to the restaurant today?" Yasin had almost forgotten to ask.

"Yes, I just spoke to them now. They asked to look through everything. Thankfully I cleaned up your room and got rid of anything you left behind before they came back. The shooter admitted to the police that he was trying to cash in on a bounty for you. I told the police that I didn't know you were sitting outside my store. They bought the story, surprisingly, but they know you're around here now."

Yasin felt overcome with fear once again. Ali noticed his anxious expression. "You need to leave as soon as possible," Ali stressed. "It's not safe for you to be here."

"I know," Yasin said. "I have a plan, but I need a portion of my next paycheck early for the last couple days of work that I did."

Ali smiled wryly. "I can do that. But what's your plan?"

"I have made an arrangement with a taxi driver here to take me to Philadelphia. He's charging me five hundred."

Yasin dug in his pocket and pulled out a bunch of crumpled bills. "I have $445 right now."

"I can give you the money," Ali said, "but are you sure that's a good idea? Philadelphia is only a few hours away. The NYPD might collaborate with their police department to search for you. I don't think running away to Philly is a long-term solution."

"I know, but do you have any better ideas?"

"I think you need to leave the country," Ali said simply.

"That's what I wanted to do all along, but it's easier said than done," Yasin groaned. "I know you want to help, but this isn't the time for brainstorming from scratch. There are probably police on their way right now to look for me, and random people with guns are trying to capture me too. I need the money. I need to get out of New York, at least."

Ali nodded and pulled out his wallet. He counted five twenty-dollar bills and handed them to Yasin.

"Thank you," Yasin said, adding it to his pile. He tried to straighten the bills out into a neater stack. He would have an extra forty-five dollars to start a new life in Philly.

Ali stood abruptly and clapped a hand to his forehead. "Wait! I just thought of something!"

Yasin stopped recounting his cash. "Yes?"

"It's a crazy idea—really crazy—but it might work."

"What is it?"

"I'm getting a big delivery in tomorrow, at six in the morning, right after Fajr. It's a truckload of imported

Algerian sodas coming from Montreal, for my grocery store, but also for the restaurant."

"And?"

"It's going back to Montreal afterwards. Empty."

"Interesting." Yasin put the cash down. "And you're thinking—"

"I'm thinking if we can find a way to hide you in the truck, you could be out of the country by midday tomorrow. Then you can't be put on trial for anything that happened here, unless the US officially requests Canada to send you back, which is unlikely. But either way, you could lay low there for years and nobody would notice you."

Yasin thought about Ali's plan. It was high risk, and high reward. If he could get to Montreal, a French-speaking province with a large African population, he could probably get set up quickly to start sending payments back to his wife and son, whom he hadn't been able to support since his arrest nearly four months ago. But if he got caught on the way, he was going straight back to prison.

"What do you have to lose?" Ali asked, watching Yasin think through the possibilities.

"Nothing," Yasin admitted. "I'm a hunted man either way."

Ali got serious. "All right, I'm going to think of how we can do this. You just lay low here. After Fajr, I'll unload the truck, come get you, and we'll find a way to hide you inside. It's a box truck, probably around sixteen feet long. There should be enough space for you to fit. And whatever you do, don't mention me. If you do end up being caught, say you broke into the van."

"Of course," Yasin said. "Understood."

"Okay, so you will hide here in the masjid until I get you in the morning?"

"Yes," Yasin said. "I want to be here tonight anyway. The imam said it could be Laylatul Qadr."

"Oh, yes," Ali said. "Make as much dua and prayer as you can tonight. Ask Allah to clear your name, so maybe you can come back, and to forgive you for your sins. And remember, He is the one in control of everything. He can make the impossible, possible."

Yasin was almost too scared to have hope that his life could somehow go back to normal. It would be a dream if he could come back to New York and work and live freely again one day. If he had the chance to do it all over again, he would have made better choices. He would have sought a more honest living than the one Suleyman set up for him. Instead of selling fake bags, he could have found Ali sooner and worked for him from the start. He never would have been sent to jail, and escaping prison wouldn't have even been a possibility. He would surround himself with good people, and try his best to lead a good life.

"I have a lot to ask Allah for," Yasin said, after reflection. "Safety, security, forgiveness. And guidance. I will wait for you in the morning, in sha Allah."

"Oh, by the way, I have something I want to give you," Ali said. "It was supposed to be your Eid present, but since this is all happening, I must give it to you now." He reached beside him and pulled out a bag that Yasin recognized.

"I bought it at that Suhoor Fest," Ali explained. From the bag he pulled out a North African style thobe. It was white with a pattern of gold vertical lines throughout it.

"It's beautiful," Yasin said, taking it into his hands. "You didn't have to do this." Yasin rose to his feet and pulled the thobe on, shaking it loose until it reached down to his ankles. He looked down and saw Ali discreetly wiping away tears. Yasin suddenly felt emotional too.

"I'm sorry to see you go already," Ali said. "It hasn't even been two weeks, but it's been a pleasure to work with you and get to know you as a brother."

Ali reached down and clasped Yasin's hand in a firm handshake, then lifted him all the way up into a full embrace.

"It's been my honor to know you too, my brother."

Chapter 30: Saif

After abruptly arresting Suleyman and reading him his rights, Detective Kaminski called in backup to transport him to the nearest precinct. Then, Saif, Elias, and Jessica jumped into their SUV and followed the car with Suleyman.

"We're going to see the Dirty Thirty in person." Elias nudged Saif in the backseat, smiling.

"I'm so confused though," Saif whispered. "Why is Kaminski so sure Suleyman tried to kill Yasin?"

"I can hear you," Detective Kaminski said, "and I'm not positive—it's a strong suspicion. But when I heard him say Yasin was dead, alarm bells rang for me. I know for sure that Yasin wasn't killed in that blast. And that's how we're gonna get Suleyman to confess."

They pulled into the parking lot on 151st Street a few minutes later. Detective Kaminski went to grab Suleyman out of the car, forcing him forward into the precinct, the rookie cops following them in. A local cop recognized her.

"Hey, Bea, long time no see—"

"I'd really like to catch up, Wilfred, but I need to question a suspect right now. Any interview rooms free?"

"Sure," the man got serious, "room three in the back."

Detective Kaminski walked Suleyman over to the interrogation room. "You three, go in from there," she ordered, pointing at a second entrance. Then she went in the main door.

Saif, Elias, and Jessica walked through the other door which opened into a clear glass window on one side, giving them a view of the room with Suleyman and Detective Kaminski. They watched her cuff him to the table and heard her offer him a drink. He asked for a Coke.

"You heard him, get the man a Coke," she said, without looking away.

"Is she talking to us?" Saif asked.

"I'll get it," Jessica said. She returned a moment later. "Someone's getting it."

After a few minutes a cop walked in with the soda, put it on the table, then left the room. For a long moment, the only sounds were the crack of the can opening and Suleyman taking loud sips.

Detective Kaminski broke the silence. "So, wanna tell me why you tried to have Yasin killed?"

"I have no idea what you're talking about," Suleyman said. "And he's not with us anymore. Have some respect for my friend."

"Suleyman, I'm not sure you're aware, but Yasin is still alive."

"That's false," Suleyman said. "But I wish he was alive, of course."

"You say he was killed in the blast at Madina Masjid, in the East Village."

"Yes, I have some friends who work down there. They told me he was staying at the mosque and he died in Hoffmeyer's attack."

"I think you and I both know that wasn't the work of Hoffmeyer."

"If it wasn't Hoffmeyer, then who was it?"

"I don't know, you tell me."

"Are you accusing me of bombing a mosque?"

"Did you?"

"No."

"Did you hire someone to do it?"

Suleyman twitched.

"So you hired someone to do it. But why? Why did you want to kill Yasin? Why did you want to kill your so-called best friend?"

"I didn't do anything. I want to speak to my lawyer."

"You don't have a lawyer."

"I don't care, I want one."

Detective Kaminski took a deep breath. "I'll leave you alone for a few minutes until you want to talk about why you tried to kill Yasin." She stood up and left the room, then quietly entered the viewing room with the others.

"He can't hear us right now," Detective Kaminski said. "So, can any of you think of a potential motive?"

"Wait, can you explain why it wasn't Hoffmeyer who bombed the mosque?" Saif inquired.

"Much of Hoffmeyer's case was under wraps, since it was elevated to an FBI investigation," Detective Kaminski explained. "I was privy to more details than most."

"So what do we not know about it?"

"Hoffmeyer had a clear method of operation. He didn't use cheap bombs; his were made with high-grade materials and impossible to track. The bomb that went off at the mosque was a homemade bomb, cobbled together by an amateur. Since nobody else was in the mosque, it must have been a targeted attack. Someone wanting to commit a hate crime à la Hoffmeyer would have detonated the bomb when the mosque was full of worshippers. And the biggest indicator of Suleyman's involvement is he's confident that Yasin died in the blast, when the official file says there were zero deaths, and one injured man who fled the scene. It seems like someone Suleyman hired to kill Yasin lied to him about completing the job."

"Oh, so that's why casualty numbers were never released for that attack," Saif realized. "I thought it was related to being an FBI case."

"It was. The FBI knew immediately that the Madina Mosque bombing was not the work of Hoffmeyer. But until now, they've assumed that it was a copycat attacker hoping to further sow chaos. They decided that until Hoffmeyer was caught, they were going to let the public think it was him, so more copycats didn't emerge. When they did catch Hoffmeyer, the case of the mosque bombing fell by the wayside and became irrelevant. Until now."

"But why did Suleyman try to get him killed, if they were close with each other before?" Jessica wondered.

"I have a theory," Saif said. "Maybe it's because Yasin knew something that Suleyman didn't want coming out."

"Is that why he called in a tip, hoping Yasin would get caught again?" Jessica added.

"You might be right," Saif said. "And when it didn't get Yasin found, he decided to take matters into his own hands and have Yasin killed instead. But what could Yasin have known?"

"Maybe it was related to the original case that got Yasin arrested," Elias said. "What was it again? Drug trafficking?"

"Yeah," Saif recalled. "He was found with several pounds of fentanyl. I think Yasin was one of those guys that sells fake bags on the streets. When they rounded up his stuff, they found the drugs inside. Maybe Suleyman framed him?"

"And weren't the drugs tied to a Dominican gang?" Jessica remembered.

"Yeah, that's why his sentence was elevated to twenty years," Saif said.

They all fell silent, then looked at Detective Kaminski, who was standing a few steps away and smiling proudly. "Good detective work, rookies," she said.

They turned to watch through the window while Detective Kaminski went back inside the room with Suleyman. "Ready to talk?" she asked.

Suleyman looked at her and made a symbol of his lips being sealed.

"We know about the Dominican gang, and the drugs you were selling for them."

Suleyman's eyes darted away, his expression betraying unease.

"Yasin told us all about it."

"You found Yasin?" Suleyman asked, his eyes growing large.

"So you admit you aren't sure he died in that blast."

"I sure to God hope he didn't." Suleyman's lip quivered, as if he wanted to know more about where Yasin was, but he held himself back from speaking.

"Well I'm happy to share the good news then. Yasin was picked up hiding in a house in Bed-Stuy today," Detective Kaminski lied.

Suleyman's index finger started to bounce on the table. "Do you have a photo?" Suleyman asked. "If my good friend is still alive I'd love to see proof."

"I'm afraid that's confidential."

Suleyman's eyes began to bulge, and he was chewing his bottom lip. "What did he say?"

"Oh, he told us all about you, and the fentanyl trade you had going on. You were hiding it in the fake merchandise weren't you? We have names of all the other street sellers you worked with."

"BS. It's his word against mine, and he's a criminal."

"Amadou spoke to us too."

Suleyman closed his eyes and his head bowed down. "Damn it Amadou!" he sucked his lip furiously. Then his face admitted defeat. "Fine. Screw it. I'll tell you about the Dominicans, but I need assurances. And I didn't commit attempted murder. You have no proof of that."

"Fine. What kind of assurances?"

"I want to walk free, if I tell you where I got the drugs. I'll tell you everything I know. But you have to also give me protection, and promise me I won't be deported. I'm on a green card now."

"If you give us material evidence that we can use to take down the gang, we might let you go free. But if you don't give us enough information—"

"Please, I'll do anything you need. I'll go undercover for you and feed you information."

"Fine," Detective Kaminski said. "We'll make a deal. Now, tell me everything you know."

Suleyman looked relieved, but his face took a dismal turn as he started to tell his story. "I first got in touch with the Trinitarios as a customer," he explained. "I used to buy weed from them every week or so to sell to my friends. As I grew my customer base, I started buying it wholesale from them, several pounds at a time, and the transactions started to get big as well. But I was smoking a lot of it myself, and giving it away to people at parties, females especially, and I was starting to lose money. But I kept reupping with my dealer, taking it on credit, until I got into a lot of debt. And that's when they started making demands."

"What kind of demands?" Detective Kaminski asked.

"They told me if I didn't start moving the harder stuff for them, they would kill me."

"And that's how you got into the fentanyl trade?"

"Yeah. They told me I didn't have to sell it, just move it around for them. And they had a plan for me. All I had to do was execute it."

"And what was their plan?"

"They knew that I managed the counterfeit bag business in Harlem. They wanted me to create a network of merchandise sellers that would move their product around as needed. They had me recruit people who were willing to work for them. We devised a plan together to choose a specific bag, a Michael Kors purse, as the mule. We picked it because I had a ton of stock for those bags, but when the brand lost some prestige, nobody was buying them on the street anymore. Why would you buy a fake Michael Kors bag on the street when you can find them at TJ Maxx?"

"I see," Detective Kaminski said, stifling a laugh after his final comment. "So you moved fentanyl pills for them through your network of bag sellers. How did this involve Yasin Bamba?"

"I never asked Yasin to join our operation. I knew he would never do it. He was already depressed about selling fake bags, because he thought it was dishonest. He would never agree to move drugs for me. But one day, I was out doing deliveries, and I had a purse full of pills, supposed to be going to someone else. That day, I saw two police officers going around busting unauthorized street sellers. I freaked out, because I had all those drugs on me. That's when I saw Yasin. I ran over to him, told him about the police, and then I dropped the purse into his pile and told him to run the opposite direction. I thought he had enough time to get away. But when I doubled back later, I looked down into the subway, and saw the police looking through his stuff. I felt so bad in the moment—"

"But you let him take the fall," Detective Kaminski concluded. "You knew he had no idea about the pills, and secretly testified against him to ensure the conviction."

"He testified against him?" Saif said to Elias and Jessica. "That's even more messed up."

Suleyman was taken aback that Detective Kaminski knew about the testimony, but didn't argue. "I feel terrible about it now," he said.

"So why try to kill him?"

"I didn't," Suleyman growled.

*He's lying…*Saif thought.

"Alright, fine," Detective Kaminski said. "We'll be in touch about collecting evidence on the Trinitario gang. Let me get the paperwork done, and you'll be free to go."

She returned to the viewing room with the others and her tough face broke into a smile. "We got him."

"I can't believe it worked," Saif exhaled while they all exchanged high fives.

Detective Kaminski then went to speak privately with her former colleague at the thirtieth precinct for a few minutes. She returned in great spirits.

"Detective Reynolds has agreed to conduct the sting operation into the Dominican gang," she said. "Apparently, they've already been investigating the local fentanyl trade for several months. Suleyman is going to be a huge asset."

Saif looked back at Suleyman as he was being uncuffed. It didn't seem fair to let him go, after everything he admitted to doing, and everything he probably did but didn't admit to. *This guy is clearly evil. Is it worth letting him go free just because he's helping on another case?* He watched in disgust as Suleyman exited the precinct.

It was now nearly two in the morning and they were all exhausted—all except Detective Kaminski.

"Let's all meet up tomorrow morning outside Captain Mancini's office and brief him on the case," she said. "Let's say, eight am?"

Saif groaned internally, but he knew he had to be in the room for the briefing. He had played an important role in this investigation, and it was a surefire way to get back on the captain's good side. "Sure, sounds good."

They all exited the precinct and Detective Kaminski dropped them off back at the 114th, and then drove off.

"See you tomorrow," Saif said to Jessica and Elias through a long yawn. He forced his legs home and immediately crashed on the sofa, just barely managing to set up his phone alarm to wake up at seven.

When he woke up nearly five hours later, Saif got dressed and groomed his hair perfectly. When he and the others were recognized by the captain in front of everyone, he was going to look good.

He strolled into the precinct a healthy fifteen minutes before eight. Captain Mancini was already in his office, but Jessica and Elias weren't there yet. He went to get coffee in the break room and found Detective Kaminski, who somehow looked like she had gotten a full night's rest.

"Looking sharp, rookie," she said. Saif started to recognize a pattern with her; she was super friendly just after solving a case, but serious and unsmiling otherwise.

"To be honest, I feel I haven't been a very good cop until this moment," Saif confided in her in the empty room. "This could be my big break."

"You've only been a cop for what, a month? Cheer up, you have a long career ahead of you. I see you being in my shoes one day."

Saif smiled. Being a detective and solving real crimes was much cooler than just being an average cop on the street.

They were soon joined by Elias and Jessica. It was two minutes to eight.

"Let's get this show on the road," Detective Kaminski said. "I'll start, but I want you all to pitch in, so the captain sees you were an important part of the case."

They walked inside his office and waited for the captain to notice them. "Ah yes, we said eight o'clock right? Take a seat. So you found Bamba, right?"

"Not exactly," Detective Kaminski replied, her confidence slightly shaken. "I told you it was about his case, but it goes much deeper than just him."

Captain Mancini furrowed his eyebrows. "It's simple. He's the last fugitive. Catch him and this case is closed. What else am I missing?"

"Sir, it's about the drugs Yasin was found with initially," Saif piped up.

Captain Mancini leaned forward and clasped his hands together. "Okay, I'm listening."

Detective Kaminski picked up again. "Originally, Yasin Bamba was found with five pounds of fentanyl in his merchandise as a street seller. We tracked the drugs to a Dominican gang in the Bronx—"

"Yes, yes, we knew all this. What else is there?"

"I'm getting there," Detective Kaminski said, starting to become flustered. "Yasin worked for a man named Suleyman, who was the distributor for a huge network of street sellers. Suleyman worked for a gang called the Trinitarios, pushing their drugs all throughout the city, hidden in purses and bags. We arrested him last night, and he confessed to everything."

"Interesting," Captain Mancini said, his face becoming visibly brighter. "The thirty has been trying to take that gang down for months."

"Exactly," Jessica added. "And we even got Suleyman to agree to work for us, as a mole into their organization."

"Good work," Captain Mancini said, "but I'm still failing to see how this gets us closer to Yasin."

"The thing is, Yasin was innocent," Elias said. "Last night, Suleyman admitted to planting the drugs in Yasin's stock right before he was arrested."

Captain Mancini leaned back into his leather chair and looked mildly impressed. "Quite a conspiracy you guys uncovered. Nice work everyone."

Jessica, Elias, and Saif exchanged celebratory glances.

"So now that this Suleyman character is caught and the thirty will commence with the sting operation, I want you back on track to find Yasin. We've received reports that he was seen on Steinway last night."

"Reports? From who?" Detective Kaminski asked.

"Some idiot who said he was a bounty hunter working for a local billionaire. We think he's lying about that, but he says he's positive that he ID'd Yasin sitting outside of a restaurant on Steinway."

"Wait, we just proved Yasin is innocent of his conviction," Saif butted in. "Shouldn't he be allowed to walk free now?"

The room fell silent. Captain Mancini fixed his gaze on Saif. "Walk free?"

"Um, yes, sir," Saif mumbled.

"You do realize he escaped a police van with six other lunatics and has been hiding from the law for the last three and half weeks, right?" His voice started low and rose the more he spoke.

"Yes, sir, but—"

"How do you think it looks, how do you think *we'd* look," and he poked his thick thumb in his chest, "if we come out to the media and say, 'Yeah, we couldn't find the last guy on the list but he's actually a nice sweet guy who can do no wrong?'"

"What do we do then?" Saif asked.

"We catch him, and we throw that low life back into prison!" Captain Mancini roared.

"That's just not fair!" Saif said, ignoring warning looks from Detective Kaminski and the others. "Suleyman did the crime, he should do the time!"

"You want to be fair, huh? Let's tally up what this guy did. He's an illegal migrant, for one. He shouldn't even be in this country. He sold counterfeit bags on the street. Another crime. And he fled custody, in an escape that killed *your* fellow cop. That's three crimes. I think the man deserves to rot in a cell for a while, don't you?"

Saif's lower lip trembled in anger. He had nothing to say back.

"Alright, back to work. Get out of my office." Captain Mancini dismissed them, and the group of four spilled out of his office one by one, into the stares of the rest of the precinct.

"Well, that didn't go as expected," Jessica huffed once the other cops had gone back to work.

"I'm going home," Saif said suddenly, turning towards the door.

"Saif, no," Jessica said. "Elias, tell him not to leave."

"Are you okay with this?" Saif turned back to look at Detective Kaminski.

She stared back without a word. But masked behind her steely expression, she too, seemed dejected.

Saif turned back to the door.

"Saif," Elias called, following him halfheartedly, but Saif didn't turn back again. He exited the precinct at a quarter past eight in the morning and reached home by eight thirty.

"You're home early? Please don't tell me you're suspended again," his mother pleaded.

"No, this is different," Saif said. He took her by the hand and led her into the living room, taking a seat on the couch. "I don't know if this job is for me," he said flatly. He wasn't sad now, or angry. He just wanted clarity.

"What happened?" his mother asked.

Saif sighed, not excited to recount what happened again, but he felt his mother's perspective might help him confirm what he was feeling. "Do you remember one of the guys who escaped, Yasin, the African one?"

She thought for a second. "Yasin, yes the Muslim one. What happened with him? Did they catch him?"

"No, not yet." Saif drew a deep breath. "Last night, I came late because we were questioning some people who used to know him. Well, we found out that he was innocent. He never sold drugs like they said originally."

"I knew it. A Muslim cannot sell drugs."

"Well, one did. His friend Suleyman."

"Audho billah. So he made this Yasin take the blame? How can someone do that to their friend?"

"I don't know, he's a horrible person," Saif said. "But anyway, when we found out the truth, I went to the captain and told him the full story, but he still won't let Yasin walk free. He says it would make the police look bad. I can't understand it. Isn't our job to catch the bad guys and protect innocent people? Am I supposed to go along with this?"

Saif's mom took his hand and her expression turned uncharacteristically firm and serious. "You have to make a choice, Saif. Your father made his. And you saw how it ended."

Saif looked at her in surprise. She never spoke this candidly about his father, or his death. Then he thought, more seriously than ever before, about his role on the force. It hadn't even been a month yet. He didn't want to seem like he gave up because he couldn't handle being a cop. Then he thought of the friends he'd made: Jessica, who was always helpful and genuine, Elias, who had never failed him as a friend, even Detective Kaminski, who was becoming a sort of mentor. If the system was broken, these were still good, hardworking cops, and he enjoyed working with them. Should he really give it all up?

His mother now looked at him with the same expression she always gave him: one of compassion and sympathy. Suddenly, something clicked in his brain. This wasn't the expression he wanted his mother to have when she gazed at him. This wasn't what her being proud looked like.

"Mama, what should I do?" When the words left his mouth, he felt a warm feeling rise in his heart. He realized he rarely asked his mother for her advice on his problems, with the intention to truly listen to what she had to say.

"My beloved son," she said in Arabic, "tonight is the night of Laylatul Qadr. This is the night when Allah promises to accept all of our pleas and prayers. Please, Saif, go to the masjid tonight for Taraweeh prayer and pray until the end, all twenty prayers."

Twenty sounded like a lot. Saif hadn't prayed at all in months. But he had no other ideas. Maybe God had the answer he was looking for all along.

"I know you care about doing what's right with Yasin. Even if you feel powerless right now, remember, Allah is in control, and He is the Most Just. Put your trust in Him."

"You're right. Thank you, Mama."

"And when you pray, don't forget your father. Pray for his forgiveness, and that he is entered into Jannah."

"Okay," Saif promised. "I will."

Chapter 31: Saif

Later that night, after eating iftar with his mother, Saif put on his father's old djellaba and bright red chechia and considered himself in the mirror. He thought the djellaba was going to be loose on him but it fit perfectly. He dug in his closet for the oud perfume someone had once given him after a umrah trip and sprayed some of it on his neck and wrists. The earthy-sweet scent seemed to calm his racing heart. He checked his phone and realized he was a few minutes late for prayer at the Al Iman mosque.

When he reached the doors of Al Iman after a brisk ten-minute walk, the building was already filled to the brim with worshippers. Isha prayer had begun. He took his shoes off in the entryway and waited for space to clear up. After a few moments, he was able to find a spot to pray in the back row and squeezed into a small space against a wall.

The imam at the mosque that night was a special guest from Egypt. During the Isha prayer, he showed flashes of his sublime vocals, but he was saving most of his energy for the Taraweeh prayers afterwards, which many people had come from all over Queens to attend.

In the short intermission between Isha and Taraweeh prayers, even more people arrived. They looked around for empty space in the prayer hall to stand. The body heat from the crowd made the entire mosque feel warm and stuffy. Volunteers went around passing out small water bottles. Others carried incense burners that filled the air with a complex woody aroma.

Though he hadn't prayed in a mosque in over a year, Saif felt deeply at home. Throughout his childhood, he had sat through boring lectures in this very mosque, but now, those memories felt tender and nostalgic.

Saif surveyed the busy crowd as he waited patiently for the Taraweeh prayers to begin. There were hundreds and hundreds of faces, some vaguely familiar, most not, but then he saw a face that made him feel embarrassed. It was Ammu Ali, whom he hadn't seen since their shouting match at his grocery store a few weeks ago. He promised himself he would make things right with Ammu Ali later.

Then, everyone stood up again, and the imam cleared his voice as he prepared to lead Taraweeh. In Arabic, he explained how Taraweeh prayers were prayed: twenty prayers, prayed two at a time.

This time, the imam read powerfully, pouring his whole heart into the words he was reciting. The crowd followed along, and even those few who didn't speak Arabic were familiar with these last few chapters of the Quran. Saif found his mind predicting verses ahead of the imam, realizing he had once memorized these chapters in his youth.

After each round of prayer ended, a handful of worshippers dropped off and went home. Each time, Saif moved forward into the next line ahead of him. Once they completed eight prayers, a significant chunk of people left the prayer hall. Saif took a sip of water from a bottle he was given. He sat for a moment on the ground, his legs appreciating the break from standing. Then he stood up again, moving up to join the remaining worshippers.

The crowd continued to grow smaller after every prayer. After sixteen, there were just three rows of people left standing, down from thirty rows at the beginning of the night. The group was mostly made up of older men now, dressed in thobes similar to the one Saif had on. Saif forced himself up again in prayer. His legs felt like jelly, and he wondered how these old men were still standing.

Two more prayers down, and Saif was now entirely exhausted. But he couldn't give up now. He reminded himself of why he was praying. He thought about his mother, and his father. He thought about his future, and what God wanted from him. He raised himself slowly to his feet. The imam got ready to lead the final two prayers.

Suddenly, the man in front of him stepped back and left towards the restrooms, leaving an empty space in the front row. Saif reached down to pick up his phone and keys from the ground in front of him. As he rose to move ahead and take the other man's place, one of the men next to the empty space turned back, looking for someone to step forward. Saif looked up at his face, and instantly froze in horror. Yasin looked back at him in confusion and then realized Saif had recognized him. Yasin's eyes grew large, and his body became stiff. He looked up at the mosque's exit. The other men behind them had already started praying, blocking his way out. Yasin looked back at Saif, swallowing nervously. The imam began to recite, his voice filling the loudspeakers, but neither Saif nor Yasin could hear it over the sound of their own heartbeats. Then, Saif took a deep breath, and he stepped forward into the empty space next to Yasin. He put his phone and keys on the ground and fixed his right foot next to Yasin's left foot, and his right shoulder beside Yasin's left shoulder. They both began to pray.

> *By the passage of time!*
> *Surely, humanity is in grave loss,*
> *Except for those who have faith, do good, urge one another to the truth, and urge one another to perseverance.*

Epilogue

Yasin scraped thick snow off the windshield of his delivery truck while the heater ran inside. Winter had started early in Montreal, and he was getting accustomed to its endless snowfall.

It had been six months since he left New York City, and when he remembered his harrowing final moments there, his heart shook in deep gratitude for his present freedom. He remembered to thank Ali and prayed for him silently.

After all, it was Ali who had orchestrated his escape using the very delivery truck Yasin drove now. Ali's contact in Montreal had hired Yasin upon his arrival, employing him in delivering goods imported from Algeria to local businesses.

When Yasin completed his route a few hours later, the sun had already gone down and it was dark and cold and windy. He parked the truck as close as possible to the entrance of their warehouse in the Little Maghreb neighborhood and went inside to submit the cash collected from the day's work.

Yasin opened the thick front doors of the warehouse and squeezed through towers of boxed and wrapped goods. In the back corner, his boss Muhsin had a private office. Yasin went into the dimly lit room and took a seat on the lone musty chair opposite Muhsin. He took out a wad of colorful Canadian dollars and set it on the heavy oak desk in front of him.

"Merci," Muhsin said. "Avant que tu partes, j'ai une lettre pour toi."

"Pour moi?" Yasin asked, surprised. He took the already opened letter from Muhsin's hands and pulled out the paper inside. It was a handwritten note. Small, neat text was crammed into the top margin.

Muhsin, please forward this message to my friend.
It is from a mutual contact of ours.
Ali

Below that, a lengthier letter was written in a less legible style.

Assalamu alaikum,

You probably don't remember me because we've never spoken to each other, but we met briefly at Masjid Al Iman the night you left. My name is Saif and I used to be a NYPD officer. My employment there began right after the famous escape, and my task was your recapture.

In the months that followed, I grappled with many feelings, many thoughts, and many reflections. It was only after you left that I spoke to Ali and learned about your story.

I had previously looked into your case, and discovered the many injustices you faced. I found Suleyman, and my colleagues and I forced him to admit to his crimes. You'll be happy to know that he is now in prison, after he failed to help with an investigation.

Alhamdulillah, with Ali's support, I am now on a different path. I went back to school and I hope to become a lawyer one day.

With this in mind, I wanted to write to you and tell you that not all hope is lost. After I become a lawyer, the case I want to be my first one, is yours. I once applied myself towards your capture, but now I hope to work towards your freedom.

In sha Allah, a day will arrive when you can rejoin us here in New York City.

Your brother,
Saif Belkacem

Yasin carefully folded the now tear-blotted letter and placed it safely in his coat pocket. "Bonne soirée, Muhsin."

"À demain, Yasin."

Yasin walked out of the office, navigated through the maze of boxes, and opened the thick doors of the warehouse. Fresh snow had covered the truck since he had arrived, and more was falling still.

He paused under the awning outside, watching the fuzzy clumps of snow descend gracefully in the light of a nearby street-lamp. He exhaled slowly. His breath twirled into visible wisps and danced in front of him. Winter in Montreal was cold, but it didn't bother him anymore.

About The Author

Badees Nouiouat is an author and documentary filmmaker from Dallas, Texas. He now lives in Astoria, New York City with his wife and young daughter. Badees previously published *The Adventures of Nur Al-Din*, followed by *The Sultan's Sword*, and hopes to continue contributing works that represent the Muslim community.

Get in touch with Badees for speaking engagements and book signings at contact.badees@gmail.com